AROUND THE WORLD IN EIGHTY DAYS
BY JULES VERNE

JULES VERNE (1828–1905). Often overlooked by English critics, Verne was a prolific writer whose work combined a vivid imagination with a gift for popularizing science and travel. He remains among the classics of nineteenth-century French literature.

Born in Nantes in 1828, Jules Verne was the eldest of five children. His father, Pierre Verne, a successful lawyer, was known to write occasional verse but encouraged his son to follow the family profession, which Verne duly did, studying law in Paris. His schooldays proved unexceptional and, apart from an unrequited love he cherished for his cousin, happy. After successfully completing his *baccalauréat* at the Lycée in Nantes in 1847, Verne went to Paris in order to study for the bar. For the next ten years he devoted himself to his real interest, writing, living an artist's existence in a succession of gloomy lodgings. During this time he received moderate success with his plays, and it is thought that about seven of his works reached the stage or print. Alexandre Dumas *père* and *fils* were instrumental in this. In 1856 Verne attended a wedding where he met his future wife, Honorine de Viane, a widow with two daughters. After his marriage in 1857 Verne became a stockbroker and for a time his interests vacillated between the *bourse* and the theatre. It was not until the success of some of his traveller's tales which he wrote for the *Musée des familles* that his true talent for imaginative travel stories emerged. The success of *Five Weeks in a Balloon* (1862) led to a partnership between Verne and the publisher Hetzel that lasted for forty years and was intended, in Hetzel's own words, 'to sum up all the geographical, geological, physical and astronomical knowledge amassed by modern science, and to rewrite the history of the world'. Between the publication of *Journey to the Centre of the Earth* in 1864 and his death Verne wrote a staggering sixty-three novels, including *From the Earth to the Moon* (1865), *Twenty Thousand Leagues under the Sea* (1869) and *Around the World in Eighty Days* (1873). Verne himself travelled widely in Europe, North Africa and America and was a keen yachtsman. He divided his time between Paris, Amiens and his yacht, but for reasons which remain a mystery he suddenly sold his yacht in 1886 and never travelled again. A month later he was shot twice by his mentally unstable nephew, leaving him permanently lame. Jules Verne died at Amiens in 1905. After his death several posthumous works appeared, but it has since been discovered that Verne's son Michel wrote large chunks of them.

Introducing the memorable figure of Phileas Fogg, *Around the World in Eighty Days* became an instant success on its publication in 1873. It remains almost unsurpassed as a piece of adventure fiction.

Readers may also find the following books of interest: William Butcher, *Verne's Journey to the Centre of the Self: Space and Time in the 'Voyages extraordinaires'* (1990); Jean Chesneaux, *The Political and Social Ideas of Jules Verne* (1972); Arhur B. Evans, *Jules Verne Rediscovered* (1988); and Andrew Martin, *The Mask of the Prophet: The Extraordinary Fictions of Jules Verne* (1990).

PENGUIN POPULAR CLASSICS

AROUND THE WORLD IN EIGHTY DAYS

JULES VERNE

*Revised and updated translation
by Jacqueline Rogers*

PENGUIN BOOKS

PENGUIN BOOKS

Published by the Penguin Group
Penguin Books Ltd, 80 Strand, London WC2R ORL, England
Penguin Putnam Inc., 375 Hudson Street, New York, New York 10014, USA
Penguin Books Australia Ltd, Ringwood, Victoria, Australia
Penguin Books Canada Ltd, 10 Alcorn Avenue, Toronto, Ontario, Canada M4V 3B2
Penguin Books India (P) Ltd, 11 Community Centre, Panchsheel Park,
New Delhi – 110 017, India
Penguin Books (NZ) Ltd, Cnr Rosedale and Airborne Roads, Albany, Auckland,
New Zealand
Penguin Books (South Africa) (Pty) Ltd, 24 Sturdee Avenue, Rosebank 2196, South Africa

Penguin Books Ltd, Registered Offices: 80 Strand, London WC2R ORL, England

www.penguin.com

First published 1873
Published in Penguin Popular Classics 1994

2

Printed in the UK by CPI Bookmarque, Croydon, CR0 4TD

ISBN 978-0-14062-368-0

CONTENTS

5

CHAPTER I

In Which Phileas Fogg and Passepartout Accept Each Other, the One as Master, the Other as Servant

M r.* Phileas Fogg lived, in 1872, at No. 7, Saville Row, Burlington Gardens, the house in which Sheridan died in 1814. He was one of the most prominent members of the London Reform Club, though he never did anything to attract attention; an enigmatic character about whom little was known except that he was a polished man of the world. People said that he resembled Byron—at least that his head was Byronic; but he was a bearded, tranquil Byron, who might live on a thousand years without growing old.

An Englishman, indeed it was more doubtful whether Phileas Fogg was a Londoner. He was never seen on 'Change, nor at the Bank, nor in the counting rooms of the "City"; no ships of which he was the owner ever came into London docks; he had no public employment; he had never been entered at any of the Inns of Court, either at the Temple, or Lincoln's Inn, or Gray's Inn; nor had his voice ever resounded in the Court of Chancery, or in the Exchequer, or the Queen's Bench, or the Ecclesiastical Courts. He certainly was not a manufacturer; nor was he a merchant or a gen-

* "Mr." in the French original.

tleman farmer. His name was unfamiliar to the scientific and learned societies, and he never was known to take part in the deliberations of the Royal Institution or the London Institution, the Artisan's Association or the Institution of Arts and Sciences. He belonged, in fact, to none of the numerous societies which swarm in the English capital, from the Harmonica Society to that of the Entomologists, founded mainly for the purpose of abolishing pernicious insects.

Phileas Fogg was a member of the Reform, and that was all.

The way in which he got admission to this exclusive club was simple enough.

He was recommended by the Barings Brothers, with whom he had an open credit. His checks were regularly paid on sight from his account, which was always flush.

Was Phileas Fogg rich? Undoubtedly. But those who knew him best could not imagine how he had made his fortune, and Mr. Fogg was the last person to whom to apply for the information. He was not lavish, nor, on the contrary, stingy; for whenever he knew that money was needed for a noble, useful, or benevolent purpose, he supplied it quietly, and sometimes anonymously. He was, in short, the least communicative of men. He talked very little, and seemed all the more mysterious for his taciturn manner. His daily habits were quite open to observation; but whatever he did was so precisely what he had always done before, that the wits of the curious were fairly puzzled.

Had he traveled? It was likely, for no one seemed to be so familiar with the world; there was no spot so secluded that he did not have an intimate acquaintance with it. He often corrected, with a few clear words, the thousand conjectures advanced by members of the club as to lost and unheard-of travelers; he would point out the true probabilities, seem as if gifted with a sort of second sight, so often did events justify his predictions. He must have traveled everywhere, at least in the spirit.

In any case it was certain that Phileas Fogg had not absented himself from London for many years. Those who had the honor of a closer acquaintance with him than the rest, declared that nobody could claim to have ever seen him anywhere else. His sole pastimes were reading the papers and playing whist. He often won at this game, which, as a silent one, harmonized with his nature; but his winnings never went into his purse, but were reserved as a fund for his charities. Mr. Fogg played, not to win, but for the sake of playing. The game was, in his eyes, a contest, a struggle with a difficulty, yet a motionless, unwearying struggle, congenial to his tastes.

Phileas Fogg was not known to have either wife or children, which happens to the most honest people; nor relatives or near friends, which is certainly more unusual. He lived alone in his house in Saville Row, whither none penetrated. A single servant sufficed to serve him. He had lunch and dinner at the club, at hours mathematically fixed, in the same room, at the same table, never taking his meals with other members, much less bringing a guest with him; and went home at exactly midnight, only to retire at once to bed. He never used the cozy rooms which the Reform provides for its members. He spent ten hours out of the twenty-four in Saville Row, either sleeping or preparing himself to go out. When he chose to take a walk, it was with a regular step in the entrance hall with its mosaic flooring, or in the circular gallery with its dome supported by twenty red porphyry Ionic columns, and illumined by blue painted windows. When he breakfasted or dined, all the resources of the club— its kitchens and pantries, its buttery and dairy— provided his table with their most succulent foods; the serious waiters, in dress coats and shoes with swan-skin soles, serving to him in special porcelain, and on the finest linen; club decanters, of a lost mold, contained his sherry, his port, and his cinnamon-spiced claret; while his beverages were refreshingly cooled with ice, brought at great cost from the American lakes.

If to live in this style is to be eccentric, it must be confessed that there is something good in eccentricity!

The mansion in Saville Row, though not sumptuous, was exceedingly comfortable. The habits of its occupant were such as to demand but little from the sole servant; but Phileas Fogg required him to be almost superhumanly prompt and regular. On this very 2d of October he had dismissed James Forster, because that luckless youth had brought him shaving water at eighty-four degrees Fahrenheit instead of eighty-six; and he was awaiting his successor, who was due at the house between eleven and half-past.

Phileas Fogg was seated squarely in his armchair, his feet close together like those of a grenadier on parade, his hands resting on his knees, his body straight, his head erect; he was steadily watching an elaborate clock which indicated the hours, the minutes, the seconds, the days, the months, and the years. At exactly half-past eleven Mr. Fogg would, according to his daily habit, leave Saville Row, and go to the Reform.

A rap at this moment sounded on the door of the drawing room where Phileas Fogg was seated, and James Forster, the dismissed servant, appeared.

"The new servant," said he.

A young man of thirty advanced and bowed.

"You are a Frenchman, I believe," asked Phileas Fogg, "and your name is John?"

"Jean, if monsieur pleases," replied the newcomer, "Jean Passepartout, a nickname which has stick with me because I have a natural aptness for going out of one business and into another. I believe I'm honest, monsieur, but, to be outspoken, I've had several trades. I've been an itinerant singer, a circus rider, when I used to vault like Leotard, and dance on a rope like Blondin. Then I got to be a professor of gymnastics, so as to make better use of my talents; and then I was a sergeant fireman in Paris, and I even have in my résumé some remarkable fires. But I left France five years ago, and, wishing to taste the sweets of domestic life, took service as a valet here in England. Finding myself out of place, and hearing that Monsieur Phileas Fogg was the most exact and settled gentleman in the United Kingdom, I have come to monsieur in the hope of living with him a tranquil life, and forgetting even the name of Passepartout.''

"Passepartout suits me,'' answered Mr. Fogg. "You come well recommended to me. You know my conditions?''

"Yes, monsieur.''

"Good. What time is it?''

"Twenty-two minutes after eleven,'' returned Passepartout, drawing an enormous silver watch from the depths of his pocket.

"You are slow,'' said Mr. Fogg.

"Pardon me, monsieur, but that's impossible.''

"You are four minutes slow. No matter; it's enough to mention the error. Now from this moment, twenty-nine minutes after eleven, A.M., this Wednesday, October 2nd, you are in my service.''

Phileas Fogg got up, took his hat in his left hand, put it on his head with an automatic motion, and went off without a word.

Passepartout heard the street door shut once; it was his new master going out. He heard it shut again; it was his predecessor, James Forster, departing in his turn. Passepartout remained alone in the house in Saville Row.

CHAPTER II

IN WHICH PASSEPARTOUT IS CONVINCED THAT HE HAS AT LAST FOUND HIS IDEAL

"To be sure," muttered Passepartout, somewhat flurried, "I've seen people at Madame Tussaud's as lively as my new master!"

Madame Tussaud's "people," let it be said, are of wax, and are much visited in London; speech is all that is wanting to make them human.

During his brief interview with Mr. Fogg, Passepartout had been carefully observing him. He appeared to be a man about forty years of age, with fine, handsome features, and a tall, well-shaped figure; his hair and whiskers were light, his forehead compact and unwrinkled, his face rather pale, his teeth magnificent. His countenance possessed in the highest degree what physiognomists call "repose in action," a quality of those who act rather than talk. Calm and phlegmatic, with a clear eye, Mr. Fogg seemed a perfect type of that English composure which Angelica Kauffmann has so skillfully represented on canvas. Seen in the various phases of his daily life, he gave the idea of being perfectly well balanced, as exactly regulated as a Leroy chronometer. Phileas Fogg was, indeed, exactitude personified, and this was betrayed even in the expression of his very hands and feet; for in men, as well as in animals, the limbs themselves are expressive of the passions.

14

He was so exact that he was never in a hurry, was always ready, and was economical in both his steps and his motions. He never took one step too many, and always went to his destination by the shortest way; he made no superfluous gestures, and was never seen to be moved or agitated. He was the most deliberate person in the world, yet always arrived on time.

He lived alone, and so to speak, outside of every social relation; and as he knew that in this world there must be friction, and since friction slows things down, he never rubbed against anybody.

As for Jean, also known as Passepartout, he was a true Parisian of Paris. For the five years he had lived in England, taking service as a valet, he had in vain searched for a master after his own heart. Passepartout was by no means one of those pert dunces depicted by Molière, with a bold gaze and a nose held high in the air; he was an honest fellow, with a pleasant face, lips a trifle protruding, soft-mannered and helpful, with a good round head, such as one likes to see on the shoulders of a friend. His eyes were blue, his complexion rubicund, his face plump enough so he could see his own cheeks, his body muscular, and his physical powers fully developed by the exercises of his younger days. His brown hair was somewhat tumbled; for while the ancient sculptors are said to have known eighteen methods of arranging Minerva's tresses, Passepartout was familiar with but one of fixing his own: three strokes of a large-tooth comb was enough to complete his morning rituals.

It would be rash to predict how Passepartout's lively nature would agree with Mr. Fogg. Would the new servant turn out as absolutely methodical as his master required? Experience alone could solve the question. Passepartout had been a sort of wanderer in his early years, and now yearned for peace. So far he had failed to find it, though he had already served in ten English houses. But he could not take root in any of these, and with chagrin he found his masters invariably whimsical and irregular, constantly running about the country, or on the lookout for adventure. His last master, young Lord Longferry, Member of Parliament, after spending his nights in the Haymarket taverns, was too often brought home in the morning on policemen's shoulders. Passepartout, eager to be able to respect the gentleman whom he served, ventured a mild remonstrance on such conduct, which on being ill received, he took his leave. Hearing that Mr. Phileas Fogg was looking for a servant, and that his life was one of unbroken regularity, that he neither traveled nor stayed from home overnight, he felt sure that this would be the place he was after. He presented himself, and was accepted, as has been seen.

At half-past eleven, then, Passepartout found himself alone in the house in Saville Row. He began its inspection without delay, looking it over from cellar to attic. So clean, well arranged, and solemn a mansion pleased him. It seemed to him like a snail's shell, lighted and warmed by gas, which sufficed for both these purposes. When Passepartout reached the second story, he recognized at once the room which he was to inhabit, and he was well pleased with it. Electric bells and speaking-tubes afforded communication with the lower stories. On the mantel stood an electric clock, precisely like that in Mr. Fogg's bedchamber, both beating the same second at the same instant. "That's good, that'll do," said Passepartout to himself.

He suddenly observed, hung over the clock, a card which, upon inspection, proved to be a program of the daily routine of the house. It included—from eight in the morning, exactly at which hour Phileas Fogg rose, till half-past eleven, when he left the house for the Reform Club—all the details of service, the tea and toast at twenty-three minutes past eight, the shaving-water at thirty-seven minutes past nine, and the hair-

combing at twenty minutes before ten. Everything was
regulated and foreseen that was to be done from half-
past eleven A.M. till midnight, the hour at which the
methodical gentleman retired.

Mr. Fogg's wardrobe was amply supplied and in the
best taste. Each pair of trousers, coat, and vest bore a
number, indicating the time of year and season at
which they were in turn to be laid out for wearing; and
the same system was applied to the master's shoes. In
short, the house in Saville Row, which must have been
a very temple of disorder and unrest under the illus-
trious but dissipated Sheridan, was coziness, comfort,
and method idealized. There was no study, nor were
there books, which would have been quite useless to
Mr. Fogg, for at the Reform two libraries, one of general literature and the other of law and politics, were
at his service. A moderate-sized safe stood in his bedroom, constructed so as to defy fire as well as burglars. Passepartout found neither arms nor hunting
weapons anywhere. Everything betrayed the most
tranquil and peaceable habits.

Having scrutinized the house from top to bottom,
he rubbed his hands, a broad smile overspread his features, and he said joyfully, "This is just what I wanted!
Ah, we shall get on together, Mr. Fogg and I! What a
domestic and regular gentleman! A real machine; well,
I don't mind serving a machine."

CHAPTER III

IN WHICH A CONVERSATION TAKES PLACE WHICH SEEMS LIKELY TO COST PHILEAS FOGG DEAR

Phileas Fogg, having shut the door of his house at half-past eleven, and having put his right foot before his left five hundred and seventy-five times, and his left foot before his right five hundred and seventy-six times, reached the Reform Club, an imposing edifice in Pall Mall, which could not have cost less than three million. He went at once to the dining room, the nine windows of which opened upon a tasteful garden, where the trees were already gilded with an autumn coloring. He took his place at his usual table, which had already been set for him. His lunch consisted of a side dish, a broiled fish with Reading sauce, a scarlet slice of roast beef garnished with mushrooms, a rhubarb and gooseberry tart, and a slice of Cheshire cheese, the whole being washed down with several cups of tea, for which the Reform is famous. He rose at thirteen minutes to one, and directed his steps toward the main salon, a sumptuous room adorned with lavishly framed paintings. A servant handed him an uncut *Times*, which he proceeded to cut with a skill which betrayed familiarity with this delicate operation. The perusal of this paper absorbed Phileas Fogg until a quarter before four, while the *Standard*, his next task, occupied him till the dinner hour. Dinner went as lunch had, and Mr. Fogg reappeared in the reading room and sat down to the *Pall Mall* at twenty minutes before six. Half an hour later several members of the Reform came in and drew up to the fireplace, where a coal fire was burning steadily. They were Mr. Fogg's usual partners at whist: Andrew Stuart, an engineer; John Sullivan and Samuel Fallentin, bankers; Thomas Flanagan, a brewer; and Gauthier Ralph, one of the directors of the Bank of England. All were rich and highly respectable, even in a club which counts among its members the princes of English trade and finance.

"Well, Ralph," said Thomas Flanagan, "what about that robbery?"

"Oh," replied Stuart, "the bank will lose the money."

"On the contrary," broke in Ralph, "I hope we may put our hands on the robber. Skillful detectives have been sent to all the principal ports of America and the Continent, and he'll be a clever fellow if he slips through their fingers."

"But have you got the robber's description?" asked Stuart.

"In the first place, he is no robber at all," returned Ralph, positively.

"What! a fellow who makes off with fifty-five thousand pounds, no robber?"

"No."

"Perhaps he's a manufacturer, then."

"The *Daily Telegraph* says that he is a gentleman."

It was Phileas Fogg, whose head now emerged from behind his newspapers, who made this remark. He bowed to his friends, and entered into the conversation. The affair which formed its subject, and which was the talk of the town, had occurred three days before at the Bank of England. A package of bank notes, valuing fifty-five thousand pounds, had been taken from the table of the principal cashier who had been engaged in registering the receipt of three shillings and sixpence. Of course he could not have his eyes everywhere. Let it be known that the Bank of England shows a touching confidence in the honesty of the public. There are neither guards nor gratings to protect its treasures, and gold, silver, and bank notes are freely exposed, at the mercy of the first comer. A keen observer of English customs relates that, being in one of the rooms of the Bank one day, he had the curiosity to examine a gold ingot weighing some seven or eight pounds. He took it up, scrutinized it, passed it to his neighbor, he to the next man, and so on until the ingot, going from hand to hand, was transferred to the end of a dark entry. It did not return to its place for half an hour. Meanwhile, the cashier had not so much as raised his head. But in the present instance things had not gone so smoothly. The package of notes not being found when five o'clock sounded from the ponderous clock in the "drawing office," the amount was passed to the account of profit and loss. As soon as the robbery was discovered, select detectives hastened off to Liverpool, Glasgow, Havre, Suez, Brindisi, New York, and other ports, inspired by the promise of a reward of two thousand pounds and five per cent on the sum that might be recovered. Detectives were also charged with narrowly watching those who arrived at or left London by rail, and a judicial examination was at once entered upon.

There were real grounds for supposing, as the *Daily Telegraph* said, that the thief did not belong to a professional band. On the day of the robbery a well-dressed gentleman of polished manners, and with a well-to-do air, had been observed going to and fro in the paying room, where the crime was committed. A description of him was easily procured and sent to the detectives; and some good minds, of whom Ralph was one, hoped that the thief would not escape. The papers and clubs were full of the affair, and everywhere people were discussing the probabilities of a successful pursuit. The Reform Club was especially agitated, one of its members being a Bank official.

Ralph was convinced the search wouldn't be in vain, for he thought that the prize offered would greatly stimulate the detectives' zeal and activity. But Stuart was far from sharing this confidence; and as they sat at the whist table, they continued to argue the matter. Stuart and Flanagan played together, while Phileas Fogg had Fallentin for his partner. As the game proceeded the conversation ceased, except between the rubbers, when it revived again.

"I maintain," said Stuart, "that the chances are in favor of the thief, who must be a shrewd fellow."

"Well, but where can he fly to?" asked Ralph. "No country is safe for him."

"Pshaw!"

"Where could he go, then?"

"Oh, I don't know that. The world is big enough."

"It was once," said Phileas Fogg, in a low tone. "Cut, sir," he added, handing the cards to Thomas Flanagan.

The discussion fell during the rubber, after which Stuart took up its thread.

"What do you mean by 'once'? Has the world grown smaller?"

"Certainly," returned Ralph. "I agree with Mr. Fogg. The world *has* grown smaller, since a man can now go around it ten times more quickly than a hundred years ago. And that is why the search for this thief will more likely succeed."

"And also why the thief can get away more easily."

"Be so good as to play, Mr. Stuart," said Phileas Fogg.

But the incredulous Stuart was not convinced, and when the hand was finished, said eagerly: "You have a strange way, Ralph, of proving that the world has grown smaller. So, because you can go around it in three months—"

"In eighty days," interrupted Phileas Fogg.

"That is true, gentlemen," added John Sullivan. "only eighty days, now that the section between Rothal and Allahabad, on the Great Indian Peninsula Railway, has been opened. Here is the estimate made by the *Daily Telegraph:*—

From London to Suez *via* Mont Cenis and Brindisi, by rail and steamboats	7 days.
From Suez to Bombay, by steamer	13 "
From Bombay to Calcutta, by rail	3 "
From Calcutta to Hong Kong, by steamer	13 "
From Hong Kong to Yokohama (Japan), by steamer	6 "
From Yokohama to San Francisco, by steamer	22 days.
From San Francisco to New York, by rail	7 "
From New York to London, by steamer and rail	9 "
Total	80 days.

"Yes, in eighty days!" exclaimed Stuart, who in his excitement made a false deal. "But that doesn't take into account bad weather, contrary winds, ship-wrecks, railway accidents, and so on."

"All included," returned Phileas Fogg, continuing to play despite the discussion.

"But suppose the Hindus or Indians pull up the rails," replied Stuart; "suppose they stop the trains, pillage the luggage vans, and scalp the passengers!"

"All included," calmly retorted Fogg, adding, as he threw down the cards, "Two trumps."

Stuart, whose turn it was to deal, gathered them up,

and went on: "You are right theoretically, Mr. Fogg, but in practice—"

"In practice also, Mr. Stuart."

"I'd like to see you do it in eighty days."

"It depends on you. Shall we go?"

"Heaven preserve me! But I would wager four thousand pounds that such a journey, made under these conditions, is impossible."

"Quite possible, on the contrary," returned Mr. Fogg.

"Well, make it, then!"

"The journey around the world in eighty days?"

"Yes."

"I should like nothing better."

"When?"

"At once. Only I warn you that I shall do it at your expense."

"It's absurd!" cried Stuart, who was beginning to be annoyed at the persistence of his friend. "Come, let's go on with the game."

"Deal over again, then," said Phileas Fogg. "There's a false deal."

Stuart took up the pack with a feverish hand; then suddenly put it down again.

"Well, Mr. Fogg," said he, "it shall be so: I will wager the four thousand on it."

"Calm down, my dear Stuart," said Fallentin. "It's only a joke."

"When I say I'll wager," returned Stuart, "I mean it."

"All right," said Mr. Fogg; and, turning to the others, he continued, "I have a deposit of twenty thousand at Baring's which I will willingly risk."

"Twenty thousand pounds!" cried Sullivan. "Twenty thousand pounds, which you would lose by a single unforeseen delay!"

"The unforeseen does not exist," quietly replied Phileas Fogg.

"But, Mr. Fogg, eighty days are only the estimate of the least possible time in which the journey can be made."

"A well-used minimum is sufficient."

"But, in order not to exceed it, you must jump mathematically from the trains upon the steamers, and from the steamers upon the trains again."

"I will jump—mathematically."

"You are joking."

"A true Englishman doesn't joke when he is talking about so serious a thing as a wager," replied Phileas Fogg, solemnly. "I will bet twenty thousand pounds against anyone who wishes, that I will go around the world in eighty days or less; in nineteen hundred and twenty hours, or a hundred and fifteen thousand two hundred minutes. Do you accept?"

"We accept," replied Messrs. Stuart, Fallentin, Sullivan, Flanagan, and Ralph, after consulting each other.

"Good," said Mr. Fogg. "The train leaves for Dover at a quarter before nine. I will take it."

"This very evening?" asked Stuart.

"This very evening," returned Phileas Fogg. He took out and consulted a pocket calendar, and added, "As today is Wednesday, the second of October, I shall be due in London, in this very room of the Reform Club, on Saturday, the twenty-first of December, at a quarter before nine P.M., or else the twenty thousand pounds, now deposited in my name at Baring's will belong to you, in fact and in right, gentlemen. Here is a check for the amount."

A memorandum of the wager was at once drawn up and signed by the six parties, during which Phileas Fogg preserved a stoic composure. He certainly did not bet to win, and had only staked the twenty thousand pounds, half of his fortune, because he foresaw that he might have to spend the other half to carry out this difficult, not to say unattainable, project. As for his antagonists, they seemed much agitated; not so much by the value of their stake, as because they had some scruples about betting under conditions so difficult to their friend.

The clock struck seven, and the party offered to stop the game so that Mr. Fogg might make his preparations for departure.

"I am always ready!" was his tranquil response. "Diamonds are trumps. Be so good as to play, gentlemen."

CHAPTER IV

IN WHICH PHILEAS FOGG ASTOUNDS PASSEPARTOUT, HIS SERVANT

Having won twenty guineas at whist, and taken leave of his friends, Phileas Fogg, at twenty-five minutes past seven, left the Reform Club.

Passepartout, who had conscientiously studied the list of his duties, was more than surprised to see his master, guilty of being off schedule, appear at this unaccustomed hour; for, according to rule, he was not due in Saville Row until precisely midnight.

Mr. Fogg went to his bedroom, and called, "Passepartout!"

Passepartout did not reply. It could not be he who was called; it was not the right hour.

"Passepartout!" repeated Mr. Fogg, without raising his voice.

Passepartout made his appearance.

"I've called you twice," observed his master.

"But it is not midnight," responded the other, showing his watch.

"I know it; I don't blame you. We start for Dover and Calais in ten minutes."

A puzzled grin overspread Passepartout's round face; clearly he had not understood his master.

"Monsieur is going to leave home?"

"Yes," returned Phileas Fogg. "We are going around the world."

Passepartout opened wide his eyes, raised his eyebrows, held up his hands, and seemed about to collapse, so overcome was he with stupefied astonishment.

"Around the world!" he murmured.

"In eighty days," responded Mr. Fogg. "So we haven't a moment to lose."

"But the trunks?" gasped Passepartout, unconsciously swaying his head from right to left.

"We'll have no trunks; only an overnight bag, with two shirts and three pairs of stockings for me, and the same for you. We'll buy our clothes on the way. Bring down my mackintosh and traveling blanket, and some good shoes, though we shall do little walking. Make haste!"

Passepartout tried to reply, but could not. He went out, went up to his own room, fell into a chair, and muttered: "That's too much! And I, who wanted to remain quiet!"

He mechanically set about making the preparations for departure. Around the world in eighty days! Was his master a fool? No. Was this a joke, then? They were going to Dover; good. To Calais; good again. After all, Passepartout, who had been away from France five years, would not be sorry to set foot on his native soil again. Perhaps they would go as far as Paris, and it would do his eyes good to see Paris once more. But surely a gentleman so sparing of his steps would stop there; no doubt—but, then, it was nonetheless true that he was going away, this person who had been so sedentary!

By eight o'clock Passepartout had packed the modest bag containing the wardrobes of his master and himself. Then, still troubled in mind, he carefully shut the door of his room, and joined Mr. Fogg.

Mr. Fogg was quite ready. Under his arm might have been observed a red-bound copy of *Bradshaw's Continental Railway Steam Transit and General Guide*, with its timetables showing the arrival and departure of streamers and railways. He took the bag, opened it, and slipped into it a goodly roll of Bank of England notes, which would be honored wherever he might go.

"You have forgotten nothing?" he asked.

"Nothing, monsieur."

"My mackintosh and my blanket?"

"Here they are."

"Good. Take this bag—" (handing it to Passepartout). "Take good care of it, for there are twenty thousand pounds in it."

Passepartout nearly dropped the bag, as if the twenty thousand pounds were in gold, and weighed him down.

Master and servant then went downstairs, the street door was double locked, and at the end of Saville Row they took a cab and drove rapidly to Charing Cross. The cab stopped before the railway station at twenty minutes past eight. Passepartout jumped off the box and followed his master, who, after paying the cabman, was about to enter the station, when a poor beggar, with a child in her arms, her naked feet smeared with mud, her head covered with a wretched bonnet, from which hung a tattered feather, and her shoulders shrouded in a ragged shawl, approached, and mournfully asked for alms.

Mr. Fogg took out the twenty guineas he had just won at whist, and handed them to the beggar, saying, "Here, my good woman. I'm glad that I met you," and passed on.

Passepartout had a moist sensation about the eyes; his master's action had won his heart.

Two first-class tickets for Paris were speedily purchased, and as Mr. Fogg was crossing the station to the train, he saw his five friends of the Reform.

"Well, gentlemen," said he, "I'm off, you see. If you examine my passport when I get back, you will be able to judge whether I have accomplished the journey agreed upon."

"Oh, that would be quite unnecessary, Mr. Fogg,"

said Ralph, politely. "We will trust your word, as a gentleman of honor."

"You do not forget when you are due in London again?" asked Stuart.

"In eighty days; on Saturday, the twenty first of December, 1872, at a quarter before nine P.M. Goodbye, gentlemen."

Phileas Fogg and his servant sat in a first-class carriage at twenty minutes before nine. Five minutes later the whistle blew and the train slowly glided out of the station.

The night was dark, and a fine, steady rain was falling. Phileas Fogg, snugly ensconced in his corner, did not open his mouth. Passepartout, not yet recovered from his stupefaction, clung mechanically to the bag, with its enormous treasure.

Just as the train was whirling through Sydenham, Passepartout suddenly uttered a cry of despair.

"What's the matter?" asked Mr. Fogg.

"Alas! In my hurry—I—forgot—"

"What?"

"To turn off the gas in my room!"

"Very well, young man," returned Mr. Fogg, coolly; "it will burn—at your expense."

CHAPTER V

In Which a New Species of Bonds Appears on the London Exchange

Phileas Fogg rightly suspected that his departure from London would create a lively sensation at the West End. The news of the bet spread through the Reform Club, and afforded an exciting topic of conversation to its members. From the Club it soon got into the papers throughout England. The boasted "tour of the world" was talked about, disputed, argued with as much warmth as if the subject were another Alabama claim. Some took sides with Phileas Fogg, but the large majority shook their heads and came out against him; it was absurd, impossible, they declared, that the tour of the world could be made, except theoretically and on paper, in this minimum of time, and with the existing means of traveling. The *Times, Standard, Morning Post,* and *Daily News,* and twenty other highly respectable newspapers declared themselves against Mr. Fogg; the *Daily Telegraph* alone hesitatingly supported him. People in general thought him a lunatic, and blamed his Reform Club friends for having accepted a wager which betrayed the mental aberration of its proposer.

Articles no less passionate than logical appeared on the question, for geography is one of the pet subjects of the English; and the columns devoted to Phileas Fogg's venture were eagerly devoured by all classes of readers. At first some rash individuals, principally women, took up his cause, which became still more popular when the *Illustrated London News* came out with his portrait, copied from a photograph in the Reform Club. A few readers of the *Daily Telegraph* even dared to say, "Why not, after all? Stranger things have come to pass."

At last a long article appeared, on the 7th of October, in the bulletin of the Royal Geographical Society, which treated the question from every point of view and demonstrated the utter folly of the enterprise.

Everything, it said, was against the travelers, every obstacle imposed alike by man and by nature. A miraculous agreement of the times of departure and arrival, which was impossible, was absolutely necessary to his success. He might, perhaps, reckon on the arrival of trains at the designated hours, in Europe, where the distances were relatively moderate; but when he calculated upon crossing India in three days, and the United States in seven, could he rely beyond misgiving upon accomplishing his task? There were accidents of machinery, trains derailing, collisions, bad weather, the blocking up by snow—were not all these against Phileas Fogg? Would he not find himself, when traveling by steamer in winter, at the mercy of the winds and fogs? Is it uncommon for the best ocean steamers to be two or three days behind time? But a single delay would suffice to fatally break the chain of communication. Should Phileas Fogg once miss, even by an hour, a steamer, he would have to wait for the next, and that would irrevocably render his attempt vain.

This article made a great deal of noise, and all the papers reprinted it and his stock went down sharply.

Everybody knows that England is the world of betting men, who are of a higher class than mere gamblers; to bet is in the English temperament. Not only the members of the Reform, but the general public, made heavy wagers for or against Phileas Fogg, who was set down in the betting books as if he were a race-horse. Bonds were issued, and made their appearance on the London Exchange; "Phileas Fogg bonds" were offered at par or at a premium, and a great business was done in them. But five days after the article in the bulletin of the Geographical Society appeared, the demand began to subside; "Phileas Fogg" declined. They were offered by packages, at first of five, then of ten, until at last nobody would take less than twenty, fifty, a hundred!

Lord Albemarle, an elderly paralytic gentleman, was now the only advocate of Phileas Fogg left. This noble lord, who was fastened to his chair, would have given his fortune to be able to go around the world, if it took ten years. He bet five thousand pounds on Phileas Fogg. When the folly as well as the uselessness of the adventure was pointed out to him, he contented himself with replying, "If the thing is feasible, the first to do it ought to be an Englishman."

The Fogg party dwindled more and more, everybody was going against him, and the bets stood a hundred and fifty and two hundred to one. And a week after his departure, an incident occurred which deprived him of backers at any price.

The commissioner of police was sitting in his office at nine o'clock one evening, when the following telegram was put into his hands:—

Suez to London.

ROWAN, COMMISSIONER OF POLICE, SCOTLAND YARD: I've found the bank robber, Phileas Fogg. Send without delay warrant of arrest to Bombay.

Fix, Detective.

The effect of this telegram was instantaneous. The honorable gentleman disappeared to give place to the bank robber. His photograph, which was hung with those of the rest of the members at the Reform Club, was minutely examined, and it corresponded, feature by feature, to the description of the robber which had been provided to the police. The mysterious habits of Phileas Fogg were recalled; his solitary ways, his sudden departure. And it seemed clear that, in undertaking a tour around the world on the pretext of a wager, he had no other end in view than to elude the detectives and throw them off his track.

CHAPTER VI

In Which Fix, the Detective, Betrays a Very Natural Impatience

The circumstances under which this telegram about Phileas Fogg was sent were as follows:—

The steamer *Mongolia*, belonging to the Peninsula and Oriental Company, built of iron, of two thousand eight hundred tons burden, and five hundred horse-power, was due at eleven o'clock A.M. on Wednesday, the 9th of October, in Suez. The *Mongolia* plied regularly between Brindisi and Bombay via the Suez Canal, and was one of the fastest steamers belonging to the company, always making more than ten knots an hour between Brindisi and Suez and nine and a half between Suez and Bombay.

Two men were promenading up and down the wharves among the crowd of natives and strangers pushing at this once-small village—now, thanks to the enterprise of M. Lesseps, a fast-growing town. One was the British consul in Suez, who, despite the prophecies of the English Government, and the unfavorable predictions of Stephenson, was in the habit of seeing, from his office window, English ships daily passing to and fro on the great canal, by which the old round-about route from England to India by the Cape of Good Hope was shortened by half. The other was a small, thin man, with a nervous, intelligent face and bright eyes peering out from under eyebrows which he was incessantly twitching. He was just now manifesting unmistakable signs of impatience, nervously pacing up and down, and unable to stand still for a moment. This was Fix, one of the detectives who had been despatched from England in search of the bank robber. It was his task to narrowly watch every passenger who arrived in Suez, and to follow up all who seemed to be suspicious characters, or bore a resemblance to the description of the criminal, which he had received two days before from the police headquarters in London. The detective was evidently stimulated by the splendid reward, and awaited with a feverish impatience, easy to understand, the arrival of the steamer *Mongolia*.

"So you say, consul," asked he for the twentieth time, "that this steamer won't be long?"

"No, Mr. Fix," replied the consul. "She was spotted yesterday in Port Said, and the rest of the way is of no account to such a craft. I repeat that the *Mongolia* has always been in advance of the time required by the company's regulations, and won the prize awarded for being ahead of time."

"Does she come directly from Brindisi?"

"Directly from Brindisi; she takes on the Indian mail there, and she left there Saturday at five P.M. Have patience, Mr. Fix, she will not be late. But really I don't see how, from the description you have, you will be able to recognize your man, even if he is on board the *Mongolia*."

"A man rather feels the presence of these fellows, consul, than recognizes them. You must have a scent for them, and a scent is like a sixth sense which combines hearing, seeing, and smelling. I've arrested more than one of these gentlemen in my time, and if my thief is on board, I'll answer for it, he'll not slip through my fingers."

"I hope so, Mr. Fix, for it was a heavy robbery."

"A magnificent robbery, consul; fifty-five thousand

pounds! We don't often have such windfalls. Burglars are getting to be so petty nowadays! A fellow gets hung for a handful of shillings!''

"Mr. Fix," said the consul, "I like your way of talking, and hope you'll succeed; but I fear you will find it far from easy. Don't you see, the description which you have there has a singular resemblance to an honest man?''

"Consul," remarked the detective, dogmatically, "great robbers *always* resemble honest folks. Fellows who have rascally faces have only one course to take, and that is to remain honest; otherwise they would be arrested off-hand. The artistic thing is to unmask honest countenances. It's no light task, I admit, but a real art.''

Mr. Fix evidently was somewhat conceited.

Little by little the scene on the quay became more animated. Sailors of various nations, merchants, ship-brokers, porters, fellahs, bustled to and fro. Obviously the arrival of the boat was close. The weather was clear and slightly chilly. The minarets of the town loomed above the houses in the pale rays of the sun. A jetty pier, some two thousand yards long, extended into the roadstead. A number of fishing smacks and coasting boats, some retaining the fantastic fashion of ancient galleys, were discernible on the Red Sea.

As he passed among the busy crowd, Fix, according to habit, scrutinized the passersby with a keen, rapid glance.

It was now half-past ten.

"The steamer doesn't come!" he exclaimed, as the port clock struck.

"She can't be far off now," answered his companion.

"How long will she stop in Suez?"

"Four hours; long enough to get in her coal. It is thirteen hundred and ten miles from Suez to Aden, at the other end of the Red Sea, and she has to take in a fresh coal supply.''

"And does she go from Suez directly to Bombay?''

"Without putting in anywhere.''

"Good,'' said Fix. "If the robber is on board, he will no doubt get off at Suez, so as to reach the Dutch or French colonies in Asia by some other route. He ought to know that he would not be safe an hour in India, which is English soil.''

"Unless,'' objected the consul, "he is exceptionally shrewd. An English criminal, you know, is always better concealed in London than anywhere else.''

This observation offered the detective food for thought, and meanwhile the consul went away to his office. Fix, left alone, was more impatient than ever, having a premonition that the robber was on board the *Mongolia*. If he had indeed left London intending to reach the New World, he would naturally take the route via India, which was less watched and more difficult to watch than that of the Atlantic. But Fix's reflections were soon interrupted by a succession of sharp whistles, which announced the arrival of the *Mongolia*. The porters and fellahs rushed down the quay, and a dozen boats pushed off from the shore to go and meet the steamer. Soon her gigantic hull appeared, passing along between the banks, and eleven o'clock struck as she anchored in the docks. She brought an unusual number of passengers, some of whom remained on deck to scan the picturesque panorama of the town, while the greater part disembarked in the boats and landed on the quay.

Fix carefully examined each face and figure which made its appearance. Presently one of the passengers, after vigorously pushing his way through the importunate crowd of porters, came up to him, and politely asked if he could point out the English consulate, at the same time showing a passport which he wished to have visaed. Fix instinctively took the passport, and

with a rapid glance read the description of its bearer.
An involuntary motion of surprise nearly escaped him,
for the description in the passport was identical with
that of the bank robber which he had received from
Scotland Yard.

"Is this your passport?" he asked.

"No, it's my master's."

"And your master is—"

"He stayed on board."

"But he must go to the consulate in person, so as
to establish his identity."

"Oh, is that necessary?"

"Quite indispensable."

"And where is the consulate?"

"There on the corner of the square," said Fix,
pointing to a house two hundred steps off.

"I'll go and get my master, who won't be much
pleased, however, to be disturbed."

The passenger bowed to Fix, and returned to the
steamer.

CHAPTER VII

WHICH ONCE MORE DEMONSTRATES
THE USELESSNESS OF PASSPORTS AS
AIDS TO DETECTIVES

The detective went down the quay and rapidly made his way to the consul's office, where he was at once ushered in to see that official.

"Consul," said he, without preamble, "I have strong reasons for believing that my man is a passenger on the *Mongolia*." And he narrated what had just passed concerning the passport.

"Well, Mr. Fix," replied the consul, "I shall not be sorry to see the rascal's face; but perhaps he won't come here—that is, if he is the person you suppose him to be. A robber doesn't quite like to leave traces of his flight behind him; and besides, he is not obliged to have his passport countersigned."

"If he is as shrewd as I think he is, consul, he will come."

"To have his passport visaed?"

"Yes. Passports are only good for annoying honest folks and aiding in the flight of rogues. I assure you this one will be in order; but I hope you will not visa it."

"Why not? If the passport is genuine, I have no right to refuse."

"Still, I must keep this man here until I can get a warrant from London to arrest him."

"Ah, that's your business. But I cannot—"

The consul did not finish his sentence, for as he spoke a knock was heard at the door, and two strangers entered, one of whom was the servant whom Fix had met on the quay. The other, who was his master, held out his passport with the request that the consul would do him the favor to visa it. The consul took the document and carefully read it, while Fix observed the stranger, or rather devoured him with his eyes from a corner of the room.

"You are Mr. Phileas Fogg?" said the consul, after reading the passport.

"I am."

"And this man is your servant?"

"He is; a Frenchman, named Passepartout."

"You are from London?"

"Yes."

"And you are going—"

"To Bombay."

"Very good, sir. You know that a visa is useless, and that no passport is required?"

"I know it, sir," replied Phileas Fogg; "but I wish to prove, by your visa, that I came by Suez."

"Very well, sir."

The consul proceeded to sign and date the passport, after which he added his official seal. Mr. Fogg paid the customary fee, coolly bowed, and went out, followed by his servant.

"Well?" queried the detective.

"Well, he looks and acts like a perfectly honest man," replied the consul.

"Possibly; but that is not the question. Do you think, consul, that this phlegmatic gentleman resembles, feature by feature, the robber whose description I have received?"

"I concede that; but then, you know, all descriptions—"

"I'll get to the bottom of this," interrupted Fix.

"The servant seems to me less mysterious than the master; besides, he's a Frenchman, and can't help talking. Excuse me for a little while, consul."

Fix started off in search of Passepartout.

Meanwhile Mr. Fogg, after leaving the consulate, returned to the quay, gave some orders to Passepartout, went off to the *Mongolia* in a boat, and went down to his cabin. He took up his notebook, which contained the following memoranda:—

"Left London, Wednesday, October 2nd, at 8:45 P.M.

"Reached Paris, Thursday, October 3rd, at 7:20 A.M.

"Left Paris, Thursday, at 8:40 A.M.

"Reached Turin by Mont Cenis, Friday, October 4th, at 6:35 A.M.

"Left Turin, Friday, at 7:20 A.M.

"Arrived at Brindisi, Saturday, October 5th, at 4 P.M.

"Sailed on the *Mongolia,* Saturday, at 5 P.M.

"Reached Suez, Wednesday, October 9th, at 11 A.M.

"Total of hours spent, 158½; or, in days, six days and a half."

These dates were inscribed in an itinerary divided into columns, indicating the month, the day of the month, and the day for the stipulated and actual arrivals at each principal point—Paris, Brindisi, Suez, Bombay, Calcutta, Singapore, Hong Kong, Yokohama, San Francisco, New York, and London—from the 2nd of October to the 21st of December; and giving a space for setting down the gain made or the loss suffered on arrival at each locality. This methodical record thus contained an account of everything needed, and Mr. Fogg always knew whether he was behind or ahead of his schedule. On this Friday, October 9th, he noted his arrival in Suez, and observed that he had as yet neither gained nor lost. He sat down quietly to lunch in his cabin, never once thinking of inspecting the town, being one of those Englishmen who are apt to see foreign countries through the eyes of their servants.

CHAPTER VIII

IN WHICH PASSEPARTOUT TALKS RATHER MORE, PERHAPS, THAN IS PRUDENT

Fix soon joined Passepartout, who was lounging and looking about on the quay, since he did not feel, like Fogg, that he was obliged not to see anything.

"Well, my friend," said the detective, coming up with him, "is your passport visaed?"

"Ah, it's you, is it, monsieur?" answered Passepartout. "Thanks, yes, the passport is in order."

"And you are looking about you?"

"Yes; but we travel so fast that I seem to be journeying in a dream. So this is Suez?"

"Yes."

"In Egypt?"

"Certainly, in Egypt."

"And in Africa?"

"In Africa."

"In Africa!" repeated Passepartout. "Just think, monsieur, I had no idea that we should go farther than Paris. And all that I saw of Paris was between twenty minutes past seven and twenty minutes before nine in the morning, between the North and the Lyons stations, through the windows of a car and in a driving rain! How I regret not having seen once more Père laChaise and the circus in the Champs Elysées!"

"You are in a great hurry, then?"

"I am not, but my master is. By the way, I must buy some shoes and shirts. We came away without trunks, only with an overnight bag."

"I will show you an excellent shop for getting what you want."

"Really, monsieur, you are very kind."

And they walked off together, Passepartout chatting volubly as they went along.

"Above all," said he, "don't let me miss the steamer."

"You have plenty of time; it's only twelve o'clock."

Passepartout pulled out his big watch. "Twelve!" he exclaimed; "why it's only eight minutes before ten."

"Your watch is slow."

"My watch? A family watch, monsieur, which has come down from my great-grandfather! It doesn't vary five minutes in the year, it's a perfect chronometer."

"I see how it is," said Fix. "You have kept London time, which is two hours behind that of Suez. You ought to regulate your watch at noon in each country."

"I! regulate my watch! Never!"

"Well, then, it will not agree with the sun."

"Too bad for the sun, monsieur. The sun will be wrong, then!"

And the good fellow returned the watch to its fob with a defiant gesture. After a few minutes' silence, Fix resumed: "You left London hastily, then?"

"I rather think so! Last Wednesday at eight o'clock in the evening, Monsieur Fogg came home from his club, and three-quarters of an hour afterwards we were off."

"But where is your master going?"

"Always straight ahead. He is going around the world."

"Around the world?" cried Fix.

"Yes, and in eighty days! He says it is on a wager; but, between us, I don't believe a word of it. That wouldn't be common sense. There's something else in the wind.''

''Ah! Mr. Fogg is a character, is he?''

''I should say he is.''

''Is he rich?''

''No doubt, for he is carrying an enormous sum in brand-new bank notes with him. And he doesn't spare the money on the way, either: he has offered a large reward to the engineer of the *Mongolia* if he gets us to Bombay well ahead of time.''

''And you have known your master a long time?''

''Why, no. I entered his service the very day we left London.''

The effect of these replies upon the already suspicious and excited detective may be imagined. The hasty departure from London soon after the robbery; the large sum carried by Mr. Fogg; his eagerness to reach distant countries; the pretext of an eccentric and foolhardy bet—all confirmed Fix in his theory. He continued to pump poor Passepartout, and learned that he really knew little or nothing of his master, who lived a solitary existence in London, was said to be rich, though no one knew where his riches came from, and was mysterious and impenetrable in his affairs and habits. Fix felt sure that Phileas Fogg would not land in Suez, but was really going on to Bombay.

''Is Bombay far from here?'' asked Passepartout.

''Pretty far. It is a ten days' voyage by sea.''

''And in what country is Bombay?''

''India.''

''In Asia?''

''Certainly.''

''Oh gosh! I was going to tell you—there's one thing that worries me—my burner!''

''What burner?''

''My gas burner, which I forgot to turn off, and which is at this moment burning—at my expense. I have calculated, monsieur, that I lose two shillings every twenty four hours, exactly sixpence more than I earn; and you will understand that the longer our journey—''

Did Fix pay any attention to Passepartout's tróuble about the gas? It is not probable. He was not listening, but was reaching a decision. Passepartout and he had now arrived at the shop, where Fix left his companion to make his purchases, after recommending him not to miss the steamer, and hurried back to the consulate. Now that he was fully convinced, Fix had quite recovered his equanimity.

"Consul," said he, "I have no longer any doubt. I have spotted my man. He passes himself off as an eccentric who is going around the world in eighty days."

"Then he's a sharp fellow," returned the consul, "and counts on returning to London after putting the police of the two continents off his track."

"We'll see about that," replied Fix.

"But are you not mistaken?"

"I am not mistaken."

"Why was this robber so anxious to prove, by the visa, that he had passed through Suez?"

"Why? I have no idea; but listen to me."

He reported in a few words the most important parts of his conversation with Passepartout.

"In short," said the consul, "appearances are wholly against this man. And what are you going to do?"

"Send a telegram to London for a warrant of arrest to be despatched instantly to Bombay, take passage on board the *Mongolia*, follow my rogue to India, and there, on English ground, arrest him politely, with my warrant in hand, and my hand on his shoulder."

Having uttered these words with a cool, careless air, the detective took leave of the consul, and went to the telegraph office, whence he set the telegram mentioned to the London police office. A quarter of an hour later found Fix, with a small bag in his hand, proceeding on board the *Mongolia;* and soon, the noble steamer rode out at full steam upon the waters of the Red Sea.

CHAPTER IX

In Which the Red Sea and the Indian Ocean Prove Propitious to the Designs of Phileas Fogg

The distance between Suez and Aden is precisely thirteen hundred and ten miles, and the regulations of the company allow the steamers one hundred and thirty-eight hours in which to cross it. The *Mongolia*, thanks to the vigorous exertions of the engineer, seemed likely, so rapid was her speed, to reach her destination considerably within that time. The greater part of the passengers from Brindisi were bound for India—some for Bombay, others for Calcutta by way of Bombay, the nearest route thither, now that a railway crosses the Indian peninsula. Among the passengers were a number of officials and military officers of various ranks, the latter being either attached to the regular British forces, or commanding the Sepoy troops and receiving high salaries ever since the central government had assumed the powers of the East India Company; for the sublieutenants got £280, brigadiers, £2400, and generals of division, £4000. What with the military men, a number of rich young Englishmen on their travels, and the hospitable efforts of the purser, the time passed quickly on the *Mongolia*. The best of fare was spread upon the cabin tables at breakfast, lunch, dinner, and the eight o'clock supper, and the ladies scrupulously changed their dresses twice a day; and the hours were whiled away, when the sea was tranquil, with music, dancing, and games.

But the Red Sea is full of caprice, and often boisterous, like most long and narrow gulfs. When the wind came in from the African or Asian coast, the *Mongolia*, with her long hull, would roll fearfully. Then the ladies speedily would disappear below; the pianos would be silent; singing and dancing suddenly would cease. Yet the good ship ploughed straight on, unhindered by wind or wave, towards the straits of Bab-el-Mandeb.

What was Phileas Fogg doing all this time? It might be thought that, in his anxiety, he would be constantly watching the changes of the wind, the disorderly raging of the billows—every chance, in short, which might force the *Mongolia* to slacken her speed, and thus interrupt his journey. But if he thought of these possibilities, he did not betray the fact by any outward sign.

Always the same impassive member of the Reform Club, whom no incident could surprise, as unvarying as the ship's chronometers, and seldom having the curiosity even to go upon the deck, he passed through the memorable scenes of the Red Sea with cold indifference. He did not care to recognize the historic towns and villages which, along its borders, raised their picturesque outlines against the sky. And he betrayed no fear of the dangers of the Arabic Gulf, which the old historians always spoke of with horror, and upon which the ancient navigators never ventured without appeasing the gods with ample sacrifices. How did this eccentric personage pass his time on the *Mongolia?* He ate his four hearty meals every day, regardless of the most persistent rolling and pitching on the part of the steamer; and he played whist.

Yes! he had found partners as enthusiastic in the game as himself. A tax collector, on the way to his post in Goa; the Rev. Decimus Smith, returning to his parish in Bombay; and a brigadier-general of the English army, who was about to rejoin his brigade in Benares, made up the party, and, with Mr. Fogg, played whist by the hour in absorbing silence.

As for Passepartout, he, too, had escaped seasickness, and took his meals conscientiously in the forward cabin. He rather enjoyed the voyage, for he was well fed and well lodged, saw the world, and consoled himself with the delusion that his master's whim would end in Bombay. He was pleased, on the day after leaving Suez, to find on deck the obliging person with whom he had chatted on the quays.

"If I am not mistaken," he said, approaching this person with his most amiable smile, "you are the gentleman who so kindly volunteered to guide me in Suez?"

"Ah! I quite recognize you. You are the servant of the strange Englishman—"

'Just so, Monsieur—"

"Fix."

"Monsieur Fix," resumed Passepartout, "I'm charmed to find you on board. Where are you bound?"

"Like you, to Bombay."

"That's capital! Have you made this trip before?"

"Several times. I am one of the agents of the Peninsula Company."

"Then you know India?"

"Why—yes," replied Fix, who spoke cautiously.

"A curious place, this India?"

"Oh, very curious. Mosques, minarets, temples, fakirs, pagodas, tigers, snakes, elephants! I hope you will have ample time to see the sights."

"I hope so, Monsieur Fix. You see, a man of sound sense ought not to spend his life jumping from a steamer upon a railway train, and from a railway train upon a steamer again, pretending to go around the world in eighty days! No; you may be sure, all these gymnastics will cease in Bombay.''

''And Mr. Fogg is getting on well?'' asked Fix, in the most natural tone in the world.

''Quite well, and I too. I eat like a famished ogre; it's the sea air.''

''But I never see your master on deck.''

''Never; he hasn't the least curiosity.''

''Do you know, Mr. Passepartout, that this supposed tour in eighty days may conceal some secret errand—perhaps a diplomatic mission?''

''To be sure, Monsieur Fix, I assure you I know nothing about it, nor would I give half a crown to find out.''

After this meeting, Passepartout and Fix got into the habit of chatting together, the latter making it a point to gain the servant's confidence. He frequently offered him a glass of whiskey or pale ale in the steamer barroom, which Passepartout never failed to accept cheerfully, and, not wanting to feel indebted, offered him a round in return, mentally pronouncing Fix the best of good fellows.

Meanwhile the *Mongolia* was pushing forward rapidly; on the 13th, Mocha, surrounded by its ruined walls whereon date trees stood out, was sighted, and on the mountains beyond were growing vast coffee fields. Passepartout was delighted to behold this famous place, and thought that, with its circular walls and dismantled fort, it looked like an immense coffee cup. The following night they passed through the Strait of Bab-el-Mandeb, which means in Arabic ''The Bridge of Tears,'' and the next day they put in at Steamer Point, northwest of Aden harbor, to take in coal. This matter of fueling steamers is a serious one at such distances from the coal mines; it costs the Peninsula Company some eight hundred thousand pounds a year. In these distant seas, coal is worth three or four pounds sterling a ton.

The *Mongolia* still had sixteen hundred and fifty miles to go before reaching Bombay, and was obliged to remain four hours at Steamer Point to coal up. But this delay, as it was foreseen, did not affect Phileas Fogg's program; besides, the *Mongolia,* instead of reaching Aden on the morning of the 15th, when she was due, arrived there on the evening of the 14th, a gain of fifteen hours.

Mr. Fogg and his servant went ashore at Aden to have the passport again visaed; Fix, unobserved, followed them. The visa procured, Mr. Fogg returned on board to resume his former habits; meanwhile Passepartout, acording to his custom, strolled about among the mixed population of Somalis, Hindus, Parsees, Jews, Arabs, and Europeans who make up the twenty-five thousand inhabitants of Aden. He gazed with wonder upon the fortifications which make this place the Gibraltar of the Indian Ocean, and the vast cisterns where the English engineers were still at work, two thousand years after the engineers of Solomon.

"Very curious, *very* curious," said Passepartout to himself, on returning to the steamer. "I see that it is by no means useless to travel, if a man wants to see something new." At six P.M. the *Mongolia* slowly moved out of the roadstead, and was soon once more on the Indian Ocean. She had a hundred and sixty-eight hours in which to reach Bombay, and the sea was favorable, the wind being in the northwest, and all sails aiding the engine. The steamer rolled but little; the ladies, in fresh dresses, reappeared on deck, and the singing and dancing were resumed. The trip was being accomplished most successfully, and Passepartout was enchanted with the congenial companion which chance had secured him in the person of the delightful Fix. On Sunday, October 20th, towards noon, they came in sight of the Indian coast; two hours later the pilot came on board. A range of hills lay against the sky in the horizon, and soon the rows of palms which adorn Bombay came distinctly into view. The steamer entered the roadstead formed by the islands in the bay, and at half-past four she hauled up at the quays of Bombay.

Phileas Fogg was finishing the thirty-third rubber of the voyage, and his partner and himself having, by a bold stroke, captured all thirteen of the tricks, concluded this fine campaign with a brilliant victory.

The *Mongolia* was only due in Bombay on the 22nd; she arrived on the 20th. For Phileas Fogg this was a gain of two days since his departure from London, and he calmly entered the fact in the itinerary, in the column of gains.

CHAPTER X

IN WHICH PASSEPARTOUT IS ONLY TOO GLAD TO GET OFF WITH THE LOSS OF HIS SHOES

Everybody knows that India, the great reversed triangle of land, with its base in the north and its appex in the south, embraces fourteen hundred thousand square miles, upon which is spread unequally a population of one hundred and eighty million. The British Crown exercises a real and despotic dominion over the larger portion of this vast country, and has a governor-general stationed at Calcutta, governors at Madras, Bombay, and in Bengal, and a lieutenant-governor at Agra.

But so-called British India only embraces seven hundred thousand square miles, and a population of from one hundred to one hundred and ten million inhabitants. A considerable portion of India is still free from British authority; and there are certain ferocious rajahs in the interior who are absolutely independent. The celebrated East India Company was all-powerful from 1756, when the English first gained a foothold on the spot where now stands the city of Madras, down to the time of the great Sepoy insurrection. It gradually annexed province after province, purchasing them from the native chiefs, whom it seldom paid, and appointed the governor-general and his subordinates, civil and military. But the East India Company has now passed away, leaving the British possessions in India directly under the control of the Crown. The aspect of the country, as well as manners and distinctions of race, is changing daily.

Formerly one was obliged to travel in India by the old cumbrous methods of going on foot or on horseback, in palanquins or unwieldy coaches; now fast steamboats ply on the Indus and the Ganges, and a great railway, with branch lines joining the main line at many points on its route, crosses the peninsula from Bombay to Calcutta in three days. This railway does not run in a direct line across India. The distance between Bombay and Calcutta, as the crow flies, is only from one thousand to eleven hundred miles; but the deflections of the road increase this distance by more than a third.

The general route of the Great Indian Peninsula Railway is as follows: leaving Bombay, it passes through Salcette, crosses to the continent opposite Tannah, goes over the chain of the Western Ghauts, runs thence northeast as far as Burhampoor, skirts the nearly independent territory of Bundelcund, goes up to Allahabad, turns thence east, meeting the Ganges at Benares, then departs from the river a little, and, going southeast by Burdivan and the French town of Chandernagor, has its terminus at Calcutta.

The passengers of the *Mongolia* went ashore at halfpast four P.M.; at exactly eight the train would start for Calcutta.

Mr. Fogg, after bidding good-bye to his whist partners, left the steamer, gave his servant several errands to do, urged him to be at the station promptly at eight, and, with his regular step, which beat to the second, like an astronomical clock, directed his steps to the passport office. As for the wonders of Bombay—its famous city hall, its splendid library, its forts and docks, its bazaars, mosques, synagogues, its Armenian churches, and the noble pagoda on Malebar Hill

with its two polygonal towers—he cared not a straw to
see them. He would not contemplate the masterpieces
of Elephanta, nor its mysterious hypogea, concealed
southeast from the docks, nor those fine remains of
Buddhist architecture, the Kanherian grottoes of the
island of Salcette.

No! nothing. Having transacted his business at the
passport office, Phileas Fogg went quietly to the railway station, where he ordered dinner. Among the
dishes served up to him, the maître d'hôtel especially
recommended a certain rabbit stew on which he prided
himself.

Mr. Fogg accordingly tasted the dish, but, despite
its spicy sauce, found it far from palatable. He rang
for the maître d'hôtel and said, fixing his clear eyes
upon him, "Is this rabbit, sir?"

"Yes, my lord," the rascal boldly replied, "rabbit
from the jungles."

"And this rabbit did not mew when he was killed?"

"Mew, my lord! what, a rabbit mew! I swear to
you—"

"Be so good, maître d'hôtel, as not to swear, but
remember this: cats were formerly considered, in India, as sacred animals. Those were the good old
days."

"For the cats, my lord?"

"Perhaps for the travelers as well!"

After which Mr. Fogg quietly continued his dinner.
Fix had gone on shore shortly after Mr. Fogg, and his
first destination was the headquarters of the Bombay
police. He made himself known as a London detective, explained his business in Bombay, and his position relative to the supposed robber, and nervously
asked if a warrant had arrived from London. It had
not reached the office; indeed, there had not yet been
time for it to arrive. Fix was sorely disappointed, and
tried to obtain an order of arrest from the director of
the Bombay police. This the director refused, as the

matter concerned the London office, which alone could legally deliver the warrant. Fix did not insist, and understood he had to resign himself to await the arrival of the important document; meanwhile he was determined not to lose sight of the mysterious rogue as long as he stayed in Bombay. He did not doubt for a moment, any more than Passepartout, that Phileas Fogg would remain there, at least until it was time for the warrant to arrive.

Passepartout, however, had no sooner heard his master's orders on leaving the *Mongolia*, then he saw at once that they were to leave Bombay as they had done Suez and Paris, and that the journey would be extended at least as far as Calcutta, and perhaps beyond there. He began to ask himself if this bet that Mr. Fogg talked about was not really in good earnest, and whether fate was not in truth forcing him, despite his love of repose, around the world in eighty days!

Having purchased the usual quota of shirts and socks, he was walking about the streets, where crowds of people of many nationalities—Europeans, Persians with pointed caps, Hindus with round turbans, Sindhis with square bonnets, Parsees with black mitres, and long-robed Armenians—were collected. It happened to be the day of a Parsee festival. These descendants of the sect of Zoroaster—the most thrifty, civilized, intelligent, and austere of the East Indians, among whom are counted the richest native merchants of Bombay—were celebrating a sort of religious carnival, with processions and shows, in the midst of which Indian dancing girls, clothed in rose-colored gauze looped up with gold and silver, danced airily, but with perfect modesty, to the sound of viols and the clanging of tambourines. It is needless to say that Passepartout watched these curious ceremonies with wide eyes and gaping mouth, and that his countenance was that of the greenest booby imaginable.

Unhappily for his master, as well as himself, his

curiosity drew him farther off than he intended to go. Indeed, having seen the Parsee carnival wind away in the distance, he was turning his steps toward the station, when he happened to go by the splendid pagoda on Malebar Hill, and was seized with the unfortunate desire to see its interior. He was quite ignorant that it is forbidden to Christians to enter certain Indian temples, and that even the faithful must not go in without first leaving their shoes outside the door. It may be said here that the wise policy of the British Government severely punishes a disregard of the practices of the native religions.

Passepartout, however, thinking no harm, went in like a simple tourist, and was soon lost in admiration of the splendid Brahmin ornamentation, when suddenly he found himself sprawling on the sacred stones. He looked up to behold three enraged priests, who fell upon him, tore off his shoes, and began to beat him with loud, savage exclamations. The agile Frenchman was soon upon his feet, and lost no time in knocking down two of his long-gowned adversaries with his fists and a vigorous application of his toes; then, rushing out of the pagoda as fast as his legs could carry him, he soon escaped the third priest who had rushed after him, rousing the crowd.

At five minutes before eight, Passepartout, hatless, shoeless, and having in the squabble lost his package of shirts and socks, rushed breathlessly into the station.

Fix, who had followed Mr. Fogg to the station, and saw that he was really going to leave Bombay, was there upon the platform. He had resolved to follow the supposed robber to Calcutta, and farther, if necessary. Passepartout did not see the detective, who stood in an obscure corner; but Fix heard him relate his adventures in a few words to Mr. Fogg.

"I hope that this will not happen again," said Phileas Fogg, coolly, as he got into the train. Poor

Passepartout, quite crestfallen, followed his master without a word. Fix was about to enter another carriage, when an idea struck him which induced him to alter his plan.

"No, I'll stay," muttered he. "An offence has been committed on Indian soil. I've got my man."

Just then the locomotive gave a sharp screech, and the train disappeared into the darkness of the night.

CHAPTER XI

In Which Phileas Fogg Secures a Curious Means of Conveyance at a Fabulous Price

The train had started punctually. Among the passengers were a number of officers, Government officials, and opium and indigo merchants whose business called them to the eastern coast. Passepartout rode in the same carriage with his master, and a third passenger occupied a seat opposite them. This was Sir Francis Cromarty, one of Mr. Fogg's whist partners on the *Mongolia*, now on his way to join his corps at Benares. Sir Francis was a tall, fair man of fifty, who had greatly distinguished himself in the last Sepoy revolt. He made India his home, only paying brief visits to England at rare intervals; and was almost as familiar as a native with the customs, history, and character of India and its people. But Phileas Fogg, who was not traveling, but only describing a circumference, did not bother to inquire into these subjects; he was a solid body, traversing an orbit around the terrestrial globe according to the laws of rational mechanics. He was at this moment calculating in his mind the number of hours spent since his departure from London, and had it been in his nature to make a useless gesture, would have rubbed his hands in satisfaction. Sir Francis Cromarty had observed the oddity of his traveling companion—although the only opportunity he had for studying him had been while he was dealing the cards, and between two rubbers—and had wondered whether a human heart really beat beneath this cold exterior, and whether Phileas Fogg had any sense of the beauties of nature. Of all the eccentric persons the brigadier-general had ever met, none was comparable to this product of the exact sciences.

Phileas Fogg had not concealed from Sir Francis his design of going around the world, nor the circumstances under which he set out. The general only saw in the wager a useless eccentricity, and a lack of sound common sense. In the way this strange gentleman was going on, he would leave the world without having done any good to himself or anybody else.

An hour after leaving Bombay the train had passed the viaducts and the island of Salcette, and had got into the open country. At Callyan they reached the junction of the branch line which descends toward southeastern India by Kandallah and Poona; and, passing Pauwell, they entered the mountains, with their basalt bases, and their summits crowned with thick and verdant forests. Phileas Fogg and Sir Francis Cromarty exchanged a few words from time to time, and now Sir Francis, reviving the conversation, observed, "Some years ago, Mr. Fogg, you would have met with a delay at this point, which would probably have lost you your wager."

"How so, Sir Francis?"

"Because the railway stopped at the base of these mountains, which the passengers were obliged to cross in palanquins or on ponies to Kandallah, on the other side."

"Such a delay would not have upset my plans in the least," said Mr. Fogg. "I have constantly foreseen the likelihood of certain obstacles."

"But, Mr. Fogg," pursued Sir Francis, "you run the risk of having some difficulty about this good fellow's adventure at the pagoda." Passepartout, his feet comfortably wrapped in his traveling-blanket, was sound asleep, and did not dream that anybody was talking about him. "The Government is very severe about that kind of offence. It takes particular care that the religious customs of the Indians should be respected, and if your servant were caught—"

"Very well, Sir Francis," replied Mr. Fogg; "if he had been caught he would have been condemned and punished, and then would have quietly returned to Europe. I don't see how the affair could have delayed his master."

The conversation fell again. During the night the train left the mountains behind, and passed Nassik, and the next day proceeded over the flat, well-cultivated country of the Khandeish, with its straggling villages, above which rose the minarets of the pagodas. This fertile territory is watered by numerous small rivers and limpid streams, mostly tributaries of the Godavery.

Passepartout, on waking and looking out, could not believe that he was actually crossing India in a railway train. It seemed to him incredible. And yet, nothing was more real. The locomotive, guided by an English engineer and fed with English coal, threw out its smoke upon cotton, coffee, nutmeg, clove, and pepper plantations, while the steam curled in spirals around groups of palm trees, in the midst of which were seen picturesque bungalows, viharis (a sort of abandoned monasteries), and marvelous temples enriched by the endless ornamentation of Indian architecture. Then they came upon vast tracts extending to the horizon, jungles with snakes and tigers, which fled at the noise of the train, and at last forests penetrated by the railway and still haunted by elephants which, with pensive eyes, gazed at the train as it passed. Beyond Malli-gaum the travelers crossed the fatal country so often stained with blood by the followers of the goddess Kali. Not far off rose Ellora, with its graceful pagodas, and the famous Aurungabad, capital of the ferocious Aureng-Zeb, now the chief town of one of the detached provinces of the Kingdom of the Nizam. Feringhea, the Thuggee chief, king of the stranglers, ruled over this region. These ruffians, united by a secret bond, strangled victims of every age in honor of the goddess Death, without ever shedding blood. There was a period when this part of the country could scarcely be traveled over without corpses being found in every direction. The English Government had succeeded in greatly diminishing these murders, though the Thuggees still existed and pursued their horrible rites.

At half-past twelve the train stopped at Burhampoor, where Passepartout was able to purchase some babouches, Indian slippers ornamented with false pearls, in which, with evident vanity, he proceeded to incase his feet. The travelers had a hasty lunch, and started off for Assurghur, after skirting for a little the banks of the small river Tapty, which empties into the Gulf of Cambray, near Surat.

It is now fitting to reveal Passepartout's thoughts. Up to his arrival in Bombay, he had entertained hopes that their journey would end there; but now that they were plainly whirling across India at full speed, a sudden change had come over his mind. His old vagabond nature returned to him; the unconventional ideas of his youth once more took possession of him. He came to regard his master's project as intended in good earnest, believed in the reality of the bet, and therefore in the tour of the world, and the necessity of making it without fail within the designated period. Already he began to worry about possible delays and accidents which might happen on the way. He felt involved in the wager, and trembled at the thought that he might have been the means of losing it by his unpardonable folly of the night before. Being much less coolheaded than Mr. Fogg, he was much more restless, counting and recounting the days gone by, cursing when the train stopped, accusing it of sluggishness, and mentally blaming Mr. Fogg for not having bribed the engineer. The good fellow was ignorant that, while it was possible by such means to hasten the rate of a steamer, it could not be done on the railway.

The train entered the passes of the Sutpour Mountains, which separate the Khandeish from Bundelcund, toward evening. The next day Sir Francis Cromarty asked Passepartout what time it was; to which, on consulting his watch, he replied that it was three in the morning. This great timepiece, always set on the Greenwich meridian, which was now some seventy-seven degrees west, was at least four hours slow. Sir Francis corrected Passepartout's time, whereupon the latter made the same remark that he had made to Fix. He tried to have him understand that the watch should be regulated in each new meridian, since he was constantly going east (that is in the face of the sun) and therefore the days were shorter by four minutes for each degree gone over. Passepartout obstinately refused to alter his watch, which he kept on London time. It was an innocent habit which could harm no one.

The train stopped, at eight o'clock, in the midst of a glade some fifteen miles beyond Rothal, where there were several bungalows and workmen's cabins. The conductor, passing beside the carriages, shouted, "Passengers will get out here!"

Phileas Fogg looked at Sir Francis Cromarty for an explanation; but the general could not tell what a halt meant in the midst of this forest of dates and acacias.

Passepartout, not less surprised, rushed out and speedily returned, crying, "Monsieur, no more railway!"

"What do you mean?" asked Sir Francis.

"I mean to say that the train isn't going on."

The general at once stepped out, while Phileas Fogg

calmly followed him, and they proceeded together to the conductor.

"Where are we?" asked Sir Francis.

"At the hamlet of Kholby."

"Do we stop here?"

"Certainly. The railway isn't finished."

"What! not finished?"

"No. There's still a matter of fifty miles to be laid from here to Allahabad, where the line begins again."

"But the papers announced the opening of the railway throughout."

"What can I say, officer? The papers were mistaken."

"Yet you sell tickets from Bombay to Calcutta," retorted Sir Francis, who was getting angry.

"No doubt," replied the conductor; "but the passengers know that they must provide means of transportation for themselves from Kholby to Allahabad."

Sir Francis was furious. Passepartout would willingly have knocked the conductor down, and did not dare to look at his master.

"Sir Francis," said Mr. Fogg, quietly, "we will, if you please, look about for some means to reach Allahabad."

"Mr. Fogg, is this a delay greatly to your disadvantage?"

"No, Sir Francis; it was foreseen."

"What! You knew that the way—"

"Not at all; but I knew that some obstacle or other would sooner or later arise on my route. Nothing, therefore, is lost. I have two days which I have already gained to sacrifice. A steamer leaves Calcutta for Hong Kong at noon, on the twenty-fifth. This is the twenty-second, and we shall reach Calcutta in time."

There was nothing to say to so confident a response.

It was but too true that the railway works stopped at this point. The papers were like some watches, which have a way of getting too fast, and had been premature in their announcement of the completion of the line. The greater part of the travelers were aware of this interruption, and leaving the train, they began to engage such vehicles as the village could provide— four-wheeled palkigharis, waggons drawn by zebus, carriages that looked like perambulating pagodas, palanquins, ponies, and whatnot.

Mr. Fogg and Sir Francis Cromarty, after searching the village from end to end, came back without having found anything.

"I shall go afoot," said Phileas Fogg.

Passepartout, who had now joined his master, made a wry grimace, as he thought of his magnificent but too frail babouches. Happily, he too had been looking about him, and, after a moment's hesitation, said, "Monsieur, I think I have found a means of conveyance."

"What?"

"An elephant! An elephant that belongs to an Indian who lives but a hundred steps from here."

"Let's go and see the elephant," replied Mr. Fogg.

They soon reached a small hut, near which, enclosed within some high fences, was the animal in question. An Indian came out of the hut, and, at their request, conducted them within the enclosure. The elephant, which its owner had reared, not as a beast of burden, but for warlike purposes, was half domesticated. The Indian had begun already, by irritating him often, and feeding him during three months on sugar and butter, in order to make him unnaturally ferocious. This method was often employed by those who train the Indian elephants for battle. Happily, however, for Mr. Fogg, the animal's instruction in this direction had not gone far, and the elephant still preserved his natural gentleness. Kiouni—this was the name of the beast—could doubtless travel rapidly for a long time, and for lack of any other means of conveyance, Mr. Fogg resolved to hire him. But elephants are far from cheap in India, as they are becoming scarce. The males, which alone are suitable for circus shows, are much sought, especially as they do not breed in captivity and therefore can only be gotten through hunting. When, therefore, Mr. Fogg proposed to the Indian to hire Kiouni, he refused point-blank. Mr. Fogg persisted, offering the excessive sum of ten pounds an hour for the loan of the beast to Allahabad. Refused. Twenty pounds? Refused also. Forty pounds? Still refused. Passepartout jumped at each bid, but the Indian declined to be tempted. Yet the offer was an alluring one, for, supposing it took the elephant fifteen hours to reach Allahabad, his owner would receive no less than six hundred pounds sterling.

Phileas Fogg, without getting in the least flurried, then proposed to purchase the animal outright, and at first offered a thousand pounds for him. The Indian, perhaps thinking he was going to make a great deal, still refused.

Sir Francis Cromarty took Mr. Fogg aside, and begged him to consider before he went any further; to which that gentleman replied that he was not in the habit of acting rashly, that a bet of twenty thousand pounds was at stake, that the elephant was absolutely necessary to him, and that he would secure him if he had to pay twenty times his value. Returning to the Indian, whose small, sharp eyes, glistening with greed, betrayed that for him it was only a question of how great a price he could obtain, Mr. Fogg offered first twelve hundred, then fifteen hundred, eighteen hundred, two thousand pounds. Passepartout, usually so rubicund, was fairly white with suspense.

At two thousand pounds the Indian yielded.

"What a price, good heaven!" cried Passepartout, "for an elephant!"

It only remained now to find a guide, which was easier. A young Parsee with an intelligent face offered his services, which Mr. Fogg accepted, promising so generous a reward as to materially stimulate his zeal. The elephant was led out and equipped. The Parsee, who was an accomplished elephant driver, covered his back with a sort of saddlecloth, and attached to each of his flanks some curiously uncomfortable seats.

Phileas Fogg paid the Indian with some bank notes which he extracted from the famous bag, a proceeding that seemed to poor Passepartout to wrench his insides. Then he offered to carry Sir Francis to Allahabad, which the brigadier gratefully accepted, as one traveler more would not be likely to tire the gigantic beast. Provisions were purchased at Kholby, and while Sir Francis and Mr. Fogg took the seats on either side, Passepartout got astride the saddlecloth between them. The Parsee perched himself on the elephant's neck, and at nine o'clock they set out from the village, the animal marching off by the shortest cut through the dense forest of palms.

CHAPTER XII

In Which Phileas Fogg and His Companions Venture Across the Indian Forests, and What Ensues

In order to shorten the journey, the guide left on his right the line where the railway was still in process of being built. This line, owing to the capricious turnings of the Vindhia Mountains, did not pursue a straight course. The Parsee, who was quite familiar with the roads and paths in the district, declared that they would gain twenty miles by striking directly through the forest.

Phileas Fogg and Sir Francis Cromarty, plunged to their necks in the peculiar seats provided for them, were horribly jostled by the swift trotting of the elephant, spurred on as he was by the skillful Parsee; but they endured the discomfort with true British calm, talking little, and scarcely able to catch a glimpse of each other. As for Passepartout, who was mounted on the beast's back, and receiving the direct force of each blow as he trod along, he was very careful, in accordance with his master's advice, to keep his tongue from between his teeth, as it would otherwise have been bitten off. The good fellow bounced from the elephant's neck to his rump, and vaulted like a clown on a springboard. Yet he laughed in the midst of his bouncing, and from time to time took a piece of sugar out of his pocket, and inserted it in Kiouni's trunk, who received it without slackening his regular trot.

After two hours the guide stopped the elephant and gave him an hour for rest, during which Kiouni, after quenching his thirst at a neighbouring pond, set to devouring the branches and shrubs around him. Sir Francis didn't regret the pause, as he was exhausted. Mr. Fogg seemed as fit as if he had just gotten out of bed. "Why, he's made of iron!" exclaimed the general, gazing admiringly at him.

"Of wrought iron," replied Passepartout, as he set about preparing a hasty lunch.

At noon the Parsee gave the signal of departure. The country soon became wild-looking. Groves of dates and dwarf palms succeeded the dense forests; then vast, dry plains, dotted with scanty shrubs and sown with great blocks of syenite. All this portion of Bundelcund, which is little frequented by travelers, is inhabited by a fanatic population, hardened in the most horrible practices of the Hindu faith. The English have not been able to secure complete dominion over this territory, which is subjected to the influence of rajahs whom it is almost impossible to reach in their inaccessible mountain retreats. The travelers several times saw bands of ferocious Indians, who, when they perceived the elephant striding across country, made angry and threatening motions. The Parsee avoided them as much as possible. Few animals were observed on the route; even the monkeys hurried from their path with contortions and grimaces which made Passepartout rock with laughter.

In the midst of his gaiety, however, one thought troubled the good servant. What would Mr. Fogg do with the elephant when he got to Allahabad? Would he carry him on with him? Impossible! The cost of transporting him would make him ruinously expensive. Would he sell him, or set him free? The estimable beast certainly deserved some consideration. Should Mr. Fogg choose to make Kiouni a present to

Passepartout, he would be very much embarrassed.
These thoughts kept worrying him.

The principal chain of the Vindhias was crossed by
eight in the evening, and another pause was made on
the northern slope, in a ruined bungalow. They had
gone nearly twenty-five miles that day, and an equal
distance still separated them from the station of Allahabad.

The night was cold. The Parsee lit a fire in the
bungalow with a few dry branches, and the warmth
was very welcome. The provisions purchased at
Kholby sufficed for supper, and the travelers ate rav-
enously. The conversation, beginning with a few dis-
connected phrases, soon gave way to loud and steady
snores. The guide watched Kiouni, who slept standing, bolstering himself against the trunk of a large
tree. Nothing occurred during the night to disturb the
slumberers, although occasional growls from pan-
thers and chatterings of monkeys broke the silence.
But the carnivores made no hostile demonstration
against the occupants of the bungalow. Sir Francis
slept heavily, like an honest soldier overcome with
fatigue. Passepartout was wrapped in uneasy dreams
of the bouncing of the day before. As for Mr. Fogg,
he slumbered as peacefully as if he had been in his
serene mansion in Saville Row.

The journey was resumed at six in the morning;
the guide hoped to reach Allahabad by evening. In
that case, Mr. Fogg would only lose a part of the
forty-eight hours saved since the beginning of the
tour. Kiouni, resuming his rapid gait, soon went
down the lower spurs of the Vindhias, and toward
noon they passed by the village of Kallenger, on the
Cani, one of the branches of the Ganges. The guide
avoided inhabited places, thinking it safer to keep to
open country, which lies along the first depressions
of the basin of the great river. Allahabad was now
only twelve miles to the northeast. They stopped un-

der a clump of bananas, the fruit of which, as healthy as bread and as succulent as cream, was amply appreciated.

At two o'clock the guide entered a thick forest which extended several miles; he preferred to travel under cover of the woods. They had not as yet had any unpleasant encounters, and the journey seemed about to be successfully accomplished, when the elephant, becoming restless, suddenly stopped.

It was then four o'clock.

"What's the matter?" asked Sir Francis, sticking out his head.

"I don't know, officer," replied the Parsee, listening attentively to a confused murmur which came through the thick branches.

The murmur soon become more distinct; it now seemed like a distant concert of human voices accompanied by brass instruments. Passepartout was all eyes and ears. Mr. Fogg patiently waited without a word. The Parsee jumped to the ground, fastened the elephant to a tree, and plunged into the thicket. He soon returned, saying, "A procession of Brahmins is coming this way. We must prevent their seeing us, if possible."

The guide unloosed the elephant and led him into a thicket, at the same time asking the travelers not to stir. He held himself ready to mount the animal at a moment's notice, should flight become necessary. But he evidently thought that the procession of the faithful would pass without perceiving them amid the thick foliage, in which they were wholly concealed.

The discordant tones of the voices and instruments drew nearer, and now droning songs mingled with the sound of the tambourines and cymbals. The head of the procession soon appeared beneath the trees, a hundred paces away; and the strange figures of this religious ceremony were easily distinguished through the branches. First came the priests, with mitres on their heads, and clothed in long lace robes. They were surrounded by men, women, and children, who sang a kind of lugubrious psalm, interrupted at regular intervals by the tambourines and cymbals. Behind them was drawn a carriage with large wheels, the spokes of which represented serpents entwined with each other. Upon the carriage, which was drawn by four richly harnessed zebus, stood a hideous statue with four arms, the body colored a dull red, with haggard eyes, dishevelled hair, protruding tongue, and lips tinted with betel. It stood upright upon the figure of a prostrate and headless giant.

Sir Francis, recognizing the statue, whispered, "The goddess Kali; the goddess of love and death."

"Of death, perhaps," muttered back Passepartout, "but of love—that ugly old hag? Never!"

The Parsee made a motion to keep silence.

A group of old fakirs was capering and making a wild ado around the statue; they were striped with ochre, and covered with cuts whence their blood issued drop by drop. Some Brahmins, clad in all the sumptuousness of Oriental apparel, and leading a woman who faltered at every step, followed. This woman was young, and as fair as a European. Her head and neck, shoulders, ears, arms, hands and toes, were covered with jewels and gems—with bracelets, earrings, and rings; while a tunic spangled with gold, and covered with a light muslin robe, betrayed the outline of her form.

The guards who followed the young woman presented a violent contrast to her, armed as they were with naked sabres hung at their waists, and long damascened pistols, and bearing a corpse on a palanquin. It was the body of an old man, gorgeously dressed in the clothes of a rajah, wearing, as in life, a turban embroidered with pearls, a robe of tissue of silk and gold, a scarf of cashmere sewed with diamonds, and the magnificent weapons of a Hindu prince. Next came the musicians and a rearguard of capering fakirs, whose cries sometimes drowned the noise of the instruments; these closed the procession.

Sir Francis watched sadly the procession, and, turning to the guide, said, "A suttee."

The Parsee nodded, and put his finger to his lips. The procession slowly wound under the trees, and soon its last ranks disappeared in the depths of the wood. The songs gradually died away; occasionally cries were heard in the distance, until at last all was silence again.

Phileas Fogg had heard what Sir Francis said, and, as soon as the procession had disappeared, asked, "What is a 'suttee'?"

"A suttee," answered the general, "is a human sacrifice, but a voluntary one. The woman you have just seen will be burned tomorrow at the dawn of day."

"Oh, the scoundrels!" cried Passepartout, who could not repress his indignation.

"And the corpse?" asked Mr. Fogg.

"Is that of the prince, her husband," said the guide; "an independent rajah of Bundelcund."

"Is it possible," resumed Phileas Fogg, his voice betraying not the least emotion, "that these barbarous customs still exist in India, and that the English have been unable to put a stop to them?"

"These sacrifices do not occur in most of India," replied Sir Francis. "But we have no power over these savage territories, and especially here in Bundelcund. The whole district north of the Vindhias is the theatre of incessant murders and pillage."

"The poor wretch!" exclaimed Passepartout, "to be burned alive!"

"Yes," returned Sir Francis, "burned alive. And

if she were not, you cannot conceive what treatmentshe would be obliged to submit to from her relatives. They would shave off her hair, feed her on a scanty allowance of rice, treat her with contempt. She would be looked upon as an vile creature, and would die in some corner, like a mangy dog. The prospect of so frightful an existence drives these poor creatures to the sacrifice much more than love or religious fanaticism. Sometimes, however, the sacrifice is really voluntary, and it requires the active interference of the Government to prevent it. Several years ago, when I was living in Bombay, a young widow asked permission of the governor to be burned along with her husband's body. As you may imagine, he refused. The woman left the town, took refuge with an independent rajah, and there carried out her sacrifice.''

While Sir Francis was speaking, the guide shook his head several times, and now said, ''The sacrifice which will take place tomorrow at dawn is not a voluntary one.''

''How do you know?''

''Everybody knows about this affair in Bundelcund.''

''But the wretched creature did not seem to be making any resistance,'' observed Sir Francis.

''That was because they had intoxicated her with fumes of hemp and opium.''

''But where are they taking her?''

''To the pagoda of Pillaji, two miles from here. She will pass the night there.''

''And the sacrifice will take place—''

''Tomorrow, at the first light of dawn.''

The guide now led the elephant out of the thicket, and leaped upon his neck. Just as he was about to urge Kiouni forward with a peculiar whistle, Mr. Fogg stopped him, and, turning to Sir Francis Cromarty, said, ''Suppose we save this woman.''

"Save the woman, Mr. Fogg!"

"I have yet twelve hours to spare; I can devote them to that."

"Why, you are a man of heart!"

"Sometimes," replied Phileas Fogg, quietly. "When I have the time."

CHAPTER XIII

IN WHICH PASSEPARTOUT RECEIVES A NEW PROOF THAT FORTUNE FAVORS THE BRAVE

The project was a bold one, full of difficulty, perhaps impracticable. Mr. Fogg was going to risk life, or at least liberty, and therefore the success of his tour. But he did not hesitate, and he found in Sir Francis Cromarty an enthusiastic ally.

As for Passepartout, he was ready for anything that might be proposed. His master's idea charmed him, for he perceived a heart, a soul, under that icy exterior. He began to love Phileas Fogg.

There remained the guide: What course would he adopt? Wouldn't he take sides with the Indians? They might not have his assistance. They must at least be assured of his neutrality.

Sir Francis frankly put the question to him.

"Officers," replied the guide, "I am a Parsee, and this woman is a Parsee. Command me as you will."

"Excellent," said Mr. Fogg.

"However," resumed the guide, "do realize that, not only shall we risk our lives, but horrible tortures, if we are captured."

"That is foreseen," replied Mr. Fogg. "I think we must wait till night before acting."

"I think so," said the guide.

The good Indian then gave some account of the victim, who, he said, was a celebrated beauty of the Parsee race and the daughter of a wealthy Bombay merchant. She had received a thoroughly English education in that city, and, from her manners and intelligence, would be thought an European. Her name was Aouda. Left an orphan, she was married against her will to the old rajah of Bundelcund. Knowing the fate that awaited her, she escaped, was captured and condemned by the rajah's relatives, who had an interest in her death, to this sacrifice from which it seemed she could not escape.

The Parsee's narrative only confirmed Mr. Fogg and his companions in their generous design. It was decided that the guide should direct the elephant toward the pagoda of Pillaji, which he accordingly approached as quickly as possible. They halted, half an hour afterward, in a grove some five hundred feet from the pagoda, where they were well concealed; but they could hear the groans and cries of the fakirs distinctly.

They then discussed the means of getting to the victim. The guide was familiar with the pagoda of Pillaji, in which, he was certain, the young woman was imprisoned. Could they enter any of its doors while the whole party of Indians was plunged in a drunken sleep, or was it safer to attempt to make a hole in the walls?

This could only be determined at the moment and the place themselves. But it was certain that the abduction must be made that night, and not at dawn when the victim was to be led to her funeral pyre. Then no human intervention could save her.

As soon as night fell, about six o'clock, they decided to make a reconnaissance around the pagoda. The cries of the fakirs were just ceasing; the Indians were deep into the drunkenness caused by liquid opium mingled with hemp, and it might be possible to slip between them to the temple.

The Parsee, leading the others, noiselessly crept through the wood, and in ten minutes they found themselves on the banks of a small stream, whence, by the light of the rosin torches, they perceived a pyre of wood, on the top of which lay the embalmed body of the rajah, which was to be burned with his wife. The pagoda, whose minarets loomed above the trees in the deepening dusk, stood a hundred steps away.

"Come!" whispered the guide.

He slipped more cautiously than ever through the brush, followed by his companions; the silence around was only broken by the low murmuring of the wind among the branches.

Soon the Parsee stopped on the borders of a glade which was lit up by torches. The ground was covered by groups of the Indians, motionless in their drunken sleep; it seemed a battlefield strewn with the dead. Men, women and children lay together.

In the background, among the trees, the pagoda of Pillaji loomed indistinctly. Much to the guide's disappointment, the guards of the rajah, lighted by torches, were watching the doors and marching to and fro with naked sabres. The priests, too, were probably watching from within.

The Parsee, now convinced that it was impossible to force an entrance to the temple, advanced no farther, but led his companions back again. Phileas Fogg and Sir Francis Cromarty also saw that nothing could be attempted in that direction. They stopped and engaged in a whispered colloquy.

"Let's wait, It is only eight now," said the brigadier, "and these guards may also go to sleep."

"It is not impossible," returned the Parsee.

They lay down at the foot of a tall tree and waited.

The time seemed to drag; the guide at times left them to investigate the edge of the wood, but the guards were watching steadily by the glare of the torches, and a dim light crept through the windows of the pagoda.

They waited till midnight; but no change took place

among the guards, and it became apparent that their yielding to sleep could not be counted on. The other plan must be carried out. An opening in the walls of the pagoda must be made. It remained to find out whether the priests were watching by the side of their victim as assiduously as were the soldiers at the door.

After a last consultation, the guide announced that he was ready for the attempt, and advanced, followed by the others. They took a roundabout way, so as to get at the pagoda on the rear. They reached the walls about half-past twelve, without having met anyone; here there was no guard, nor were there either windows or doors.

The night was dark. The moon, on the wane, scarcely left the horizon and was covered with heavy clouds; the height of the trees deepened the darkness.

It was not enough to reach the walls. An opening in them must be made, and to attain this purpose the party only had their pocketknives. Happily the temple walls were built of brick and wood, which could be penetrated with little difficulty. After one brick had been taken out, the rest would yield easily.

They set noiselessly to work, and the Parsee on one side and Passepartout on the other began to loosen the bricks, so as to make an opening two feet wide. They were getting on rapidly, when suddenly a cry was heard in the interior of the temple, followed almost instantly by other cries replying from the outside. Passepartout and the guide stopped. Had they been heard? Was the alarm being given? Common prudence urged them to retire, and they did so, followed by Phileas Fogg and Sir Francis. They again hid in the wood, and waited till the disturbance, whatever it might be, ceased, holding themselves ready to resume their attempt without delay. But, awkwardly enough, the guards now appeared at the rear of the temple, and settled there to prevent all approach.

It would be difficult to describe the disappointment

of the party, thus interrupted in their work. They now could not reach the victim; how, then, could they save her? Sir Francis shook his fist, Passepartout was beside himself, and the guide gnashed his teeth with rage. The tranquil Fogg waited, without betraying any emotion.

"We have nothing to do but to go away," whispered Sir Francis.

"Nothing but to go away," echoed the guide.

"Stop," said Fogg. "I am only due at Allahabad tomorrow before noon."

"But what can you hope to do?" asked Sir Francis. "In a few hours it will be daylight, and—"

"The chance which now seems lost may present itself at the last moment."

Sir Francis would have liked to read Phileas Fogg's mind.

What was this cool Englishman thinking of? Was he planning to make a rush for the young woman at the very moment of the sacrifice, and boldly snatch her from her executioners?

This would be utter madness, and it was hard to admit that Fogg was that mad. Sir Francis consented, however, to remain to the end of this terrible drama. The guide led them to the rear of the glade, where they were able to observe the sleeping groups.

Meanwhile, Passepartout, who had perched himself on the lower branches of a tree, was pondering an idea which had at first struck him like a flash, and which was now firmly lodged in his brain.

He had begun by saying to himself, "What folly!" and now he was repeating, "Why not, after all? It's a chance—perhaps the only one; and with such fools!"

Thinking thus, he slipped, with the suppleness of a serpent, to the lowest branches, the ends of which bent almost to the ground.

The hours passed, and the lighter shades now announced the approach of day, though it was not yet light. This was the moment. The slumbering multitude became animated, the tambourines sounded, songs and cries arose; the hour of the sacrifice had come. The doors of the pagoda swung open, and a bright light escaped from its interior, in the midst of which Mr. Fogg and Sir Francis caught sight of the victim. She seemed, having shaken off the stupor of intoxication, to be striving to escape from her executioner. Sir Francis's heart throbbed; and convulsively seizing Mr. Fogg's hand, found in it an open knife. Just at this moment the crowd began to move. The young woman had again fallen into a stupor, caused by the fumes of hemp. She passed among the fakirs, who escorted her with their wild, religious cries.

Phileas Fogg and his companions, mingling in the rear ranks of the crowd, followed; and in two minutes they reached the banks of the stream and stopped fifty paces from the pyre, upon which still lay the rajah's corpse. In the semi-obscurity they saw the victim, quite senseless, stretched out beside her husband's body. Then a torch was brought, and the wood, soaked with oil, instantly took fire.

At this moment Sir Francis and the guide seized Phileas Fogg, who, in an instant of mad generosity, was about to rush upon the pyre. But he had quickly pushed them aside, when the whole scene suddenly changed. A cry of terror arose. The whole multitude prostrated themselves, terrorstricken, on the ground.

The old rajah was not dead, then, since he rose of a sudden, like a spectre, took up his wife in his arms, and descended from the pyre in the midst of the clouds of smoke, which only heightened his ghostly appearance.

Fakirs, soldiers, and priests, seized with instant terror, lay there, with their faces on the ground, not daring to lift their eyes and behold such a prodigy.

The inanimate victim was borne along by the vigorous arms which were carrying her, and in which she

did not seem a burden. Mr. Fogg and Sir Francis stood
erect, the Parsee bowed his head, and Passepartout
was, no doubt, scarcely less stupefied.

The resuscitated rajah approached Sir Francis and
Mr. Fogg, and, in an abrupt tone, said, "Let us be
off!"

It was Passepartout himself, who had slipped upon
the pyre in the midst of the smoke and, taking advantage of the still overhanging darkness, had delivered
the young woman from death! It was Passepartout who,
playing his part with a happy audacity, was passing
through the crowd amid the general terror.

A moment after, all four of the party were disappearing in the woods, and the elephant was bearing
them away at a rapid pace. But the cries and noise,
and a bullet which whizzed through Phileas Fogg's hat,
informed them that the trick had been discovered.

The old rajah's body, indeed, now appeared upon
the burning pyre; and the priests, recovered from their
terror, perceived that an abduction had taken place.
They hastened into the forest, followed by the soldiers, who fired a volley after the fugitives; but the
latter rapidly increased the distance between them and
soon found themselves beyond the reach of the bullets
and arrows.

CHAPTER XIV

In Which Phileas Fogg Descends the Whole Length of the Beautiful Valley of the Ganges Without Ever Thinking of Seeing It

The rash exploit had been accomplished. An hour later Passepartout was still laughing at his success. Sir Francis pressed the fearless fellow's hand, and his master said, "Well done!" which, from him, was high commendation. Passepartout replied that all the credit of the affair belonged to Mr. Fogg. As for him, he had only been struck with a "queer" idea; and he laughed to think that for a few moments he, Passepartout, the ex-gymnast, ex-sergeant fireman, had been the spouse of a charming woman, a venerable, embalmed rajah! As for the young Indian woman, she had been unconscious throughout of what had happened. Now, wrapped up in a traveling-blanket, she was reposing in one of the seats.

The elephant, thanks to the skillful guidance of the Parsee, was advancing rapidly through the still darksome forest, and, an hour after leaving the pagoda, was rushing through a vast plain. They made a halt at seven o'clock, the young woman being still in a state of complete prostration. The guide made her drink a little brandy and water, but the drowsiness which stupefied her could not yet be shaken off. Sir Francis, who was familiar with the effects of the intoxication produced by the fumes of hemp, reassured his companions on her account. But he was more disturbed at the prospect of her future fate. He told Phileas Fogg that, should Mrs.* Aouda remain in India, she would inevitably fall again into the hands of her executioners. These fanatics were scattered throughout the country, and would, despite the English police, recover their victim in Madras, Bombay, or Calcutta. She would only be safe by leaving India for ever.

Phileas Fogg replied that he would reflect upon the matter.

The station at Allahabad was reached about ten o'clock, and the interrupted line of railway being resumed, would enable them to reach Calcutta in less than twenty-four hours. Phileas Fogg would thus be able to arrive in time to take the steamer which left Calcutta the next day, October 25th, at noon, for Hong Kong.

The young woman was placed in one of the waiting rooms of the station, while Passepartout was charged with purchasing for her various clothes, a dress, a shawl, and some furs; for which his master gave him unlimited credit. Passepartout started off immediately, and found himself in the streets of Allahabad, that is, the "City of God," one of the most venerated in India, being built at the junction of the two sacred rivers Ganges and Jumna, the waters of which attract pilgrims from every part of the peninsula. The Ganges, according to the legends of the Ramayana, rises in heaven, whence, owing to Brahma's agency, it descends to the earth.

Passepartout made it a point, as he made his purchases, to take a good look at the city. It was formerly defended by a noble fort, which has since become a

*"Mrs." in the French original

state prison; its commerce has dwindled away, and Passepartout in vain looked about him for such a store as he used to frequent in Regent Street. At last he came upon an elderly, crusty Jew, who sold second-hand articles, and from whom he purchased a dress of Scotch material, a large cloak, and a fine otterskin coat, for which he did not hesitate to pay seventy-five pounds. He then returned triumphantly to the station.

The influence to which the priests of Pillaji had subjected Mrs. Aouda began gradually to yield, and she became more herself, so that her fine eyes resumed all their soft Indian expression.

When the poet-king, Ucaf Uddaul, celebrates the charms of the queen of Ahmehnagara, he speaks thus:—

"Her shining tresses, divided in two parts, encircle the harmonious contour of her white and delicate cheeks, brilliant in their glow and freshness. Her ebony brows have the form and charm of the bow of Kama, the god of love, and beneath her long silken lashes the purest reflections of the celestial light swim, as in the sacred lakes of Himalaya, in the black pupils of her great clear eyes. Her teeth, fine, even, and white, glitter between her smiling lips like dewdrops in a passion-flower's half-enveloped breast. Her delicately formed ears, her vermilion hands, her little feet, curved and tender as the lotus-bud, glitter with the brilliancy of the loveliest pearls of Ceylon, the most dazzling diamonds of Golconda. Her narrow and supple waist, which you could span with your fingers, sets forth the outline of her rounded figure and the beauty of her bosom, where youth in its flower displays the wealth of its treasures; and beneath the silken folds of her tunic she seems to have been modeled in pure silver by the godlike hand of Vicvarcarma, the immortal sculptor."

It is enough to say, without applying this poetical rhapsody to Mrs. Aouda, that she was a charming woman, in all the European acceptance of the phrase. She spoke English with great purity, and the guide had not exaggerated in saying that the young Parsee had been transformed by her upbringing.

The train was about to start from Allahabad, and Mr. Fogg proceeded to pay the guide the price agreed upon for his service, and not a farthing more; which astonished Passepartout, who remembered all that his master owed to the guide's devotion. He had, indeed, risked his life in the adventure at Pillaji, and if he should be caught afterwards by the Indians, he would with difficulty escape their vengeance. Kiouni, also, must be disposed of. What should be done with the elephant, which had been so dearly purchased? Phileas Fogg had already made up his mind in this matter.

"Parsee," he said to the guide, "you have been helpful and devoted. I have paid for your help, but not for your devotion. Would you like to have this elephant? He is yours."

The guide's eyes glistened.

"Your honour is giving me a fortune!" cried he.

"Take him, guide," returned Mr. Fogg, "and I shall still be your debtor."

"Good!" exclaimed Passepartout; "take him, friend. Kiouni is a brave and faithful beast." And, going up to the elephant, he gave him several lumps of sugar, saying, "Here, Kiouni, here, here."

The elephant grunted out his satisfaction, and, clasping Passepartout around the waist with his trunk, lifted him as high as his head. Passepartout, not in the least alarmed, caressed the animal, which replaced him gently on the ground.

Soon after, Phileas Fogg, Sir Francis Cromarty, and Passepartout, settled in a carriage with Mrs. Aouda, who had the best seat, were whirling at full speed towards Benares. It was a run of eighty miles, and was accomplished in two hours. During the journey, the young woman fully recovered her senses. What was her astonishment to find herself in this carriage, on the railway, dressed in European clothes, and with travelers who were quite strangers to her! Her companions first set about fully reviving her with a little liquor, and then Sir Francis narrated to her what had passed, dwelling upon the courage of Phileas Fogg who had not hesitated to risk his life to save her, and recounting the happy sequel of the venture, the result of Passepartout's rash idea. Mr. Fogg said nothing; while Passepartout, bashful, kept repeating that "it wasn't worth telling."

Aouda thanked her deliverers effusively, rather with tears than words; her fine eyes interpreted her gratitude better than her lips. Then, as her thoughts strayed back to the scene of the sacrifice, and recalled the dangers which still menaced her, she shuddered with terror.

Phileas Fogg understood what was going on in Mrs. Aouda's mind, and offered, in order to reassure her, to escort her to Hong Kong, where she might remain safely until the affair was hushed up—an offer which she eagerly and gratefully accepted. She had, it seems, a Parsee relation who was one of the principal merchants of Hong Kong, which is wholly an English city, though on an island on the Chinese coast.

At half-past twelve the train stopped in Benares. The Brahmin legends assert that this city is built on the site of the ancient Casi, which, like Mahomet's tomb, was once suspended between heaven and earth; though the Benares of today, which the Orientalists call the Athens of India, stands quite unpoetically on the solid earth. Passepartout caught glimpses of its brick houses and clay huts, which gave an aspect of desolation to the place, as the train entered it.

Benares was Sir Francis Cromarty's destination, the troops he was rejoining being encamped some miles north of the city. He bade adieu to Phileas Fogg, wishing him all success and expressing the hope that

he would come that way again in a less original but
more profitable fashion. Mr. Fogg pressed his fingers
lightly. The parting of Mrs. Aouda, who did not forget what she owed Sir Francis, betrayed more
warmth; and, as for Passepartout, he received a
hearty hand-shake from the general.

The railway, on leaving Benares, passed for a while
along the valley of the Ganges. Through the windows
of their carriage the travelers had glimpses of the di-
versified landscape of Behar, with its mountains
clothed in verdure, its fields of barley, wheat, and corn,
its jungles peopled with green alligators, its neat villages, and its still thickly leaved forests. Elephants were
bathing in the waters of the sacred river, and groups
of Indians, despite the advanced season and chilly air,
were performing solemnly their pious ablutions. These
were fervent Brahmins, the bitterest foes of Buddhism,
their deities being Vishnu, the solar god, Shiva, the
divine impersonation of natural forces, and Brahma,
the supreme ruler of priests and legislators. What
would these divinities think of India, anglicised as it
is to-day, with steamers whistling and scudding along
the Ganges, frightening the gulls which float upon its
surface, the turtles swarming along its banks, and the
faithful lying upon its shores?

The panorama passed before their eyes like a flash,
save when the steam concealed it fitfully from the
view; the travelers could scarcely discern the fort of
Chupenie, twenty miles southwest from Benares, the
ancient stronghold of the rajahs of Behar; or Ghazipur
and its famous rosewater factories; or the tomb of Lord
Cornwallis, rising on the left bank of the Ganges; the
fortified town of Buxar, or Patna, a large manufactur-
ing and trading place, where is held the principal
opium market of India; or Monghir, a more than European town, for it is as English as Manchester or Bir-
mingham, with its iron foundries, edge-tool factories,

and high chimneys puffing clouds of black smoke toward the sky.

Night came on; the train passed on at full speed, in the midst of the roaring of the tigers, bears, and wolves which fled before the locomotive; and the marvels of Bengal, Golconda, ruined Gour, Murshedabad, the ancient capital, Burdwan, Hugly, and the French town of Chandernagor, where Passepartout would have been proud to see his country's flag flying, were hidden from their view in the darkness.

Calcutta was reached at seven in the morning, and the boat was only leaving for Hong Kong at noon; so that Phileas Fogg had five hours before him.

According to his itinerary, he was due in Calcutta on the 25th of October, and that was the exact date of his actual arrival. He was therefore neither behind nor ahead of time. The two days gained between London and Bombay had been lost, as has been seen, in the journey across India. But it is not to be supposed that Phileas Fogg regretted them.

CHAPTER XV

In Which the Bag of Bank Notes Becomes Lighter by Thousands of Pounds

The train entered the station, and Passepartout, jumping out first, was followed by Mr. Fogg, who helped his fair companion to step onto the platform. Phileas Fogg intended to proceed at once to the Hong Kong steamer, in order to get Mrs. Aouda comfortably settled for the voyage. He was unwilling to leave her while they were still in this dangerous country.

Just as he was leaving the station a policeman came up to him, and said, "Mr. Phileas Fogg?"

"I am."

"Is this man your servant?" added the policeman, pointing to Passepartout.

"Yes."

"Be so good, both of you, as to follow me."

Mr. Fogg betrayed no surprise whatever. The policeman was a representative of the law, and law is sacred to an Englishman. Passepartout tried to reason about the matter, but the policeman tapped him with his stick, and Mr. Fogg made him a signal to obey.

"May this young lady go with us?" asked he.

"She may," replied the policeman.

Mr. Fogg, Aouda, and Passepartout were conducted to a "palkighari," a sort of four-wheeled carriage drawn by two horses, and were driven away. No one spoke during the twenty minutes which elapsed before they reached their destination.

They first passed through the "black town," with its narrow streets, its miserable, dirty huts, and squalid population; then through the "European town," brightened up by brick houses, shaded by coconut trees and bristling with masts, where, although it was early morning, elegantly dressed horsemen and handsome carriages were passing back and forth.

The carriage stopped before a modest-looking house, which, however, did not have the appearance of a private house. The policeman had his prisoners—for so, truly, they might be called—get off and led them into a room with barred windows, and said, "You will appear before Judge Obadiah at half-past eight."

He then retired, and closed the door.

"Why, we are prisoners!" exclaimed Passepartout, falling into a chair.

Mrs. Aouda, with an emotion she tried to conceal, said to Mr. Fogg. "Sir, you must leave me to my fate! It is on my account that you receive this treatment; it is for having saved me!"

Phileas Fogg contented himself with saying that it was impossible. It was quite unlikely that he should be arrested for preventing a suttee. The complainants would not dare present themselves with such a charge. There was some mistake. Moreover, he would not in any event abandon Mrs. Aouda, but would escort her to Hong Kong.

"But the steamer leaves at noon!" observed Passepartout nervously.

"We shall be on board by noon," replied his master, placidly.

It was said so positively that Passepartout could not help muttering to himself, "Parbleu, that's certain! Before noon we shall be on board." But he was by no means reassured.

At half-past eight the door opened, the policeman

appeared, and, requesting them to follow him, led the way to an adjoining hall. It was evidently a courtroom, and a crowd of Europeans and natives already occupied the rear.

Mr. Fogg and his two companions sat on a bench opposite the desks of the magistrate and his clerk. Immediately after, Judge Obadiah, a fat, round man, followed by the clerk, entered. He proceeded to take down a wig which was hanging on a nail, and hurriedly put it on his head.

"The first case," said he; then, putting his hand to his head, he exclaimed, "Hey! This is not my wig!"

"No, your worship," returned the clerk, "it is mine."

"My dear Mr. Oysterpuff, how can a judge give a wise sentence in a clerk's wig?"

The wigs were exchanged.

Passepartout was getting nervous, for the hands on the big clock over the judge seemed to go round with terrible rapidity.

"The first case," repeated Judge Obadiah.

"Phileas Fogg?" said Oysterpuff.

"I am here," replied Mr. Fogg.

"Passepartout?"

"Present!" answered Passepartout.

"Good," said the judge. "We have been looking for you, prisoners, for two days on all the trains from Bombay."

"But of what are we accused?" asked Passepartout impatiently.

"You are about to be informed."

"I am an English subject, sir," said Mr. Fogg, "and I have the right—"

"Have you been ill treated?"

"Not at all."

"Very well; let the complainants come in."

A door was swung open by order of the judge, and three Indian priests entered.

"That's it," muttered Passepartout; "these are the rogues who were going to burn our young lady."

The priests stood in front of the judge, and the clerk proceeded to read in a loud voice a complaint of sacrilege against Phileas Fogg and his servant, who were accused of having violated a place held sacred by the Brahmin religion.

"You hear the charge?" asked the judge.

"Yes, sir," replied Mr. Fogg, consulting his watch, "and I admit it."

"You admit it?"

"I admit it, and I wish to hear these priests admit, in their turn, what they were going to do at the pagoda of Pillaji."

The priests looked at each other; they did not seem to understand what was said.

"Yes," cried Passepartout, warmly; "at the pagoda of Pillaji, where they were about to burn their victim."

The judge stared with astonishment, and the priests were stupefied.

"What victim?" said Judge Obadiah. "Burn whom? In Bombay itself?"

"Bombay?" cried Passepartout.

"Certainly. We are not talking of the pagoda of Pillaji, but of the pagoda of Malebar Hill, in Bombay."

"And as proof," added the clerk, "here are the desecrator's very shoes, which he left behind him."

Whereupon he placed a pair of shoes on his desk.

"My shoes!" cried Passepartout, in his surprise permitting this imprudent exclamation to escape him.

The confusion of master and servant, who had quite forgotten the affair in Bombay, for which they were now detained in Calcutta, may be imagined.

Fix, the detective, had foreseen the advantage which Passepartout's escapade gave him, and, delaying his departure for twelve hours, had consulted the priests of Malebar Hill. Knowing that the English authorities dealt very severely with this kind of misdemeanour, he promised them a goodly sum in damages, and sent them forward to Calcutta by the next train. Owing to the delay caused by the rescue of the young widow, Fix and the priests reached the Indian capital before Mr. Fogg and his servant, the magistrates having been already warned by a telegram to arrest them should they arrive. Fix's disappointment when he learned that Phileas Fogg had not made his appearance in Calcutta may be imagined. He made up his mind that the robber had stopped somewhere on the route and taken refuge in the southern provinces. For twenty-four hours Fix watched the station with feverish anxiety; at last he was rewarded by seeing Mr. Fogg and Passepartout arrive, accompanied by a young woman, whose presence he was wholly at a loss to explain. He hastened for a policeman; and this was how the party came to be arrested and brought before Judge Obadiah.

Had Passepartout been a little less preoccupied, he would have noticed the detective in a corner of the courtroom watching the proceedings with an interest easily understood; the warrant had failed to reach him in Calcutta, as it had done in Bombay and Suez.

Judge Obadiah had unfortunately caught Passepartout's rash exclamation, which the poor fellow would have given the world to take back.

"The facts are admitted?" asked the judge.

"Admitted," replied Mr. Fogg, coolly.

"Inasmuch," resumed the judge, "as the English law protects equally and sternly the religions of the Indian people, and as the man Passepartout has admitted that he violated the sacred pagoda of Malebar Hill, in Bombay, on the 20th of October, I condemn the said Passepartout to imprisonment for fifteen days and a fine of three hundred pounds."

"Three hundred pounds!" cried Passepartout, startled at the largeness of the sum.

"Silence!" shouted the constable.

"And inasmuch," continued the judge, "as it is not proved that the act was not done by the connivance of the master with the servant, and as the master in any case must be held responsible for the acts of his paid servant, I condemn Phileas Fogg to a week's imprisonment and a fine of one hundred and fifty pounds."

Fix rubbed his hands softly with satisfaction; if Phileas Fogg could be detained in Calcutta a week, it would be more than time for the warrant to arrive. Passepartout was stupefied. This sentence was ruining his master. A wager of twenty thousand pounds lost, because he, like a true sightseer, had gone into that abominable pagoda!

Phileas Fogg, as self-composed as if the judgment did not in the least concern him, did not even frown while it was being pronounced. Just as the clerk was calling the next case, he rose, and said, "I offer bail."

"You have that right," returned the judge.

Fix's blood ran cold, but he resumed his composure when he heard the judge announce that the bail required for each prisoner would be one thousand pounds.

"I will pay it at once," said Mr. Fogg, taking a roll of bank bills from the bag which Passepartout had by him and placing them on the clerk's desk.

"This sum will be returned to you upon your release from prison," said the judge. "Meanwhile, you are out on bail."

"Come!" said Phileas Fogg to his servant.

"But let them at least give me back my shoes!" cried Passepartout, angrily.

"Ah, these are pretty expensive shoes!" he muttered, as they were handed to him. "More than a thousand pounds apiece; besides, they pinch my feet."

Mr. Fogg, offering his arm to Mrs. Aouda, then departed, followed by the crestfallen Passepartout. Fix still nourished hopes that the robber would not, after all, leave the two thousand pounds behind him, but would decide to serve out his week in jail, and rushed forth on Mr. Fogg's traces. That gentleman took a carriage, which stopped soon on one of the quays.

The *Rangoon* was moored half a mile off in the harbor, its signal of departure hoisted at the masthead.

Eleven o'clock struck; Mr. Fogg was an hour ahead. Fix saw them leave the carriage and push off in a boat for the steamer, and stamped his feet with disappointment.

"The rascal is off, after all!" he exclaimed. "Two thousand pounds sacrificed! He's a prodigal as a thief! I'll follow him to the end of the world if necessary; but at the rate he is going, the stolen money soon will be exhausted."

The detective was not far wrong in making this conjecture. Since leaving London, what with traveling-expenses, bribes, the purchase of the elephant, bails, and fines, Mr. Fogg had already spent more than five thousand pounds on the way, and the percentage of the sum recovered from the bank robber promised to the detectives was rapidly diminishing.

CHAPTER XVI

In Which Fix Does Not Seem to Understand in the Least What Is Said to Him

The *Rangoon*—one of the Peninsula and Oriental Company's boats plying in the Chinese and Japanese seas—was a propeller-driven iron steamer, weighing about seventeen hundred and seventy tons, and with engines of four hundred horsepower. She was as fast, but not as comfortable, as the *Mongolia,* and Aouda was not as well provided for on board as Phileas Fogg could have wished. However, it was only a trip from Calcutta to Hong Kong of three thousand five hundred miles, taking from ten to twelve days, and the young woman was not difficult to please.

During the first days of the journey Mrs. Aouda became better acquainted with her protector, and constantly showed her deep gratitude for what he had done. The phlegmatic gentleman listened to her, apparently at least, with coldness, neither his voice nor his manner betraying the slightest emotion; but he seemed to be always on the watch that nothing should be wanting to Mrs. Aouda's comfort. He visited her regularly each day at certain hours, not so much to talk himself as to sit and hear her talk. He treated her with the strictest politeness, but with the casual grace of an automaton, the movements of which had been arranged for this purpose. Aouda did not quite know

what to make of him, though Passepartout had given
her some hints of his master's eccentricity, and made
her smile by telling her of the wager which was send-
ing him around the world. After all, she owed Phileas
Fogg her life, and she always looked at him through
her gratitude.

Aouda confirmed the Parsee guide's narrative of
her touching history. She did, indeed, belong to the
highest of the native races of India. Many of the Parsee merchants have made great fortunes there by dealing in cotton; and one of them, Sir Jametsee Jeejeebhoy,
was made a baronet by the English government. Aouda
was a relative of this great man, and it was his cousin,
Jeejeeh, whom she hoped to join in Hong Kong.
Whether she would find a protector in him she could
not tell; but Mr. Fogg tried to calm her anxieties and
to assure her that everything would be mathematically—he used the very word—settled.

Did the young woman understand this horrible
word? One doesn't know. Aouda would fasten her great
eyes, "clear as the sacred lakes of the Himalaya,"
upon him; but the intractable Fogg, as reserved as
ever, did not seem at all inclined to throw himself into
this lake.

The first few days of the voyage passed prosper-
ously, amid favorable weather and propitious winds,
and they soon came in sight of the great Andaman,
the principal of the islands in the Bay of Bengal, with
its picturesque Saddle Peak, two thousand four hundred feet high, looming above the waters. The steamer
passed along near the shores, but the savage Papuans,
who are in the lowest scale of humanity, but are not,
as has been asserted, cannibals, did not make their
appearance.

The panorama of the islands, as they steamed by
them, was superb. Vast forests of palms, arecs, bamboo, teakwood, gigantic mimosa, and treelike ferns
covered the foreground, while behind, the graceful

outlines of the mountains were traced against the sky.
And along the coasts swarmed thousands the precious
swallows whose nests provide the tables of the Celestial Empire with an exotic dish. The varied landscape
afforded by the Andaman Islands soon was passed,
however, and the *Rangoon* rapidly approached the
Straits of Malacca, which give access to the China
seas.

What was detective Fix, so unluckily drawn on from
country to country, doing all this while? He had managed to embark on the *Rangoon* in Calcutta without
being seen by Passepartout, after leaving orders that,
if the warrant should arrive, it should be forwarded to
him in Hong Kong; and he hoped to conceal his presence until the end of the voyage. It would have been
difficult to explain why he was on board without awak-
ening Passepartout's suspicions, who thought him still
in Bombay. But necessity impelled him, nevertheless,
to renew his acquaintance with the good servant, as
will be seen.

All the detective's hopes and wishes were now cen-
tered on Hong Kong. The steamer's stay in Singapore
would be too brief to enable him to take any steps
there. The arrest must be made in Hong Kong, or the
robber would probably escape him forever. Hong Kong
was the last English ground on which he would set
foot; beyond, China, Japan, America offered Fogg an
almost certain refuge. If the warrant should at last
make its appearance in Hong Kong, Fix could arrest
him and hand him to the local police, and there would
be no further trouble. But beyond Hong Kong, a simple warrant would be of no avail; an extradition warrant would be necessary, and that would result in
delays and obstacles, of which the rascal would take
advantage to elude justice.

Fix thought over these probabilities during the long
hours which he spent in his cabin, and kept repeating to himself, "Now, either the warrant will be in

Hong Kong, in which case I shall arrest my man, or it will not be there; and this time it is absolutely necessary that I should delay his departure. I have failed in Bombay, and I have failed in Calcutta: if I fail in Hong Kong, my reputation is lost. Cost what it may, I *must* succeed! But how shall I prevent his departure, if that should turn out to be my last resource?''

Fix made up his mind that, if worst came to worst, he would make a confidant of Passepartout, and tell him what kind of a fellow his master really was. Passepartout was not Fogg's accomplice, he was very certain of this. The servant, enlightened by his disclosure, and afraid of being himself implicated in the crime, would doubtless become an ally of the detective. But this method was a dangerous one, only to be employed when everything else had failed. A word from Passepartout to his master would ruin all. The detective was extremely puzzled. But suddenly a new idea struck him. The presence of Aouda on the *Rangoon,* in company with Phileas Fogg, gave him new material for reflection.

Who was this woman? What combination of events had made her Fogg's traveling companion? They had evidently met somewhere between Bombay and Calcutta, but where? Has they met accidentally, or had Fogg gone into the interior purposely in quest of this charming woman? Fix was fairly puzzled. He asked himself whether there had not been a wicked abduction. This idea so impressed itself upon his mind that he determined to make use of the supposed intrigue. Whether the young woman was married or not, he would be able to create such difficulties for Mr. Fogg in Hong Kong that he could not escape by paying any amount of money.

But could he wait till they reached Hong Kong? Fogg had an abominable way of jumping from one boat to another, and, before anything could be done, he might be already far away.

Fix decided that he must warn the English authorities, and signal the *Rangoon* before her arrival. This was easy to do, since the steamer stopped in Singapore, which is connected by wire to Hong Kong. He finally resolved, moreover, before acting more positively, to question Passepartout. It would not be difficult to make him talk. And, as there was no time to lose, Fix prepared to make himself known.

It was now the 30th of October, and on the following day the *Rangoon* was due in Singapore.

Fix emerged from his cabin and went on deck. Passepartout was promenading up and down in the forward part of the steamer. The detective rushed forward with every appearance of extreme surprise, and exclaimed, "You here, on the *Rangoon?*"

"What, Monsieur Fix, are you on board?" returned the really astonished Passepartout, recognizing his crony of the *Mongolia*. "Why, I left you in Bombay, and here you are, on the way to Hong Kong! Are you going around the world too?"

"No, no," replied Fix; "I shall stop in Hong Kong—for at least a few days."

"Hum!" said Passepartout, who seemed for an instant perplexed. "But how is it I have not seen you on board since we left Calcutta?"

"Oh, a trifle of seasickness—I've been staying in my cabin. The Gulf of Bengal does not agree with me as well as the Indian Ocean. And how is Mr. Fogg?"

"As well and as punctual as ever, not a day behind time! But, Monsieur Fix, you don't know that we have a young lady with us."

"A young lady?" replied the detective, not seeming to comprehend what was said.

Passepartout thereupon recounted Aouda's history, the affair at the Bombay pagoda, the purchase of the elephant for two thousand pounds, the rescue, the arrest and sentence of the Calcutta court, and the restoration of Mr. Fogg and himself to liberty on bail.

Fix, who was familiar with the last events, seemed to be equally ignorant of all that Passepartout related. The latter was charmed to find so interested a listener.

"But does your master propose to take this young woman to Europe?"

"Not at all. We are simply going to place her under the protection of one of her relatives, a rich merchant in Hong Kong."

"Nothing to be done there," said Fix to himself, concealing his disappointment. "A glass of gin, Mr. Passepartout?"

"Willingly, Monsieur Fix. We must at least have a drink to our meeting on board the *Rangoon.*"

CHAPTER XVII

SHOWING WHAT HAPPENS ON THE VOYAGE FROM SINGAPORE TO HONG KONG

From that day on, the detective and Passepartout met frequently on deck, though Fix was reserved, and did not attempt to induce his companion to divulge any more facts concerning Mr. Fogg. He caught a glimpse of that mysterious gentleman once or twice; but Mr. Fogg usually confined himself to the *Rangoon's* main salon where he kept Mrs. Aouda company, or, according to his inveterate habit, took a hand at whist.

Passepartout began very seriously to conjecture what strange chance kept Fix on the same route that his master was pursuing. It was really worth considering why this certainly very amiable and agreeable person, whom he had first met in Suez, had then encountered on board the *Mongolia,* who disembarked in Bombay, announcing it as his destination, and yet now turned up so unexpectedly on the *Rangoon,* was following Mr. Fogg's tracks step by step. What was Fix's object? Passepartout was ready to wager his babouches—which he carefully kept—that Fix would also leave Hong Kong at the same time with them, and probably on the same steamer.

Passepartout might have pondered for a century without hitting upon the detective's real purpose. He never could have imagined that Phileas Fogg was being tracked around the globe as a robber. But as it is in human nature to attempt the solution of every mystery, Passepartout suddenly discovered an explanation of Fix's movements, which was in truth far from unreasonable. Fix, he thought, could only be an agent of Mr. Fogg's friends at the Reform Club, sent to follow him up, and to ascertain that he really went around the world as had been agreed upon.

"It's clear!" repeated the good servant to himself, proud of his shrewdness. "He's a spy sent to keep us in view! That isn't quite the thing, either, to be spying on Mr. Fogg, who is so honorable a man! Ah, gentlemen of the Reform, this shall cost you dear!"

Passepartout, enchanted with his discovery, resolved to say nothing to his master, lest he should be justly offended at this mistrust on the part of his adversaries. But he determined to chaff Fix, when he had the chance, with mysterious allusions, which, however, need not betray his real suspicions.

During the afternoon of Wednesday, October 30th, the *Rangoon* entered the Strait of Malacca, which separates the peninsula of that name from Sumatra. The mountainous and craggy islets hid the beauties of this noble island from the view of the travelers. The *Rangoon* dropped anchor in Singapore the next day at four A.M., to receive coal, having gained half a day on the prescribed time of her arrival. Phileas Fogg noted this gain in his journal, and then, accompanied by Mrs. Aouda, who betrayed a desire for a walk on shore, disembarked.

Fix, who suspected Mr. Fogg's every movement, followed them cautiously, without being himself noticed. Meanwhile, Passepartout, laughing to himself at Fix's maneuvers, went about his usual errands.

The island of Singapore is not imposing in aspect, for there are no mountains; yet its appearance is not without attractions. It is a park checkered by pleasant highways and avenues. A handsome carriage, drawn by a sleek pair of New Holland horses, carried Phileas Fogg and Mrs. Aouda into the midst of rows of palms with brilliant foliage, and of clove trees whereof the cloves form the heart of a half-open flower. Pepper plants replaced the prickly hedges of European fields; sago bushes, large ferns with gorgeous branches, varied the aspect of this tropical clime; while nutmeg trees in full foliage filled the air with a penetrating perfume. Agile and grinning bands of monkeys were not wanting in the forests, nor were tigers in the jungles.

After a two hours drive through the country, Mrs. Aouda and Mr. Fogg returned to the town, which is a vast collection of heavy-looking, irregular houses, surrounded by charming gardens rich in tropical fruits and plants. At ten o'clock they reembarked, closely followed by the detective, who had kept them constantly in sight.

Passepartout, who had been purchasing several dozen mangoes—a fruit as large as good-sized apples, of a dark-brown color outside and a bright red within, and whose white pulp, which melts in the mouth, affords gourmets a delicious sensation—was waiting for them on deck. He was only too glad to offer some mangoes to Aouda, who gracefully thanked him for them.

At eleven o'clock the *Rangoon* rode out of Singapore harbor, and in a few hours the high mountains of Malacca, with their forests inhabited by the most beautifully furred tigers in the world, were lost to view. Singapore is some thirteen hundred miles from the island of Hong Kong, which is a little English colony near the Chinese coast. Phileas Fogg hoped to accomplish the journey in six days, so as to be in time for the steamer which would leave on the 6th of November for Yokohama, the principal Japanese port.

The *Rangoon* had a large load of passengers, many

of whom had gone on board in Singapore, among them a number of Indians, Ceylonese, Chinamen, Malays, and Portuguese, mostly second-class travelers.

The weather, which had hitherto been fine, changed with the last quarter of the moon. The sea rolled heavily, and the wind at intervals rose almost to a storm, but happily blew from the southwest, and thus helped the steamer's progress. The captain as often as possible put up his sails, and under the double action of steam and sail, the vessel made rapid progress along the coasts of Anam and Cochin China. Owing to the defective construction of the *Rangoon,* however, unusual precautions became necessary in unfavorable weather. The loss of time which resulted from this cause, while it nearly drove Passepartout out of his mind, did not seem to affect his master in the least. Passepartout blamed the captain, the engineer, and the crew, and cursed all those who carry passengers. Perhaps the thought of the gas, which was remorselessly burning at his expense in Saville Row, had something to do with his hot impatience.

"You are in a great hurry, then," said Fix to him one day, "to reach Hong Kong?"

"A very great hurry!"

"Mr. Fogg, I suppose, is anxious to catch the steamer for Yokohama?"

"Terribly anxious."

"You believe in this peculiar journey around the world, then?"

"Absolutely. Don't you, Mr. Fix?"

"I? I don't believe a word of it."

"You're a sly dog!" said Passepartout, winking at him.

This expression rather disturbed Fix, without his knowing why. Had the Frenchman guessed his real purpose? He knew not what to think. But how could Passepartout have discovered that he was a detective?

Yet, in speaking as he did, the man evidently meant more than he expressed.

Passepartout went still further the next day; he could not hold his tongue.

"Mr. Fix," said he, in a bantering tone, "shall we be so unfortunate as to lose you when we get to Hong Kong?"

"Why," responded Fix, a little embarrassed, "I don't know; perhaps—"

"Ah, if you would only go on with us! An agent of the Peninsular Company, you know, can't stop on the way! You were only going to Bombay, and here you are in China. America is not far off, and from America to Europe is only a step."

Fix looked intently at his companion, whose countenance was as serene as possible, and laughed with him. But Passepartout persisted in chaffing him by asking him if he made much by his present occupation.

"Yes, and no," returned Fix; "there is good and bad luck in such things. But you must understand that I don't travel at my own expense."

"Oh, I am quite sure of that!" cried Passepartout, laughing heartily.

Fix, fairly puzzled, went down to his cabin and gave himself up to his reflections. He was evidently suspected; somehow or other the Frenchman had found out that he was a detective. But had he warned his master? What part was he playing in all this: was he an accomplice or not? Was the game, then, up? Fix spent several hours turning these things over in his mind, sometimes thinking that all was lost, then persuading himself that Fogg was ignorant of his presence, and then undecided what course it was best to take.

Nevertheless, he preserved his coolness of mind, and at last resolved to deal plainly with Passepartout. If he did not find it practicable to arrest Fogg in Hong

Kong, and if Fogg made preparations to leave that last foothold of English territory, he, Fix, would tell Passepartout all. Either the servant was the accomplice of his master, and in that case the master knew of his operations, and he should fail; or else the servant knew nothing about the robbery, and then his interest would be to abandon the robber.

Such was the situation between Fix and Passepartout. Meanwhile Phileas Fogg moved about above them in the most majestic and unconscious indifference. He was passing methodically in his orbit around the world, regardless of the lesser stars which gravitated around him. Yet there was nearby what the astronomers would call an errant star, which might have produced disturbances in this gentleman's heart. But no! the charms of Aouda failed to act, to Passepartout's great surprise; and the disturbances, if they existed, would have been more difficult to calculate than those of Uranus which led to the discovery of Neptune.

Every day it was an increasing wonder to Passepartout, who read in Aouda's eyes the depths of her gratitude to his master. Phileas Fogg had enough heart to behave as a hero, but as a lover, no! As to the sentiment which this journey might have awakened in him, there was clearly no trace of such a thing; while poor Passepartout existed in perpetual trances.

One day he was leaning on the railing of the engine-room, and was observing the engine, when a sudden pitch of the steamer threw the propeller out of the water. The steam came hissing out of the valves. Passepartout was indignant.

"The valves are not sufficiently charged!" he exclaimed. "We are not going. Oh, these English! If this was an American craft, we should blow up, perhaps, but we should at all events go faster!"

CHAPTER XVIII

In Which Phileas Fogg, Passepartout, and Fix Each Goes About His Business

The weather was bad during the latter days of the voyage. The wind, obstinately remaining in the northwest, blew a gale, and slowed the steamer. The *Rangoon* rolled heavily, and the passengers became impatient of the long, monstrous waves which the wind raised before their path. A sort of tempest arose on the 3rd of November, the squall knocking the vessel about with fury and the waves running high. The *Rangoon* reefed all her sails, and even the rigging proved too much, whistling and shaking amid the squall. The steamer was forced to proceed slowly, and the captain estimated that she would reach Hong Kong twenty hours behind time, and more if the storm lasted.

Phileas Fogg gazed at the tempestuous sea, which seemed to be struggling especially to delay him, with his habitual tranquility. He never changed countenance for an instant, though a delay of twenty hours, by making him too late for the Yokohama boat, would almost inevitably cause the loss of the wager. But this calm man manifested neither impatience nor annoyance. It seemed as if the storm were a part of his program, and had been foreseen. Mrs. Aouda was amazed to find him as calm as he had been from the first time she saw him.

Fix did not look at the state of things in the same light. The storm greatly pleased him. His satisfaction would have been complete had the *Rangoon* been forced to retreat before the violence of wind and waves. Each delay filled him with hope, for it became more and more probable that Fogg would be obliged to remain some days in Hong Kong. And now the heavens themselves, with the gusts and squalls, became his allies. It mattered not that they made him seasick—he made no account of this inconvenience; and while his body was writhing under their effects, his spirit bounded with hopeful exultation.

Passepartout was enraged beyond expression by the unpropitious weather. Everything had gone so well till now! Earth and sea had seemed to be at his master's service; steamers and railways obeyed him; wind and steam united to speed his journey. Had the hour of adversity come? Passepartout was as excited as if the twenty thousand pounds were to come from his own pocket. The storm exasperated him, the gale made him furious, and he longed to lash the obstinate sea into obedience. Poor fellow! Fix carefully concealed from him his own satisfaction, for, had he betrayed it, Passepartout could scarcely have restrained himself from personal violence.

Passepartout remained on deck as long as the tempest lasted, being unable to remain quiet below, and taking it into his head to aid the progress of the ship by lending a hand with the crew. He overwhelmed the captain, officers, and sailors with all sorts of questions and they could not help laughing at his impatience. He wanted to know exactly how long the storm was going to last; whereupon he was referred to the barometer, which seemed to have no intention of rising. Passepartout shook it, but with no perceptible effect; for neither shaking nor maledictions could prevail upon it to change its mind.

On the 4th, however, the sea subsided, and the storm

lessened its violence. The wind veered south and was once more favorable. Passepartout brightened up with the weather. Some of the sails were unfurled, and the *Rangoon* resumed its trip with marvelous speed.

The time lost could not, however, be regained. Land was not sighted until five o'clock on the morning of the 6th; the steamer was due on the 5th. Phileas Fogg was twenty-four hours behind, and the Yokohama steamer would of course be missed.

The pilot went on board at six, and took his place on the bridge, to guide the *Rangoon* through the channels to the port of Hong Kong. Passepartout longed to ask him if the steamer had left for Yokohama. But he dared not, for he wished to preserve the spark of hope till the last moment. He had confided his anxiety to Fix, who—the sly rascal!—tried to console him by saying that Mr. Fogg would be in time if he took the next boat; but this only enraged Passepartout.

Mr. Fogg, bolder than his servant, did not hesitate to approach the pilot, and tranquilly ask him if he knew when a steamer would leave Hong Kong for Yokohama.

"At high tide tomorrow morning," answered the pilot.

"Ah!" said Mr. Fogg, without betraying any astonishment.

Passepartout, who heard what had happened, would willingly have kissed the pilot, while Fix would have been glad to twist his neck.

"What is the steamer's name?" asked Mr. Fogg.

"The *Carnatic.*"

"Ought she not to have gone yesterday?"

"Yes, sir; but they had to repair one of her boilers, and so her departure was postponed till tomorrow."

"Thank you," returned Mr. Fogg, who went down with his automatonlike walk to the salon.

Passepartout clasped the pilot's hand and shook it

heartily in his delight, exclaiming, "Pilot, you are a good man!"

The pilot probably does not know to this day why his responses won him this enthusiastic greeting. He went back to the bridge, and guided the steamer through the flotilla of junks, tankas, and fishing boats which crowd the harbor of Hong Kong.

At one o'clock the *Rangoon* was at the quay, and the passengers were going ashore.

Chance had strangely favored Phileas Fogg, for, if the *Carnatic* not been forced to lie over to repair her boilers, she would have left on the 6th of November, and the passengers for Japan would have been obliged to await a week for the sailing of the next steamer. Mr. Fogg was, it is true, twenty-four hours behind; but this could not seriously imperil the remainder of his tour.

The steamer which crossed the Pacific from Yokohama to San Francisco made a direct connection with that from Hong Kong, and it could not sail until the latter reached Yokohama; and if Mr. Fogg was twenty-four hours late on reaching Yokohama, this time would no doubt be easily regained in the voyage of twenty-two days across the Pacific. He found himself, then, about twenty-four hours behind, thirty-five days after leaving London.

The *Carnatic* was announced to leave Hong Kong at five the next morning. Mr. Fogg had sixteen hours in which to attend to his business there, which was to deposit Aouda safely with her wealthy relative.

On landing, he conducted her to a palanquin, in which they went to the Club Hotel. A room was reserved for the young woman, and Mr. Fogg, after seeing that she had what she needed, set out in search of her cousin Jejeeh. He instructed Passepartout to remain at the hotel until his return, that Mrs. Aouda might not be left entirely alone.

Mr. Fogg went to the Exchange, where, he was certain, every one would know so wealthy and considerable a person as the Parsee merchant. Meeting a broker, he made the inquiry, to learn that Jejeeh had left China two years before, and, retiring from business with an immense fortune, had taken up his residence in Europe—in Holland, the broker thought, with the merchants of which country he had principally traded. Phileas Fogg returned to the hotel, begged a moment's conversation with Mrs. Aouda, and, without more ado, told her that Jejeeh was no longer in Hong Kong, but probably in Holland.

Mrs. Aouda at first said nothing. She passed her hand across her forehead, and reflected a few moments. Then, in her sweet, soft voice, she said, "What ought I to do, Mr. Fogg?"

"It is very simple," responded the gentleman. "Go on to Europe."

"But I cannot intrude—"

"You do not intrude, nor do you in the least interfere with my project. Passepartout!"

"Monsieur."

"Go to the *Carnatic,* and reserve three cabins."

Passepartout, delighted that the young woman, who was very gracious to him, was going to continue the journey with them, went off at a brisk gait to obey his master's order.

CHAPTER XIX

IN WHICH PASSEPARTOUT TAKES TOO GREAT AN INTEREST IN HIS MASTER, AND WHAT COMES OF IT

Hong Kong is an island which came into the possession of the English by the treaty of Nankin after the war of 1842. It is now an important city and an excellent port. The island is situated at the mouth of the Canton River, and is separated by about sixty miles from the Portuguese town of Macao, on the opposite bank. Hong Kong has beaten Macao in the struggle for the Chinese trade, and now the greater part of the transportation of Chinese goods finds its depot at the former place. Docks, hospitals, wharves, a Gothic cathedral, a government house, macadamized streets give to Hong Kong the appearance of a town in Kent or Surrey transferred by some strange magic to its antipodes.

Passepartout wandered, with his hands in his pockets, toward the Victoria port, gazing as he went at the curious palanquins and other modes of conveyance and the groups of Chinese, Japanese, and Europeans who passed to and fro in the streets. Hong Kong seemed to him not unlike Bombay, Calcutta, and Singapore, since, like them, it betrayed everywhere the evidence of English supremacy. At the Victoria port he found a confused mass of ships of all nations, English, French, American, and Dutch, men-of-war and trading vessels, Japanese and Chinese junks, sempas, tankas, and flower boats, which formed so many floating parterres. Passepartout noticed in the crowd a number of the natives who seemed very old and were dressed in yellow. On going into a barber's to get shaved, he learned that these ancient men were all at least eighty years old, at which age they were permitted to wear yellow, which is the Imperial color. Passepartout, without exactly knowing why, thought this very funny.

On reaching the quay where they were to embark on the *Carnatic*, he was not surprised to find Fix pacing back and forth. The detective seemed very much disappointed.

"Things are not going well," muttered Passepartout, "for the gentlemen of the Reform Club!" He went up to Fix with a merry smile, as if he had not perceived that gentleman's annoyance. The detective had, indeed, good reasons to curse the bad luck which pursued him. The warrant had not come! It was certainly on the way, but as certainly it could not now reach Hong Kong for several days. Since this was the last English territory on Mr. Fogg's route, the robber would escape unless he could manage to detain him.

"Well, Monsieur Fix," said Passepartout, "have you decided to go on with us as far as America?"

"Yes." returned Fix, through his clenched teeth.

"Good!" exclaimed Passepartout, laughing heartily. "I knew you could not part from us. Come and reserve your berth."

They entered the steamer office and secured cabins for four persons. The clerk, as he gave them the tickets, informed them that, the repairs on the *Carnatic* having been completed, the steamer would leave that very evening, and not next morning as had been announced.

"That will suit my master all the better," said Passepartout. "I will go and let him know."

Fix now decided to make a bold move; he resolved to tell Passepartout all. It seemed to be the only possible means of keeping Phileas Fogg several days longer in Hong Kong. He accordingly invited his companion into a tavern which caught his eye on the quay.

On entering, they found themselves in a large room handsomely decorated, at the end of which was a large camp bed furnished with cushions. Several persons lay upon this bed in a deep sleep. At the small tables which were arranged about the room some thirty customers were drinking English beer, porter, gin, and brandy, and at the same time smoking long red clay pipes stuffed with little balls of opium mingled with essence of rose. From time to time one of the smokers, overcome with the narcotic, would slip under the table, whereupon the waiters, taking him by the head and feet, picked him up and laid him on the bed. The bed already held twenty of these stupefied smokers.

Fix and Passepartout saw that they were in a smoking-house haunted by those wretched, cadaverous, idiotic creatures to whom every year the English merchants sell one million four hundred thousand pounds of the miserable drug called opium to the tune of millions spent on one of the most despicable vices which afflict humanity! The Chinese government has in vain attempted to deal with the evil by stringent laws. It passed gradually from the rich, to whom it was at first exclusively reserved, to the lower classes, and then its ravages could not be stopped. Opium is smoked everywhere, at all times, by men and women, in the Celestial Empire; and, once accustomed to it, the victims cannot dispense with it except by suffering horrible stomach pains. A great smoker can smoke as many as eight pipes a day; but he dies in five years. It was in one of these dens that Fix and Passepartout, in search of a friendly drink, found themselves. Passepartout had no money, but willingly accepted Fix's in-

vitation in the hope of returning the favor at some
future time.

They ordered two bottles of port, to which the
Frenchman did ample justice, while Fix observed him
with close attention. They chatted about the journey,
and Passepartout was especially merry at the idea that
Fix was going to go on with them. When the bottles
were empty, however, he rose to go and tell his master
of the change in the time of the sailing of the *Carnatic.*

Fix caught him by the arm, and said, "Wait a moment."

"What for, Mr. Fix?"

"I want to have a serious talk with you."

"A serious talk!" cried Passepartout, drinking up
the little wine that was left in the bottom of his glass.
"Well, we'll talk about it tomorrow; I haven't time
now."

"Stay! What I have to say concerns your master."

Passepartout, at this, looked attentively at his companion. Fix's face seemed to have a singular expression. He resumed his seat.

"What is it that you have to say?"

Fix placed his hand upon Passepartout's arm and,
lowering his voice, said, "You have guessed who I
am?"

"Parbleu!" said Passepartout, smiling.

"Then I'm going to tell you everything—"

"Now that I know everything, my friend! Ah! that's
too much. But go on, go on anyway. First, though, let
me tell you that those gentlemen have put themselves
to a useless expense."

"Useless!" said Fix. "So you say. It's clear that you
don't know how large the sum is."

"Of course I do," returned Passepartout. "Twenty
thousand pounds."

"Fifty-five thousand!" answered Fix, pressing his
companion's hand.

"What!" cried the Frenchman. "Has Monsieur Fogg dared—fifty-five thousand pounds! Well, there's all the more reason for not losing an instant," he continued, getting up hastily.

Fix pushed Passepartout back in his chair, after having ordered a flask of brandy, and resumed: "Fifty-five thousand pounds; and if I succeed, I get two thousand pounds. If you'll help me, I'll let you have five hundred of them."

"Help you?" cried Passepartout, whose eyes were standing wide open.

"Yes; help me keep Mr. Fogg here for two or three days."

"Why, what are you saying? These gentlemen are not satisfied with following my master and suspecting his honor, but they must try to put obstacles in his way! I am embarrassed for them!"

"What do you mean?"

"I mean that it is a piece of shameful trickery. They might as well strip Mr. Fogg and put his money in their pockets!"

"That's just what we count on doing."

"It's a conspiracy, then," cried Passepartout, who became more and more excited as he drank absent-mindedly the brandy Fix was serving him. "A real conspiracy! And gentlemen, too. Bah!"

Fix began to be puzzled.

"Members of the Reform Club!" continued Passepartout. "You must know, Monsieur Fix, that my master is an honest man, and that, when he makes a wager, he tries to win it fairly!"

"But who do you think I am?" asked Fix, looking at him intently.

"Parbleu! An agent of the members of the Reform Club, sent out here to interrupt my master's journey. But, though I found you out some time ago, I've taken good care to say nothing about it to Mr. Fogg."

"He knows nothing, then?"

"Nothing," replied Passepartout, again, emptying his glass.

The detective passed his hand across his forehead, hesitating before he spoke again. What should he do? Passepartout's mistake seemed sincere, but it made his design more difficult. It was evident that the servant was not the master's accomplice as Fix had been inclined to suspect.

"Well," said the detective to himself, "as he is not an accomplice, he will help me."

He had no time to lose: Fogg must be detained in Hong Kong; so he resolved to make a clean breast of it.

"Listen to me," said Fix abruptly. "I am not, as you think, an agent of the members of the Reform Club—"

"Bah!" retorted Passepartout, looking at him mockingly.

"I am a police detective, sent out here by the London office."

"You, a detective?"

"I will prove it. Here is my commission."

Passepartout was speechless with astonishment when Fix displayed this document, the genuineness of which could not be doubted.

"Mr. Fogg's wager," resumed Fix, "is only a pretext, of which you and the gentlemen of the Reform are dupes. He had a motive for securing your innocent complicity."

"But why?"

"Listen. On the 28th of last September a robbery of fifty-five thousand pounds was committed at the Bank of England by a person whose description was fortunately secured. Here is this description; it answers exactly to that of Mr. Phileas Fogg."

"What nonsense!" cried Passepartout, striking the table with his fist. "My master is the most honorable of men!"

"How can you tell? You know scarcely anything about him. You went into his service the day he came away. And he left on a foolish pretext, without trunks, and carrying a large amount in banknotes. And yet you are bold enough to assert that he is an honest man!"

"Yes, yes," repeated the poor fellow, mechanically.

"Would you like to be arrested as his accomplice?"

Passepartout, overcome by what he had heard, held his head between his hands, and did not dare to look at the detective. Phileas Fogg, the savior of Aouda, that brave and generous man, a robber! And yet how many presumptions there were against him! Passepartout was trying to reject the suspicions which forced themselves upon his mind; he did not wish to believe that his master was guilty.

"Well, what do you want of me?" said he, at last, with effort.

"See here," replied Fix; "I have tracked Mr. Fogg to this place, but as yet I have failed to receive the warrant of arrest for which I sent to London. You must help me to keep him here in Hong Kong—"

"I! But I—"

"I will share with you the two thousand pounds reward offered by the Bank of England."

"Never!" replied Passepartout, who tried to rise, but fell back, exhausted in mind and body.

"Mr. Fix," he stammered, "even should what you say be true—if my master is really the robber you are seeking—which I deny—I have been, am, in his service; I have seen his generosity and goodness; and I will never betray him—not for all the gold in the world. I come from a village where they don't behave that way!"

"You refuse?"

"I refuse."

"Consider that I've said nothing," said Fix; "and let us drink."

Passepartout felt himself yielding more and more to the effects of the liquor. Fix, seeing that he must, at all cost, be separated from his master, wished to entirely overcome him. Some pipes full of opium lay upon the table. Fix slipped one into Passepartout's hand. He took it, put it between his lips, lit it, drew several puffs, and his head, becoming heavy under the influence of the narcotic, fell upon the table.

"At last!" said Fix, seeing Passepartout unconscious. "Mr. Fogg will not be informed of the time of the *Carnatic*'s departure; and, if he is, he will have to go without this cursed Frenchman!"

And, after paying his bill, Fix left the tavern.

CHAPTER XX

IN WHICH FIX COMES FACE TO FACE WITH PHILEAS FOGG

During this scene at the opium-house Mr. Fogg, unconscious of the danger he was in of losing the steamer, was quietly escorting Mrs. Aouda about the streets of the English quarter, making the necessary purchases for the long voyage before them. It was all very well for an Englishman like Mr. Fogg to go around the world with a bag; a lady could not be expected to travel comfortably under such conditions. He performed his task with characteristic serenity, and invariably replied to the remonstrances of his fair companion, who was embarrassed by his patience and generosity—

"It is in the interest of my journey—a part of my program."

The purchases made, they returned to the hotel, where they dined at a sumptuously served table d'hôte; after which Mrs. Aouda, shaking hands with her protector after the English fashion retired to her room for rest. Mr. Fogg absorbed himself throughout the evening in the perusal of the *Times* and *Illustrated London News*.

Had he been capable of being astonished at anything, it would have been not to see his servant return at bedtime. But, knowing that the steamer was not to leave for Yokohama until the next morning, he did not disturb himself about the matter. When Passepartout did not appear the next morning to answer his master's bell, Mr. Fogg, not betraying the least vexation, just took his bag, called Mrs. Aouda, and sent for a palanquin.

It was then eight o'clock; at half-past nine, it being then high tide, the *Carnatic* would leave the harbor. Mr. Fogg and Mrs. Aouda got into the palanquin, their luggage following on a wheelbarrow, and half an hour later stepped upon the quay whence they were to embark. Mr. Fogg then learned that the *Carnatic* had sailed the evening before. He had expected to find not only the steamer, but his servant, and was forced to give up both; but no sign of disappointment appeared on his face, and he merely remarked to Aouda, "It is an incident, madam; nothing more."

At this moment a man who had been observing him attentively approached. It was Fix, who, bowing, addressed Mr. Fogg: "Were you not, like me, sir, a passenger on the *Rangoon,* which arrived yesterday?"

"I was, sir," replied Mr. Fogg coolly. "But I have not the honor—"

"Pardon me; I thought I should find your servant here."

"Do you know where he is, sir?" asked Mrs. Aouda anxiously.

"What!" responded Fix, feigning surprise. "Is he not with you?"

"No," said Mrs. Aouda. "He has not reappeared since yesterday. Could he have gone on board the *Carnatic* without us?"

"Without you, madam?" answered the detective. "Excuse me, did you intend to sail on the *Carnatic?*"

"Yes, sir."

"So did I, madam, and I am excessively disappointed. The *Carnatic,* its repairs being completed, left Hong Kong twelve hours before the stated time, without any notice being given; and we must now wait a week for another steamer.''

As he said ''a week'' Fix felt his heart leap for joy. Fogg detained in Hong Kong a week! There would be time for the warrant to arrive, and fortune at last was with the agent of the law. His horror may be imagined when he heard Mr. Fogg say, in his placid voice, ''But there are other vessels besides the *Carnatic,* it seems to me, in the harbor of Hong Kong.''

And, offering his arm to Mrs. Aouda, he directed his steps toward the docks in search of some craft about to leave. Fix, stupefied, followed; it seemed as if he were attached to Mr. Fogg by an invisible thread. Chance, however, appeared really to have abandoned the man it had hitherto served so well. For three hours Phileas Fogg wandered about the docks, with the determination, if necessary, to charter a vessel to carry him to Yokohama; but he could only find vessels which were loading or unloading, and which therefore could not set sail. Fix began to hope again.

But Mr. Fogg, far from being discouraged, was going to continue his search even if he had to resort to Macao, when he was accosted by a sailor on one of the wharves.

''Is your honor looking for a boat?''

''Have you a boat ready for sail?''

''Yes, your honor; a pilot boat—No. 43—the best in the harbor.''

''Does she go fast?''

''Between eight and nine knots the hour. Will you look at her?''

''Yes.''

''Your honor will be satisfied with her. Is it for a sea excursion?''

''No; for a voyage.''

''A voyage?''

''Yes; will you agree to take me to Yokohama?''

The sailor leaned on the railing, opened his eyes wide, and said, "Is your honor joking?"

"No. I have missed the *Carnatic,* and I must get to Yokohama by the 14th at the latest, to take the boat for San Francisco."

"I am sorry," said the sailor, "but it is impossible."

"I offer you a hundred pounds per day, and an additional reward of two hundred pounds if I reach Yokohama in time."

"Are you in earnest?"

"Very much so."

The pilot walked away a little distance, and gazed out to sea, evidently struggling between the desire to gain a large sum and the fear of venturing so far. Fix was in mortal suspense.

Mr. Fogg turned to Mrs. Aouda and asked her, "You would not be afraid, would you, madam?"

"Not with you, Mr. Fogg," was her answer.

The pilot now returned, shuffling his hat in his hands.

"Well, pilot?" said Mr. Fogg.

"Well, your honor," replied he," I could not risk myself, my men, or my little boat of scarcely twenty tons on so long a voyage at this time of year. Besides, we could not reach Yokohama in time, for it is sixteen hundred and sixty miles from Hong Kong."

"Only sixteen hundred," said Mr. Fogg.

"It's the same thing."

Fix breathed more freely.

"But," added the pilot, "it might be done another way."

Fix ceased to breathe at all.

"How?" asked Mr. Fogg.

"By going to Nagasaki at the extreme south of Japan, or even to Shanghai, which is only eight hundred miles from here. In going to Shanghai we would not be forced to sail wide of the Chinese coast, which would be a great advantage, as the currents run north, and would help us."

"Pilot," said Mr. Fogg, "I must take the American steamer at Yokohama, and not in Shanghai or Nagasaki."

"Why not?" returned the pilot. "The San Francisco steamer does not start from Yokohama. It puts in at Yokohama and Nagasaki, but it starts from Shanghai."

"You are sure of that?"

"Perfectly."

"And when does the boat leave Shanghai?"

"On the 11th, at seven in the evening. We have, therefore, four days before us, that is ninety-six hours; and in that time, if we are lucky and have a southwest wind, and the sea is calm, we can make those eight hundred miles to Shanghai."

"And you could go—"

"In an hour; as soon as provisions could be got aboard and the sails put up."

"It is a bargain. Are you the master of the boat?"

"Yes; John Bunsby, master of the *Tankadere.*"

"Would you like a deposit?"

"If it would not put your honor out—"

"Here are two hundred pounds on account. Sir," added Phileas Fogg, turning to Fix, "if you would like to take advantage—"

"Thanks, sir; I was about to ask the favor."

"Very well. In half an hour we shall go on board."

"But poor Passepartout?" urged Aouda, who was much disturbed by the servant's disappearance.

"I shall do all I can to find him," replied Phileas Fogg.

While Fix, feverish, nervous, raging, went to the pilot boat, the others directed their course to the police station in Hong Kong. Phileas Fogg there gave Passepartout's description, and left a sum of money to be spent to repatriate him. The same formalities having been gone through at the French consulate, and the palanquin having stopped at the hotel for the luggage, which had been sent back there, they returned to the wharf.

It was not three o'clock; and pilot boat No. 43, with its crew on board, and its provisions stored away, was ready for departure.

The *Tankadere* was a neat little craft of twenty tons, as gracefully built as if she were a racing yacht. Her shining copper sheathing, her galvanized ironwork, her deck, white as ivory, betrayed the pride taken by John Bunsby in keeping her in fine shape. Her two masts leaned a trifle backward; she carried brigantine, foresail, storm jib, and standing jib, and was well rigged for running before the wind; and she seemed capable of brisk speed, which, indeed, she had already proved by gaining several prizes in pilot boat races. The crew of the *Tankadere* was composed of John Bunsby, the master, and four hardy mariners, who were familiar with the Chinese seas. John Bunsby himself, a man of forty-five or thereabouts, vigorous, sunburnt, with sparkling eyes, an energetic face and a determined look, would have inspired confidence in the most timid.

Phileas Fogg and Aouda went on board. Fix was already there. Below deck was a square cabin, of which the walls bulged out in the form of cots above a circular divan; in the center was a table equipped with a swinging lamp. The accommodation was confined, but neat.

"I am sorry to have nothing better to offer you," said Mr. Fogg to Fix, who bowed without responding.

The detective had a feeling akin to humiliation in taking advantage of Mr. Fogg's kindness.

"It's certain," thought he, "though rascal as he is, he is a polite one!"

The sails and the English flag were hoisted at ten minutes past three. Mr. Fogg and Aouda, who were seated on deck, cast a last glance at the quay, in the hope of seeing Passepartout. Fix was not without his fears since chance might have directed the steps of the unfortunate servant, whom he had so badly treated, in this direction; in which case an explanation the reverse of satisfactory to the detective would have ensued. But the Frenchman did not appear, and, without doubt, was still lying under the stupefying influence of the opium.

John Bunsby, master, at last gave the order to start, and the *Tankadere*, taking the wind under her brigantine, foresail, and standing jib, bounded briskly forward over the waves.

CHAPTER XXI

In Which the Master of the Tankadere Runs Great Risk of Losing a Reward of Two Hundred Pounds

This voyage of eight hundred miles was a perilous venture on a craft of twenty tons, and at that time of the year. The Chinese seas are usually boisterous, subject to terrible gales of wind, and especially during the equinoxes; and it was now early November.

It would clearly have been to the master's advantage to carry his passengers to Yokohama, since he was paid a certain sum per day; but he would have been rash to attempt such a voyage, and it was imprudent even to attempt to reach Shanghai. But John Bunsby believed, probably with reason, in the *Tankadere,* which rode on the waves like a seagull.

Late in the day they passed through the capricious channels of Hong Kong, and the *Tankadere,* impelled by favorable winds, conducted herself admirably.

"I do not need, pilot," said Phileas Fogg, when they got into the open sea, "to advise you to use all possible speed."

"Trust me, your honor. We are carrying all the sail the wind will let us. The poles would add nothing, and are only used when we are going into port."

"It's your trade, not mine, pilot, and I trust you."

Phileas Fogg, with body erect and legs wide apart, standing like a sailor, was gazing calmly at the swelling waters. The young woman, who was seated at the stern, was profoundly affected as she looked out upon the ocean, darkening now with the twilight, on which she had ventured in so frail a vessel. Above her head rustled the white sails, which seemed like great white wings. The boat, carried forward by the wind, seemed to be flying in the air.

Night came. The moon was entering her first quarter, and her insufficient light would soon die out in the mist on the horizon. Clouds were rising from the east, and already overcast a part of the sky.

The pilot had hung out his lights, which was very necessary in these seas crowded with vessels bound landward. Collisions are common occurrences, and, at the speed she was going, the least shock would shatter the gallant little craft.

Fix, seated in the bow, gave himself up to meditation. He kept apart from his fellow travelers, knowing Mr. Fogg's taciturn tastes; besides, he did not quite like to talk to the man whose favors he had accepted. He was thinking, too, of the future. It seemed certain that Fogg would not stop at Yokohama, but would at once take the boat for San Francisco; and the vast extent of America would insure him immunity and safety. Fogg's plan appeared to him the simplest in the world.

Instead of sailing directly from England to the United States, like a common villain, he had crossed three quarters of the globe, so as to gain the American continent more surely; and there, after throwing the police off his track, he would quietly enjoy himself with the fortune stolen from the bank. But, once in the United States, what should he, Fix, do? Should he abandon this man? No, a hundred times no! Until he had secured his extradition, he would not lose sight of him for an hour. It was his duty, and he would fulfil it to the end. At all events, there was one thing to be thankful for: Passepartout was not with his master; and it was important, especially after the confidences Fix had imparted to him, that the servant and the master should not see each other.

Phileas Fogg was also thinking of Passepartout, who had so strangely disappeared. Looking at the matter from every point of view, it did not seem to him impossible that, by some mistake, the man might have embarked on the *Carnatic* at the last moment; and this was also Mrs. Aouda's opinion, who regretted very much the loss of the honest servant to whom she owed so much. They might then find him at Yokohama; for if the *Carnatic* was carrying him thither, it would be easy to find out if he had been on board.

A brisk breeze arose about ten o'clock; but, though it might have been prudent to take in a reef, the pilot, after carefully examining the sky, let the craft remain rigged as before. The *Tankadere* bore sail admirably, as she drew a great deal of water, and everything was prepared for high speed in case of a gale.

Mr. Fogg and Aouda went down into the cabin at midnight, having been already preceded by Fix, who had lain down on one of the cots. The pilot and crew remained on deck all night.

At sunrise the next day, which was November 8th, the boat had gone more than one hundred miles. The log indicated a mean speed of between eight and nine knots. The *Tankadere* still carried all sail, and was accomplishing her greatest capacity for speed. If the wind held as it was, the chances would be in her favor. During the day she kept along the coast, where the currents were favorable; the coast, irregular in profile, and visible sometimes across the clearings, was at most five miles distant. The sea was less boisterous, since the wind came off land—a fortunate circumstance for the boat, which would suffer, owing to its small tonnage, by a heavy surge on the sea.

The breeze subsided a little toward noon, and set in

from the southwest. The pilot put up his poles, but took them down again within two hours, as the wind was beginning to blow again.

Mr. Fogg and Aouda, happily unaffected by the roughness of the sea, ate with a good appetite. Fix was invited to share their meal and had to accept but it did annoy him. To travel at this man's expense and live upon his provisions did not seem loyal to him. Still, he was obliged to eat, and so he ate.

When the meal was over, he took Mr. Fogg aside, and said, "Sir,"—this "sir" scorched his lips, and he had to control himself to avoid collaring this "gentleman"—"sir, you have been very kind to give me a passage on this boat. But, though my means will not let me act as grandly as you do, I must ask to pay my share—"

"Let us not speak of that, sir," replied Mr. Fogg.

"But, if I insist—"

"No, sir," repeated Mr. Fogg, in a tone which did not admit of a reply. "This enters into my general expenses."

Fix, as he bowed, had a stifled feeling, and going forward, where he stretched out, did not open his mouth for the rest of the day.

Meanwhile they were progressing well, and John Bunsby was in high hope. He several times assured Mr. Fogg that they would reach Shanghai in time; to which that gentleman responded that he counted upon it. The crew set to work in good earnest, inspired by the reward to be gained. There was not a sheet which was not tightened, not a sail which was not vigorously hoisted; not a lurch could be charged to the man at the helm. They worked as desperately as if they were contesting in a Royal Yacht regatta.

By evening, the log showed that two hundred and twenty miles had been accomplished from Hong Kong, and Mr. Fogg might hope that he would be able to reach Yokohama without recording any delay in his journal. In which case, the only misadventure which had overtaken him since he left London would not seriously affect his journey.

The *Tankadere* entered the Straits of Fo-Kien, which separate the island of Formosa from the Chinese coast, in the small hours of the night, and crossed the Tropic of Cancer. The sea was very rough in the straits, full of eddies formed by the countercurrents, and the chopping waves broke her course, while it became very difficult to stand on deck.

At daybreak the wind began to blow hard again, and the sky seemed to predict a gale. The barometer announced a speedy change, the mercury rose and fell capriciously; the sea also, in the southeast, raised long surges which indicated a tempest. The sun had set the evening before in a red mist, in the midst of the phosphorescent scintillations of the ocean.

John Bunsby long examined the threatening aspect of the sky, muttering indistinctly between his teeth. At last he said in a low voice to Mr. Fogg, "Shall I speak out to your honor?"

"Of course."

"Well, we are going to have a squall."

"Is the wind north or south?" asked Mr. Fogg quietly.

"South. Look! a typhoon is coming up."

"Glad it's a typhoon from the south, for it will carry us forward."

"Oh, if you take it that way," said John Bunsby, "I've nothing more to say." John Bunsby's suspicions were confirmed. At a less advanced season of the year the typhoon, according to a famous meteorologist, would have passed away like a luminous cascade of electric flame; but in the winter equinox, it was to be feared that it would burst upon them with great violence.

The pilot took his precautions in advance. He reefed all sail, the pole masts were dispensed with; all hands went forward to the bows. A single triangular sail, of strong canvas, was hoisted as a storm jib, so as to hold the wind from behind. Then they waited.

John Bunsby had requested his passengers to go below; but this imprisonment in so narrow a space, with little air, and the boat bouncing in the gale, was far from pleasant. Neither Mr. Fogg, Fix, nor Mrs. Aouda consented to leave the deck.

The storm of rain and wind descended upon them toward eight o'clock. With but its bit of sail, the *Tankadere* was lifted like a feather by a wind an idea of whose violence can scarcely be imagined. To compare her speed to four times that of a locomotive going on full steam would be far from the truth.

The boat scudded thus northward during the whole day, borne on by monstrous waves, always, fortunately, preserving a speed equal to theirs. Twenty times she seemed almost to be submerged by these mountains of water which rose behind her; but the adroit management of the pilot saved her. The passengers were often bathed in spray, but they submitted to it philosophically. Fix cursed it, no doubt; but Aouda, with her eyes fastened upon her protector, whose coolness amazed her, showed herself worthy of him, and bravely weathered the storm. As for Phileas Fogg, it seemed just as if the typhoon were a part of his program.

Up to this time the *Tankadere* had always held her course to the north; but toward evening the wind, veering three quarters, bore down from the northwest. The boat, now lying in the trough of the waves, shook and rolled terribly; the sea struck her with fearful violence. At night the tempest increased in violence. John Bunsby saw the approach of darkness and the rising of the storm with dark misgivings. He thought awhile, and then asked his crew if it was not time to put into port. After a consultation he approached Mr.

Fogg, and said, "I think, your honor, that we should do well to make for one of the ports on the coast."

"I think so too."

"Ah!" said the pilot. "But which one?"

"I know of but one," returned Mr. Fogg, tranquilly.

"And that is—"

"Shanghai."

The pilot, at first, did not seem to understand; he could scarcely realize so much determination and tenacity. Then he cried, "Well—yes! Your honor is right. To Shanghai!"

So the *Tankadere* kept steadily on her northward track.

The night was really terrible. It was a miracle that the craft did not founder. Twice it would have been all over with her, if the ropes had failed. Mrs. Aouda was exhausted, but did not utter a complaint. More than once Mr. Fogg rushed to protect her from the violence of the waves.

Day reappeared. The tempest still raged with undiminished fury; but the wind now returned to the southeast. It was a favorable change, and the *Tankadere* again bounded forward on this mountainous sea, though the waves crossed each other, and imparted shocks and countershocks which would have crushed a craft less solidly built. From time to time the coast was visible through the broken mist, but no vessel was in sight. The *Tankadere* was alone upon the sea.

There were some signs of a calm at noon, and these became more distinct as the sun went down toward the horizon. The tempest had been as brief as terrific. The passengers, thoroughly exhausted, could now eat a little and take some rest.

The night was comparatively quiet. Some of the sails were again hoisted, and the speed of the boat was very good. The next morning at dawn they sighted the coast, and John Bunsby was able to assert that they were within one hundred miles of Shanghai. A hundred miles, and only one day to cross them! That very evening Mr. Fogg had to arrive in Shanghai, if he did not want to miss the steamer to Yokohama. Had there been no storm, during which several hours were lost, they would be at this moment within thirty miles of their destination.

The wind grew decidedly calmer, and happily the sea fell with it. All sails were now hoisted, and at noon the *Tankadere* was within forty-five miles of Shanghai. There remained yet six hours in which to accomplish that distance. All on board feared that it could not be done and every one—Phileas Fogg, no doubt, excepted—felt his heart beat with impatience. The boat must keep up an average of nine knots an hour, and the wind was becoming calmer every moment! It was a capricious breeze, coming from the coast, and after it passed, the sea would be smooth again. Still, the *Tankadere* was so light, and her fine sails caught the fickle zephyrs so well, that, with the aid of the current, John Bunsby found himself at six o'clock not more than ten miles from the mouth of Shanghai River. Shanghai itself is situated at least twelve miles up the stream. At seven they were still three miles from Shanghai. The pilot swore an angry oath; the reward of two hundred pounds was evidently going to escape him. He looked at Mr. Fogg. Mr. Fogg was perfectly tranquil; and yet his whole fortune was at this moment at stake.

At this moment, also, a long black funnel, crowned with wreaths of smoke, appeared on the edge of the waters. It was the American steamer, leaving for Yokohama at the appointed time.

"Curses!" cried John Bunsby, pushing back the rudder with a desperate jerk.

"Signal her!" said Phileas Fogg quietly.

A small brass cannon stood on the forward deck of the *Tankadere*, for making signals in the fog. It was loaded to the muzzle; but just as the pilot was about to apply a red-hot coal to the touchhole, Mr. Fogg said, "Hoist your flag!"

The flag was run up at halfmast, and, this being the signal of distress, it was hoped that the American steamer, noticing it, would change her course a little, so as to join the pilot boat.

"Fire!" said Mr. Fogg. And the booming of the little cannon resounded in the air.

CHAPTER XXII

IN WHICH PASSEPARTOUT FINDS OUT THAT, EVEN AT THE ANTIPODES, IT IS CONVENIENT TO HAVE SOME MONEY IN ONE'S POCKET

The *Carnatic*, setting sail from Hong Kong at half-past six on the 7th of November, was going at full steam towards Japan. She was carrying a large cargo and a well-filled cabin of passengers. Two state-rooms in the rear were, however, unoccupied—those which had been reserved by Phileas Fogg.

The next day a passenger, with glazed-over eyes, staggering gait, and dishevelled hair, was seen to emerge from second class, and to totter to a seat on deck.

It was Passepartout; and what had happened to him was as follows.

Shortly after Fix left the opium den, two waiters had lifted the unconscious Passepartout, and had carried him to the bed reserved for the smokers. Three hours later, pursued even in his dreams by a fixed idea, the poor fellow awoke, and struggled against the stupefying influence of the narcotic. The thought of a duty unfulfilled shook off his torpor, and he hurried from the abode of drunkenness. Staggering and holding himself up by keeping against the walls, falling down and creeping up again, and irresistibly impelled by a kind of instinct, he kept crying out, "The *Carnatic!* the *Carnatic!*"

The steamer lay puffing alongside the quay, about to set sail. Passepartout had but few steps to go; and, rushing upon the plank, he crossed it, and fell unconscious on the deck, just as the *Carnatic* was moving off. Several sailors, who were evidently accustomed to this sort of scene, carried the poor Frenchman down into a second class cabin, and Passepartout did not awake until they were one hundred and fifty miles away from China. Thus he found himself the next morning on the deck of the *Carnatic,* and eagerly inhaling the exhilarating sea breeze. The pure air sobered him up. He began to collect his senses, which he found a difficult task; but at last he recalled the events of the evening before, Fix's revelation, and the opium house.

"It is evident," said he to himself, "that I have been abominably drunk! What will Mr. Fogg say? At least I have not missed the steamer, which is the most important thing."

Then, thinking of Fix, "As for that rascal, I hope we are well rid of him, and that he has not dared, as he proposed, to follow us on board the *Carnatic.* A detective on the track of Mr. Fogg, accused of robbing the Bank of England! Pshaw! Mr. Fogg is no more a robber than I am a murderer."

Should he divulge Fix's real errand to his master? Would it do to tell the part the detective was playing? Would it not be better to wait until Mr. Fogg reached London again, and then impart to him that an agent of the metropolitan police had been following him around the world, and have a good laugh over it? No doubt. At least, it was worth considering. The first thing to do was to find Mr. Fogg, and apologize for his singular behavior.

Passepartout got up and proceeded, as well as he could with the rolling of the steamer, to the after deck.

He saw no one who resembled either his master or Mrs. Aouda. "Good!" muttered he. "Mrs. Aouda has not got up yet, and Mr. Fogg has probably found some partners at whist."

He went down to the salon. Mr. Fogg was not there. Passepartout had only, however, to ask the purser the number of his master's stateroom. The purser replied that he did not know any passenger by the name of Fogg.

"I beg your pardon," said Passepartout persistently. "He is a tall gentleman, quiet, and not very talkative, and has with him a young lady—"

"There is no young lady on board," interrupted the purser. "Here is a list of the passengers; you may see for yourself."

Passepartout scanned the list, but his master's name was not upon it. All at once an idea struck him.

"Ah! am I on the *Carnatic*?"

"Yes."

"On the way to Yokohama?"

"Certainly."

Passepartout had for an instant feared that he was on the wrong boat; but, though he was really on the *Carnatic,* his master was not there.

He fell thunderstruck on a seat. He saw it all now. He remembered that the time of sailing had been changed, that he should have informed his master of that fact, and that he had not done so. It was his fault, then, that Mr. Fogg and Mrs. Aouda had missed the steamer. Yes, but it was still more the fault of the traitor who, in order to separate him from his master, and detain the latter in Hong Kong, had inveigled him into getting drunk! He now saw the detective's trick. At this moment Mr. Fogg was certainly ruined, his bet was lost, and he was perhaps arrested and imprisoned! At this thought Passepartout tore his hair. Ah, if Fix ever came within his reach, what a settling of accounts there would be!

After his first depression, Passepartout became calmer, and began to study his situation. It was certainly not an enviable one. He found himself on the way to Japan, and what should he do when he got there? His pocket was empty; he had not a solitary shilling—not so much as a penny! His passage had fortunately been paid for in advance. He now had five or six days in which to decide upon his future course. The way he ate and drank cannot be described. He ate for Mr. Fogg, for Mrs. Aouda, and for himself. He helped himself as generously as if Japan were a desert, where nothing to eat was to be found.

At dawn on the 13th the *Carnatic* entered the port of Yokohama. This is an important way station in the Pacific, where all the mail steamers, and those carrying travelers between North America, China, Japan, and the Oriental islands, put in. It is situated in the bay of Yeddo, and at but a short distance from that second capital of the Japanese Empire, and the residence of the Tycoon, the civil Emperor, before the Mikado, the spiritual Emperor, absorbed his office in his own.

The *Carnatic* anchored at the quay near the customhouse, in the midst of a crowd of ships bearing the flags of all nations.

Passepartout went timidly ashore on this so curious territory of the Sons of the Sun. He had nothing better to do than, taking chance for his guide, to wander aimlessly through the streets of Yokohama. He found himself at first in a thoroughly European quarter, the houses having low fronts, and being adorned with verandas, beneath which he caught glimpses of elegant peristyles. This quarter occupied, with its streets, squares, docks and warehouses, all the space between the "promontory of the Treaty" and the river. Here, as in Hong Kong and Calcutta, were mixed crowds of all races—Americans and English, Chinamen and Dutchmen, mostly merchants ready to buy or sell anything. The Frenchman felt himself as much alone among them as if he had dropped down in the midst of Hottentots,

He had, at least, one resource—to call on the French and English consuls at Yokohama for assistance. But he shrank from telling the story of his adventures, intimately connected as it was with that of his master: and, before doing so, he determined to exhaust all other means of aid. As chance did not favor him in the European quarter, he entered that inhabited by the native Japanese, determined, if necessary, to push on to Yeddo.

The Japanese quarter of Yokohama is called Benten, after the goddess of the sea, who is worshipped on neighboring islands. There Passepartout beheld beautiful fir and cedar groves, sacred gates of a singular architecture, bridges half-hid in the midst of bamboos and reeds, temples shaded by immense cedar trees, holy retreats where were sheltered Buddhist priests and disciples of Confucius, and interminable streets, where a perfect harvest of rose-tinted and red-cheeked children, who looked as if they had been cut out of Japanese screens, and who were playing in the midst of short-legged poodles and yellowish cats, might have been gathered.

The streets were crowded with people. Priests were passing in processions, beating their dreary tambourines; police and customhouse officers with pointed hats encrusted with lacquer, and carrying two sabres hung at their waists; soldiers clad in blue cotton with white stripes, and bearing guns; the Mikado's guards, enveloped in silken doublets, hauberks, and coats of mail; and numbers of military folk of all ranks—for the military profession is as much respected in Japan as it is despised in China—went hither and thither in groups and pairs. Passepartout saw, too, begging friars, long-robed pilgrims, and simple civilians, with their sleek and jet-black hair, big heads, long busts, slender legs, short stature, and complexions varying from copper-color to a dead white, but never yellow, like the Chinese, from whom the Japanese widely differ. He did not fail to observe the curious equipages—carriages and palanquins, barrows supplied with sails, and litters made of bamboo; nor the women—whom he thought not especially pretty—who took little steps with their little feet, whereon they wore canvas shoes, straw sandals, and wooden clogs, and who displayed slanted eyes, flat chests, teeth fashionably blackened, and gowns crossed with silken scarfs, tied in an enormous knot behind—an ornament which the modern Parisian ladies seem to have borrowed from the Japanese women.

Passepartout wandered for several hours in the midst of this motley crowd, looking in at the windows of the rich and curious shops, the jewelry establishments glittering with quaint Japanese ornaments, the restaurants decked with streamers and banners, the teahouses, where the odorous beverage was being drunk with "saki," a liquor concocted from the fermentation of rice, and the comfortable smoking houses, where they were puffing, not opium, which is almost unknown in Japan, but a very fine tobacco. He went on till he found himself in the fields, in the midst of vast rice plantations. There he saw dazzling camelias expanding themselves, with flowers which were giving forth their last colors and perfumes, not on bushes, but on trees; and within bamboo enclosures, cherry, plum, and apple trees, which the Japanese cultivate rather for their blossoms than their fruit, and which queerly-fashioned grinning scarecrows protect from the sparrows, pigeons, ravens, and other voracious birds. On the branches of the cedars were perched large eagles; amid the foliage of the weeping willows were herons, solemnly standing on one leg; and everywhere were crows, ducks, hawks, wild birds, and a multitude of cranes, which the Japanese consider sacred, and which to their minds symbolize long life and prosperity.

As he was strolling along, Passepartout noticed some violets among the shrubs.

"Good!" said he; "I'll have some supper."

But, on smelling them, he found that they were odorless.

"No luck there," he thought.

The good fellow had certainly eaten as hearty a breakfast as possible before leaving the *Carnatic;* but as he had been walking about all day, his stomach felt very empty.

He observed that the butchers' stalls contained neither mutton, goat, nor pork; and knowing also that it is a sacrilege to kill cattle, which are preserved solely for farming, he made up his mind that meat was far from plentiful in Yokohama—nor was he mistaken. Instead of butcher's meat, his stomach would have been satisfied with a quarter of wild boar or deer, a partridge, or some quails, some game or some fish, which, with rice, the Japanese eat almost exclusively. But he had to put up a good front, and to postpone the meal he craved till the following morning. Night came, and Passepartout reentered the native quarter, where he wandered through the streets, lit by multicolored lanterns, looking on at the dancers who were executing skillful steps and bounds, and the astrologers who stood in the open air with their telescopes. Then he came to the harbor, which was lit up by the rosin torches of the fishermen, who were fishing from their boats.

The streets at last became quiet, and the patrol, the officers of which, in their splendid uniforms and surrounded by their suites, looked like embassadors, followed the bustling crowd. Each time a company went by, Passepartout chuckled, and said to himself, "Good! another Japanese embassy departing for Europe!"

CHAPTER XXIII

In Which Passepartout's Nose Becomes Outrageously Long

The next morning poor, exhausted, famished, Passepartout said to himself that he must get something to eat at all costs, and the sooner he did so the better. He might, indeed, sell his watch; but he would have starved first.

Now or never he must use the strong, if not melodious voice which nature had bestowed upon him. He knew several French and English songs, and resolved to try them upon the Japanese, who must be lovers of music, since they were forever pounding on their cymbals, tam-tams, and tambourines, and could not help but appreciate European talent.

It was, perhaps, rather early in the morning to get up a concert, and the audience, prematurely aroused from their slumbers, might not, possibly, pay their entertainer with coin bearing the Mikado's features. Passepartout therefore decided to wait several hours; and, as he was walking along, it occurred to him that he would seem rather too well-dressed for a wandering artist. The idea struck him to change his garments for clothes more in harmony with his project. He might also get a little money to satisfy the immediate cravings of hunger. The resolution taken, it remained to carry it out.

After a long search Passepartout discovered a native dealer in old clothes, to whom he applied for an exchange. The man liked the European costume, and soon enough Passepartout was leaving dressed in an old Japanese coat, and a sort of one-sided turban, faded with long use. A few small pieces of silver, moreover, jingled in his pocket.

"Good!" he thought. "I will imagine I am at the Carnival!"

His first concern, after being thus "Japanized," was to enter a teahouse of modest appearance, and, to dine upon half a bird and a little rice, like a man for whom dinner was as yet a problem to be solved.

"Now," he thought, when he had eaten heartily, "I mustn't lose my head. I can't sell this costume again for one still more Japanese. I must consider how to leave this country of the Sun, of which I'll have disastrous memories, as quickly as possible."

It occurred to him to visit the steamers which were about to leave for America. He would offer himself as a cook or servant, to pay for his passage and meals. Once in San Francisco, he would find some means of going on. The difficulty was, how to cross the four thousand seven hundred miles of the Pacific which lay between Japan and the New World.

Passepartout was not the man to let an idea go begging, and directed his steps towards the docks. But, as he approached them, his project, which at first had seemed so simple, began to grow more and more impracticable. What need would they have of a cook or servant on an American steamer, and what confidence would they put in him, dressed as he was? What references could he give?

As he was reflecting in this manner, his eyes fell upon an immense poster which a sort of clown was carrying through the streets. This poster, which was in English, read as follows:—

ACROBATIC JAPANESE TROUPE,
HONORABLE WILLIAM BATULCAR,

PROPRIETOR,
LAST PERFORMANCES
PRIOR TO THEIR DEPARTURE FOR
THE UNITED STATES
OF THE
LONG NOSES! LONG NOSES!
UNDER THE DIRECT PATRONAGE OF THE
GOD TINGOU!
GREAT ATTRACTION!

"The United States!" said Passepartout; "that's just what I want!"

He followed the clown, and soon found himself once more in the Japanese quarter. A quarter of an hour later he stopped before a large cabin adorned with several clusters of streamers, the exterior walls of which were designed to represent, in violent colors and without perspective, a troupe of jugglers.

This was the Honorable William Batulcar's establishment. That gentleman was a sort of Barnum, the director of a troupe of jugglers, clowns, acrobats, highwire walkers, and gymnasts, who, according to the poster, was giving its last performances before leaving the Empire of the Sun for the States of the Union.

Passepartout entered and asked for Mr. Batulcar, who appeared in person.

"What do you want?" said he to Passepartout, whom he at first took for a native.

"Would you like a servant, sir?" asked Passepartout.

"A servant!" cried Mr. Batulcar, caressing the thick gray beard which hung from his chin. "I already have two who are obedient and faithful, have never left me, and serve me as long as I feed them—and here they are," added he, holding out his two robust arms, furrowed with veins as large as the strings of a bass viol.

"So I can be of no use to you?"

"None."

"The devil! I should so like to cross the Pacific with you!"

"Ah!" said the Honorable Mr. Batulcar. "You are no more a Japanese than I am a monkey! Why are you dressed up in that way?"

"A man dresses as he can."

"That's true. You are a Frenchman, aren't you?"

"Yes; a Parisian of Paris."

"Then you ought to know how to make faces."

"Why," replied Passepartout, a little vexed that his nationality should cause this question, "we Frenchmen know how to make faces, it is true—but not any better than the Americans do."

"True. Well, if I can't take you as a servant, I can as a clown. You see, my friend, in France they exhibit foreign clowns, and in foreign parts French clowns."

"Ah!"

"You are pretty strong, eh?"

"Especially after a good meal."

"And you can sing?"

"Yes," returned Passepartout, who had formerly sung in the streets.

"But can you sing standing on your head, with a top spinning on your left foot, and a sabre balanced on your right?"

"Humph! I think so," replied Passepartout, recalling the exercises of his younger days.

"Well, that's enough," said the Honorable William Batulcar.

The deal was settled then and there.

Passepartout had at last found something to do. He was engaged to act in the celebrated Japanese troupe. It was not a very dignified position, but within a week he would be on his way to San Francisco.

The performance, so noisily announced by the Honorable Mr. Batulcar, was to start at three o'clock, and soon the deafening instruments of a Japanese orchestra resounded at the door. Passepartout, though he had not been able to study or rehearse a part, was designated to lend the aid of his sturdy shoulders in the great exhibition of the "human pyramid," executed by the Long Noses of the god Tingou. This "great attraction" was to close the performance.

Before three o'clock the large shed was invaded by the spectators. Europeans and natives, Chinese and Japanese, men, women, and children, rushed upon the narrow benches and into the boxes opposite the stage. The musicians took up a position inside, and were vigorously performing on their gongs, tam-tams, flutes, bones, tambourines, and immense drums.

The performance was much like all acrobatic displays; but one must admit that the Japanese are the first acrobats in the world.

One, with a fan and some bits of paper, performed the graceful trick of the butterflies and the flowers. Another traced in the air a series of blue words, with the odorous smoke of his pipe, composing a compliment to the audience. A third juggled with some lighted candles, which he extinguished successively as they passed his lips, and relit again without interrupting for an instant his juggling. Another reproduced the most singular combinations with a spinning top; in his hands the revolving tops seemed to be animated with a life of their own in their interminable whirling; they ran over pipe stems, the edges of sabres, wires, and even hairs stretched across the stage; they turned around on the edges of large glasses, crossed bamboo ladders, dispersed into all the corners and produced strange musical effects by the combination of their various pitches of tone. The jugglers tossed them in the air, threw them like shuttlecocks with wooden battledores, and yet they kept on spinning; they put them into their pockets, and took them out still whirling as before.

It is useless to describe the astonishing performances of the acrobats and gymnasts. The tricks on ladders, poles, balls, barrels, and the like were executed with wonderful precision.

But the principal attraction was the exhibition of the Long Noses, a show Europe doesn't know yet.

The Long Noses formed a peculiar company, under the direct patronage of the god Tingou. Attired after the fashion of the Middle Ages, they bore upon their shoulders a splendid pair of wings. But what especially distinguished them was the long noses which were fastened to their faces, and the uses which they made of them. These noses were made of bamboo, and were five, six, and even ten feet long, some straight, others curved, some ribboned, and some having imitation warts upon them. It was upon these appendages, fixed tightly on their noses, that they performed their tricks. A dozen of these disciples of Tingou lay flat upon their backs, while others, straight as lightning rods, came and frolicked on their noses, jumping from one to another, and performing the most skilful leaps and somersaults.

As a last scene, a "human pyramid" was announced, in which fifty Long Noses were to represent the Chariot of Juggernaut. But, instead of forming a pyramid by mounting each other's shoulders, the artists were to group themselves on top of the noses. It happened that the performer who had hitherto formed the base of the Chariot had left the troupe, and as, to fill this part, only strength and adroitness were necessary, Passepartout had been chosen to take his place.

The poor fellow really felt wretched when—melancholy memory of his youth!—he donned his medieval costume, adorned with multicolored wings, and fastened to his natural feature a false nose six feet long. But he cheered up when he thought that this nose was winning him something to eat.

He went upon the stage, and took his place beside the others who were to compose the base of the Chariot of Juggernaut. They all stretched themselves on the floor, their noses pointing to the ceiling. A second group of artists disposed themselves on these long appendages, then a third above these, then a fourth, until a human monument reaching to the very cornices of the theatre soon arose on top of the noses. This elicited loud applause, in the midst of which the orchestra was just striking up a deafening air, when the pyramid tottered, the balance was lost, one of the lower noses vanished from the pyramid, and human monument was shattered like a castle built of cards!

It was Passepartout's fault. Abandoning his position, leaping over the footlights without the aid of his wings, and clambering up to the right-hand gallery, he fell at the feet of one of the spectators, crying, "Ah, my master! my master!"

"You here?"

"Myself."

"Very well; then let us go to the steamer, young man!"

Mr. Fogg, Mrs. Aouda, and Passepartout rushed through the lobby of the theatre to the outside, where they encountered the Honorable Mr. Batulcar, furious with rage. He demanded damages for the "breakage" of the pyramid. Phileas Fogg appeased him by giving him a handful of bank notes.

At half-past six, the very hour of departure, Mr. Fogg and Aouda, followed by Passepartout, who in his hurry had retained his wings and his nose six feet long, stepped upon the American steamer.

CHAPTER XXIV

During Which Mr. Fogg and Party Cross the Pacific Ocean

What had happened when the pilot boat came in sight of Shanghai will be easily guessed. The signals made by the *Tankadere* had been noticed by the captain of the Yokohama steamer, who, seeing the flag at half-mast, had directed his course toward the little craft. Phileas Fogg, after paying the stipulated price of his passage to John Bunsby, and rewarding him with the additional sum of five hundred and fifty pounds, went aboard the steamer with Mrs. Aouda and Fix. They started at once for Nagasaki and Yokohama.

They reached their destination on the morning of the November 14th. Phileas Fogg lost no time in going on board the *Carnatic,* where he learned, to Mrs. Aouda's great delight—and perhaps to his own, though he betrayed no emotion—that Passepartout, a Frenchman, had actually arrived on her the day before.

The San Francisco steamer was scheduled to leave that very evening, and it became necessary to find Passepartout, if possible, without delay. Mr. Fogg applied in vain to the French and English consuls, and, after wandering a long time through the streets, began to despair of finding his missing servant. Chance, or perhaps a kind of premonition, at last led him into the Honorable Mr. Batulcar's theater. He certainly would not have recognized Passepartout in the eccentric medieval costume; but the latter, lying on his back, had seen his master in the gallery. He could not help starting, which so changed the position of his nose as to bring the "pyramid" pell-mell upon the stage.

All this Passepartout learned from Mrs. Aouda, who told him what had taken place on the voyage from Hong Kong to Shanghai on the *Tankadere,* in company with one Mr. Fix.

Passepartout did not flinch on hearing this name. He thought that the time had not yet come to divulge to his master what had taken place between the detective and himself. In the account he gave of his absence, he simply apologized for having been overtaken by drunkenness, in smoking opium at a tavern in Hong Kong.

Mr. Fogg listened coolly to this narrative, without speaking a word. He then gave his servant enough money to obtain on board clothing more in harmony with his position. Within an hour the Frenchman had cut off his nose and parted with his wings, and kept nothing that recalled the disciple of the god Tingou.

The steamer which was about to depart from Yokohama to San Francisco belong to the Pacific Mail Steamship Company, and was named the *General Grant.* She was a large paddle-wheel steamer of two thousand five hundred tons, well equipped and very fast. The massive walking beam rose and fell above the deck; at one end a piston rod worked up and down; and at the other was a connecting rod which, in changing the rectilinear motion to a circular one, was directly connected with the shaft of the paddles. The *General Grant* was rigged with three masts, giving a large capacity for sails, and thus powerfully aiding the steam power. By making twelve knots an hour, she would cross the ocean in twenty-one days. Phileas Fogg was therefore justified in hoping that he would reach San Francisco by the 2nd of December, New York by the 11th, and London on the 20th—thus gaining several hours on the fatal date of the 21st of December.

There were many passengers on board, among them English, many Americans, a large number of Coolies on their way to California, and several East Indian officers, who were spending their vacation in going around the world. Nothing of importance happened on the voyage. The steamer, sustained on its large paddles, rolled but little, and the "Pacific" almost justified its name. Mr. Fogg was as calm and taciturn as ever. His young companion felt more and more attached to him by other ties than gratitude. His silent but generous nature impressed her more than she thought, and it was almost unconsciously that she yielded to emotions which did not seem to have the least effect upon her protector.

Besides, Mrs. Aouda took the keenest interest in his plans, and became impatient at any incident which seemed likely to endanger his journey. She often chatted with Passepartout, who did not fail to perceive the state of the lady's heart. Being the most faithful of servants, he talked incessantly of Phileas Fogg's honesty, generosity and devotion. He took pains to calm Aouda's doubts of a successful outcome of the journey, telling her that the most difficult part was over, that now they were beyond the fantastic countries of Japan and China, and were fairly on their way to civilized places again. A railway train from San Francisco to New York, and a transatlantic steamer from New York to Liverpool, would doubtless bring them to the end of this impossible journey around the world within the period agreed upon.

On the ninth day after leaving Yokohama, Phileas Fogg had crossed exactly one-half of the terrestrial globe. The *General Grant* passed, on the 23rd of November, the one hundred and eightieth meridian, and was at the very antipodes of London. Mr. Fogg had, it is true, exhausted fifty-two of the eighty days in which he was to complete the tour, and there were only twenty-eight left. But, though he was only half-way according to the meridians, he had really gone over two-thirds of the whole journey; for he had been obliged to make long circuits from London to Aden, from Aden to Bombay, from Calcutta to Singapore, and from Singapore to Yokohama. If he had followed the fiftieth parallel, which is that of London, the whole distance would only have been about twelve thousand miles. However he was forced, by the irregular methods of locomotion, to travel twenty-six thousand miles, of which he had, on the 23rd of November, accomplished seventeen thousand five hundred. And now the course was a straight one, and Fix was no longer there to put obstacles in his way!

It happened also, on the 23rd of November, that Passepartout made a joyful discovery. It will be remembered that the obstinate fellow had insisted on keeping his famous family watch at London time, and on considering the time of the countries he had passed through as quite false and unreliable. Now, on this day, though he had not changed the hands, he found that his watch exactly agreed with the ship's chronometers. His triumph was understandable. He would have liked to know what Fix would say if he were aboard!

"The rogue told me a lot of stories," repeated Passepartout, "about the meridians, the sun, and the moon! Moon, indeed! moonshine more likely! If one listened to that sort of people, a pretty sort of time one would keep! I was sure that the sun would some day set itself by my watch!"

Passepartout was not aware that, if the face of his watch had been divided into twenty-four hours like the Italian clocks, he would have no reason for exultation. For the hands of his watch, when it was nine in the morning on board, would have indicated nine o'clock in the evening, that is the twenty-first hour after midnight—precisely the difference between London time and that of the one hundred and eightieth meridian. But if Fix had been able to explain this purely physical effect, Passepartout would not have accepted it, even if he had understood it. Moreover, if the detective had been on board at that moment, Passepartout would have discussed with him quite a different subject, and in an entirely different manner.

Where was Fix at that moment?

He was actually on board the *General Grant*.

On reaching Yokohama, the detective, leaving Mr. Fogg, whom he expected to meet again during the day, had gone at once to the English consulate, where he at last found the warrant of arrest. It had followed him from Bombay, and had come by the *Carnatic*, on which he himself was supposed to be. Fix's disappointment may be imagined. The warrant was now useless! Mr. Fogg had left English ground, and it was now necessary to procure his extradition!

"Well," thought Fix, after a moment of anger, "my warrant is not good here, but it will be in England. The rogue evidently intends to return to his own country, thinking he has thrown the police off his track. Good! I will follow him across the Atlantic. As for the money, Heaven grant there may be some left! But the fellow has already spent in traveling, rewards, trials, bail, elephants, and all sorts of expenses, more than five thousand pounds. Yet, after all, the Bank is rich!"

His plan decided on, he went on board the *General Grant*, and was there when Mr. Fogg and Mrs. Aouda arrived. To his utter amazement, he recognized Passepartout, despite his medieval disguise. He quickly concealed himself in his cabin to avoid an awkward explanation, and hoped—thanks to the number of passengers—to remain unnoticed by Mr. Fogg's servant.

On that very day, however, he met Passepartout face to face on the forward deck. The latter, without a word, made a rush for him, grasped him by the throat, and, much to the amusement of a group of Americans who immediately began to bet on him, rained a perfect volley of blows on the detective which proved the great superiority of French over English fighting skill.

When Passepartout had finished, he found himself relieved and comforted. Fix got up in a somewhat rumpled condition, and, looking at his adversary, coolly said, "Are you done?"

"For the time—yes."

"Then let me have a word with you."

"But I—"

"In your master's interest."

Passepartout seemed to be mastered by Fix's coolness, for he quietly followed him, and they sat down apart from the rest of the passengers.

"You have given me a thrashing," said Fix. "Good; I expected it. Now, listen to me. Up to this point I have been Mr. Fogg's adversary. I am now on his side."

"Aha!" cried Passepartout; "you are convinced he is an honest man?"

"No," replied Fix coolly, "I think he is a rascal. Sh! don't budge, and let me speak. As long as Mr. Fogg was on English ground, it was in my interest to detain him there until my warrant of arrest arrived. I did everything I could to hold him back. I sent the Bombay priests after him, I got you drunk in Hong Kong, I separated you from him, and I made him miss the Yokohama steamer."

Passepartout listened, with closed fists.

"Now," resumed Fix, "Mr. Fogg seems to be going back to England. Well, I will follow him there. But from now on I will keep obstacles out of his way with as much zeal as I have done up to this time to put them in his path. I've changed my game, you see, and simply because it is in my interest to change it. Your interest is the same as mine. For it is only in England that you will know whether you are in the service of a criminal or an honest man."

Passepartout had listened very attentively to Fix, and was convinced that he spoke with entire good faith.

"Are we friends?" asked the detective.

"Friends?—no," replied Passepartout; "but allies, perhaps. At the least sign of treason, however, I'll twist your neck."

"Agreed," said the detective quietly.

Eleven days later, on the 3rd of December, the *General Grant* entered the bay of the Golden Gate and reached San Francisco.

Mr. Fogg had neither gained nor lost a single day.

CHAPTER XXV

In Which a Slight Glimpse Is Had of San Francisco

It was seven in the morning when Mr. Fogg, Mrs. Aouda and Passepartout set foot upon the American continent, if this name can be given to the floating quay upon which they disembarked. These quays, rising and falling with the tide, facilitate the loading and unloading of vessels. Alongside them were clippers of all sizes, steamers of all nationalities, and the steamboats, with several decks rising one above the other, which ply on the Sacramento and its tributaries. There were also heaped up the products of a commerce which extends to Mexico, Chili, Peru, Brazil, Europe, Asia, and all the Pacific islands.

Passepartout, in his joy on reaching the American continent, thought he would express it by executing a somersault in fine style. But unfortunately he landed on some worm-eaten planks and almost fell through them. Embarrassed by the manner in which he thus "set foot" upon the New World, he uttered a loud cry, which so frightened the innumerable cormorants and pelicans that are always perched upon these movable quays, that they flew noisily away.

Mr. Fogg, on reaching shore, proceeded to find out at what time the first train left for New York, and learned that this was at six o'clock P.M. He had, therefore, an entire day to spend in the capital of California. Taking a carriage for three dollars, he and Mrs.

Aouda entered it, while Passepartout climbed on the seat beside the driver, and they set out for the International Hotel.

From his exalted position Passepartout with curiosity observed the wide streets, the rows of low houses, the Anglo-Saxon Gothic churches, the great docks, the palatial wooden and brick warehouses, the numerous conveyances, omnibuses, horse-cars and upon the sidewalks, not only Americans and Europeans, but Chinese and Indians. Passepartout was surprised at all he saw. San Francisco was no longer the legendary city of 1849—a city of bandits, assassins, and arsonists, who had flocked in crowds in pursuit of gold; a paradise of outlaws, where they gambled for gold dust, a revolver in one hand and a bowie knife in the other. It was now a great commercial emporium.

The lofty tower of its City Hall overlooked the whole panorama of the streets and avenues, which intersected each other at right angles, and in the midst of which appeared pleasant, lush squares, while beyond lay the Chinese quarter, seemingly imported from the Celestial Empire in a toy box. Sombreros and red shirts and plumed Indians were rarely to be seen; but there were silk hats and black coats everywhere, worn by a multitude of frenetically active, gentlemanlike men. Some of the streets—especially Montgomery Street, which is to San Francisco what Regent Street is to London, the Boulevard des Italiens to Paris, and Broadway to New York—were lined with splendid and spacious stores which displayed the products of the entire world.

When Passepartout reached the International Hotel, it did not seem to him as if he had left England at all.

The ground floor of the hotel was occupied by a large bar, a sort of buffet freely open to all passersby, who might partake of dried beef, oyster soup, biscuits, and cheese, without charge. Payment was made only for the ale, porter, or sherry which was drunk.

This seemed "very American" to Passepartout. The hotel/restaurant was comfortable. Mr. Fogg and Mrs. Aouda settled themselves at a table, and were copiously served on very small plates by black waiters.

After breakfast, Mr. Fogg, accompanied by Mrs. Aouda, started for the English consulate to have his passport visaed. As he was going out, he met Passepartout, who asked him if it would not be wise, before taking the train, to purchase dozens of Enfield rifles and Colt revolvers. He had been listening to stories of attacks upon the trains by the Sioux and Pawnees. Mr. Fogg thought it a useless precaution, but told him to do as he thought best, and went on to the consulate.

He had not proceeded two hundred steps, however, when, "by the greatest chance in the world," he met Fix. The detective seemed wholly taken by surprise. What! Had he and Mr. Fogg crossed the Pacific together, and not met on the steamer! In any case Fix felt honored to see once again the gentleman to whom he owed so much. As his business recalled him to Europe, he should be delighted to continue the journey in such pleasant company.

Mr. Fogg replied that the honor would be his. And the detective—who was determined not to lose sight of him—begged permission to accompany them in their walk about San Francisco—a request which Mr. Fogg readily granted.

They soon found themselves on Montgomery Street, where a great crowd was gathered. The sidewalks, the streetcar rails, the shop doors, the windows of the houses, and even the roofs, were full of people. Men were going about carrying large posters, and flags and streamers were floating in the wind; loud cries were heard on all sides.

"Hurrah for Camerfield!"

"Hurrah for Mandiboy!"

It was a political meeting, or so Fix guessed as he

said to Mr. Fogg, "Perhaps we had better not mingle with the crowd. There may be danger in it."

"Yes," answered Mr. Fogg, "and blows, even if they are political, are still blows."

Fix smiled at this remark. And in order to be able to see without being jostled about, the party took up a position on the top of a flight of steps situated at the upper end of Montgomery Street. Opposite them, on the other side of the street, between a coal wharf and a petroleum warehouse, a large platform had been erected in the open air, towards which the current of the crowd seemed to be directed.

What was the purpose of this meeting? Phileas Fogg could not imagine. Was it to nominate some high official—a governor or member of Congress? It was not improbable, so agitated was the multitude before them.

Just at this moment there was an unusual stir in the crowd. All the hands were raised in the air. Some, tightly closed, seemed to disappear suddenly in the midst of the cries—an energetic way, no doubt, of casting a vote. The crowd swayed back. The banners and flags wavered, disappeared an instant, then reappeared in tatters. The undulations of the human surge reached the steps, while all the heads floundered on the surface like a sea agitated by a squall. Many of the black hats disappeared, and the greater part of the crowd seemed to have diminished in height.

"It is evidently a meeting," said Fix, "and its object must be an exciting one. I should not wonder if it were about the *Alabama*, despite the fact that that question is settled."

"Perhaps," replied Mr. Fogg simply.

"At least, there are two champions in the presence of each other, the Honorable Mr. Camerfield and the Honorable Mr. Mandiboy."

Mrs. Aouda, leaning upon Mr. Fogg's arm, was observing the tumultuous scene with surprise, while Fix was going to ask a man near him what the cause of it all was when before the man could reply, a fresh agitation arose. Hurrahs and excited shouts were heard. The staffs of the banners began to be used as offensive weapons. Fists flew about in every direction. Blows were exchanged from the tops of the carriages and omnibuses which had been blocked up in the crowd. Boots and shoes went whirling through the air, and Mr. Fogg thought he even heard the crack of revolvers mingling in the din. The mob approached the stairway, and flowed over the lower step. One of the parties had evidently been pushed back; but the mere onlookers could not tell whether Mandiboy or Camerfield had gained the upper hand.

"It would be prudent for us to leave," said Fix, who was anxious that Mr. Fogg should not receive any injury, at least until they got back to London. "If there is any question about England in all this, and we are recognized, I fear we will be in trouble."

"An English subject—" began Mr. Fogg.

He did not finish his sentence, for a terrific hubbub now arose on the terrace behind the flight of steps where they stood, and there were frantic shouts of, "Hurrah for Mandiboy! Hip, hip, hurrah!"

It was a band of voters coming to the rescue of their allies, and taking the Camerfield forces in flank. Mr. Fogg, Mrs. Aouda, and Fix found themselves between two fires; it was too late to escape. The torrent of men, armed with loaded canes and sticks, was irresistible. Phileas Fogg and Fix were roughly hustled in their attempts to protect their fair companion; the former, as cool as ever, tried in vain to defend himself with the weapons which nature has placed at the end of every Englishman's arm. A big brawny fellow with a red beard, flushed face, and broad shoulders, who seemed to be the chief of the band, raised his clenched fist to strike Mr. Fogg, whom he would have given a crushing blow if Fix had not rushed in and received it in his place. An enormous bump immediately appeared under the detective's silk hat, which was completely smashed in.

"Yankee!" exclaimed Mr. Fogg, darting a contemptuous look at his opponent.

"Englishman!" returned the other. "We will meet again!"

"When you please."

"What is your name?"

"Phileas Fogg. And yours?"

"Colonel Stamp Proctor."

The human tide now swept by, after overturning Fix, who speedily got upon his feet again, though with tattered clothes. Happily, he was not seriously hurt. His traveling overcoat was divided into two unequal parts, and his trousers resembled those which certain Indians put on only after having taken off the seat. Mrs. Aouda had escaped unharmed, and Fix alone bore marks of the fray in his black and blue bruise.

"Thanks," said Mr. Fogg to the detective, as soon as they were out of the crowd.

"No thanks are necessary," replied Fix, "but let us go."

"Where?"

"To a tailor."

Such a visit was, indeed, opportune. The clothing of both Mr. Fogg and Fix was in rags, as if they had themselves been actively engaged in the contest between Camerfield and Mandiboy. An hour after, they were once more suitably attired, and with Mrs. Aouda returned to the International Hotel.

Passepartout was waiting for his master, armed with half a dozen six-barreled revolvers. When he saw Fix with Mr. Fogg, he knit his brows. But Mrs. Aouda in a few words told him of their adventure, and he recovered his serenity. Fix evidently was no longer an enemy, but an ally; he was faithfully keeping his word.

Dinner over, the coach which was to convey the passengers and their luggage to the station drew up to the door. As he was getting in, Mr. Fogg said to Fix, "You have not seen this Colonel Proctor again?"

"No."

"I will come back to America to find him," said Phileas Fogg calmly. "It would not be right for an Englishman to permit himself to be treated in that way without retaliating."

The detective smiled, but did not reply. It was clear that Mr. Fogg was one of those Englishmen who, while they do not tolerate dueling at home, fight abroad when their honor is attacked.

At a quarter before six the travelers reached the station, and found the train ready to depart. As he was about to enter it, Mr. Fogg called a porter, and said to him, "My friend, was there not some trouble today in San Francisco?"

"It was a political meeting, sir," replied the porter.

"But I thought there was a great deal of disturbance in the streets."

"It was only a meeting assembled for an election."

"The election of a general-in-chief, no doubt?" asked Mr. Fogg.

"No, sir, of a justice of the peace."

Phileas Fogg got into the train, which started off at full speed.

CHAPTER XXVI

IN WHICH PHILEAS FOGG AND PARTY TRAVEL BY THE PACIFIC RAILROAD

"From ocean to ocean"—so say the Americans, and these four words should make up the general designation of the "great trunk line" which crosses the entire width of the United States. The Pacific Railroad is, however, really divided into two distinct lines: the Central Pacific, between San Francisco and Ogden, and the Union Pacific, between Ogden and Omaha. Five main lines connect Omaha with New York.

New York and San Francisco are thus united by an uninterrupted metal ribbon, which measures no less than three thousand seven hundred and eighty-six miles. Between Omaha and the Pacific the railway crosses a territory which is still inhabited by Indians and wild beasts, and a large stretch of land which the Mormons, after they were driven from Illinois in 1845, began to colonize.

The journey from New York to San Francisco took, formerly, under the most favourable conditions, at least six months. It is now accomplished in seven days.

It was in 1862 that, in spite of the Southern Members of Congress, who wished a more southerly route, it was decided to lay the road between the forty-first and forty-second parallels. President Lincoln himself determined the starting point should be in Omaha, in Nebraska. The work was started at once, and pursued with true American energy. The rapidity with which it went on did not harm its good execution. The road grew a mile and a half a day across the prairies. A locomotive, running on the rails laid down the evening before, brought the rails to be laid the next day, and advanced upon them as fast as they were put in place.

The Pacific Railroad is joined by several branches in Iowa, Kansas, Colorado, and Oregon. On leaving Omaha, it passes along the left bank of the Platte River as far as the junction of its northern branch, follows its southern branch, crosses the Laramie territory and the Wasatch Mountains, turns at the Great Salt Lake, and reaches Salt Lake City, the Mormon capital, plunges into the Tuilla Valley, across the American Desert, Cedar and Humboldt Mountains, the Sierra Nevada, and descends, via Sacramento, to the Pacific—its grade, even in the Rocky Mountains, never exceeds one hundred and twelve feet to the mile.

Such was the road to be traveled through in seven days, which would enable Phileas Fogg—at least, so he hoped—to take the Atlantic steamer in New York on the 11th for Liverpool.

The car which he occupied was a sort of long omnibus on eight wheels, and with no compartments in the interior. It was supplied with two rows of seats, perpendicular to the direction of the train on either side of an aisle which led to the toilets provided in each car. Throughout the train, the cars were joined by platforms and the passengers were able to pass from one end of the train to the other. It was supplied with sitting room cars, balcony cars, restaurant cars, and smoking cars. Theater cars alone were wanting, and they will have these some day.

Books and news dealers, sellers of edibles, drinks, and cigars, who seemed to have plenty of customers, were continually circulating in the aisles.

The train left Oakland station at six o'clock. It was already night, cold and cheerless, the sky being overcast with clouds which seemed to threaten snow. The train did not proceed rapidly. Counting the stops, it did not run more than twenty miles an hour, which was a sufficient speed, however, to enable it to reach Omaha within its designated time.

There was little conversation in the car, and soon many of the passengers were asleep. Passepartout found himself beside the detective, but he did not talk to him. After recent events, their relations with each other had grown somewhat cold; there could no longer be mutual sympathy or intimacy between them. Fix's manner had not changed; but Passepartout was very reserved, and ready to strangle his former friend on the slightest provocation.

Snow began to fall an hour after they started, a fine snow, however, which happily could not delay the train. Nothing could be seen from the windows but a vast, white sheet, against which the smoke of the locomotive appeared.

At eight o'clock a steward entered the car and announced that bedtime had arrived. In a few minutes the car was transformed into a dormitory. The backs of the seats were thrown back, berths carefully packed were rolled out by an ingenious system, cabins were suddenly improvised, and each traveler soon had at his disposition a comfortable bed, protected from curious eyes by thick curtains. The sheets were clean and the pillows soft. It only remained to go to bed and sleep—which everybody did—while the train sped on across the State of California.

The country between San Francisco and Sacramento is not very hilly. The Central Pacific, taking Sacramento for its starting point, extends eastward to meet the road from Omaha. The line from San Francisco to Sacramento runs in a northeast direction along the American River, which empties into San Pablo Bay. The one hundred and twenty miles between these cities was accomplished in six hours, and towards midnight, while fast asleep, the travelers passed through Sacramento. So no one saw that important city, the seat of the State government, with its fine quays, its broad streets, its noble hotels, squares, and churches.

The train, on leaving Sacramento, and passing the stations of Junction, Roclin, Auburn, and Colfax, entered the range of the Sierra Nevada. Cisco was reached at seven in the morning; and an hour later the dormitory was transformed into an ordinary car, and the travelers could observe the picturesque beauties of the mountain region through the windows. The railway track wound in and out among the passes, now approaching the mountain sides, now suspended over precipices, avoiding abrupt angles by bold curves, plunging into narrow gorges, which seemed to have no outlet. The locomotive, its great lantern casting a reddish light, with its sharp bell, and its cowcatcher extended like a spur, mingled its shrieks and bellowings with the noise of torrents and cascades, and twined its smoke among the branches of the pines.

There were few or no bridges or tunnels on the route. The railway turned around the sides of the mountains, and did not attempt to violate nature by taking the shortest cut from one point to another.

The train entered the State of Nevada through the Carson valley about nine o'clock, going always northeast; and at midday reached Reno, where there was a delay of twenty minutes for lunch.

From this point the railway, running along Humboldt River, passed northward for several miles by its banks; then it turned eastward, and kept by the river until it reached the Humboldt Range, nearly at the extreme eastern limit of Nevada.

Having had lunch, Mr. Fogg and his companions got back to their seats in the car, and observed the varied landscape which unfolded as they passed along: the vast prairies, the mountains lining the horizon, and the creeks with their foaming streams. Sometimes a great herd of buffaloes, gathered together in the distance, would appear like a movable dam. These numberless beasts often form an insurmountable obstacle to the passage of the trains; thousands of them have been seen passing over the track for hours at a time in compact ranks. The locomotive is then forced to stop and wait till the road is once more clear.

This happened, indeed, to the train in which Mr. Fogg was traveling. About three o'clock, a herd of ten or twelve thousand head of buffalo blocked the railroad. The locomotive slackened its speed, and tried to clear the way with its cowcatcher, but the mass of animals was too great. The buffaloes marched along with a tranquil gait, uttering now and then deafening bellowings. There was no use in interrupting them, for, having taken a particular direction, nothing could moderate and change their course. They were a torrent of living flesh which no dam could contain.

The travelers gazed on this curious spectacle from the platforms. Phileas Fogg, who had the most reason of all to be in a hurry, remained in his seat, and waited philosophically until it should please the buffaloes to get out of the way.

Passepartout was furious at the delay they caused, and longed to fire his loaded revolvers at them.

"What a country!" he cried. "Mere cattle stop the trains, and go by in a procession, just as if they were not impeding travel! Parbleu! I should like to know if Mr. Fogg foresaw *this* mishap in his program! And here's an engineer who doesn't dare to run the locomotive into this herd of beasts!"

The engineer did not try to overcome the obstacle, and he was wise. He would have crushed the first buffaloes with the cowcatcher, no doubt; but the locomotive, however powerful, would soon have been stopped, the train would inevitably have been thrown off the track, and would then have been helpless.

The best course was to wait patiently, and regain the

lost time by greater speed when the obstacle was removed. The procession of buffaloes lasted three full hours, and it was night before the track was clear. The last ranks of the herd were now passing over the rails, while the first had already disappeared below the southern horizon.

It was eight o'clock when the train crossed the passes of the Humboldt Range, and half-past nine when it penetrated Utah, the region of the Great Salt Lake, the singular colony of the Mormons.

CHAPTER XXVII

IN WHICH PASSEPARTOUT UNDERGOES, AT A SPEED OF TWENTY MILES AN HOUR, A COURSE OF MORMON HISTORY

During the night of the 5th of December, the train ran southeast for about fifty miles; then rose an equal distance in a northeast direction, toward the Great Salt Lake.

Passepartout, about nine o'clock, went out upon the platform to enjoy the air. The weather was cold, the heavens gray, but it was not snowing. The disc of the sun, enlarged by the mist, seemed an enormous ring of gold, and Passepartout was amusing himself by calculating its value in pounds sterling, when he was diverted from his interesting study by a strange-looking character who made his appearance on the platform.

This character, who had taken the train at Elko, was tall and dark, with a black moustache, black stockings, a black silk hat, a black waistcoat, black trousers, a white cravat, and dogskin gloves. He might have been taken for a clergyman. He went from one end of the train to the other and tacked to the door of each car a handwritten notice in manuscript.

Passepartout came near and read one of these notices, which stated that Elder William Hitch, Mormon missionary, taking advantage of his presence on train

No. 48, would deliver a lecture on Mormonism, in car No. 117, from eleven to twelve o'clock; and that he invited all who wanted instruction concerning the mysteries of the religion of the "Latter Day Saints" to attend.

"I'll go," said Passepartout to himself. He knew nothing of Mormonism except the custom of polygamy, which is its foundation.

The news quickly spread through the train, which contained about one hundred passengers, thirty of whom at most, attracted by the notice, filled car No. 117. Passepartout took one of the seats. Neither Mr. Fogg nor Fix cared to attend.

At the appointed hour Elder William Hitch rose, and, in an irritated voice, as if he had already been contradicted, said, "I tell you that Joe Smith is a martyr, that his brother Hiram is a martyr, and that the persecutions of the United States Government against the prophets will also make a martyr of Brigham Young. Who dares to say the contrary?"

No one ventured to contradict the missionary, whose excited tone contrasted curiously with his naturally calm appearance. No doubt his anger arose from the hardships to which the Mormons were actually subjected. The government had just succeeded, with some difficulty, in subduing these independent fanatics to its rule. It had made itself master of Utah, and subjected that territory to the laws of the Union, after imprisoning Brigham Young on a charge of rebellion and polygamy. The disciples of the prophet had since redoubled their efforts, and resisted, by words at least, the authority of Congress. Elder Hitch, as is seen, was trying to make proselytes even on the railway trains.

Then, emphasizing his words with his loud voice and frequent gestures, he related the history of the Mormons from Biblical times: how in Israel, a Mormon prophet of the tribe of Joseph published the annals of the new religion and bequeathed them to his son Morom; how, many centuries later, a translation of this precious book, which was written in Egyptian, was made by Joseph Smith, Jr., a Vermont farmer, who revealed himself as a mystical prophet in 1825; and how, in short, the celestial messenger appeared to him in an illuminated forest, and gave him the annals of the Lord.

Several of the audience, not being much interested in the missionary's narrative, here left the car; but Elder Hitch, continuing his lecture, related how Smith Jr., with his father, two brothers, and a few disciples, founded the church of the "Latter Day Saints," which, adopted not only in America, but in England, Norway, Sweden, and Germany, counts many artisans, as well as men engaged in the liberal professions, among its members; how a colony was established in Ohio, a temple erected there at a cost of two hundred thousand dollars, and a town built at Kirkland; how Smith became an enterprising banker and received from a simple mummy showman a papyrus scroll written by Abraham and several famous Egyptians.

The Elder's story became somewhere wearisome, and his audience grew gradually smaller, until it was reduced to twenty passengers. But this did not disconcert William Hitch, who proceeded with the story of Joseph Smith's bankruptcy in 1837, and how his ruined creditors rolled him in tar and feathers; his reappearance some years afterwards, more honorable and honored than ever, at Independence, Missouri, the chief of a flourishing colony of three thousand disciples, and his pursuit thence by outraged Gentiles, and flight into the far West.

Ten listeners only were now left, among them honest Passepartout, who was all ears. Thus he learned that, after long persecutions, Smith reappeared in Illinois, and in 1839 founded a community at Nauvoo, on the Mississippi, numbering twenty-five thousand souls, of which he became mayor, chief justice, and general-in-chief; that he announced himself, in 1843, as a candidate for the Presidency of the United States; and that finally, being ambushed in Carthage, he was thrown into prison, and assassinated by a band of masked men.

Passepartout was now the only person left in the car, and the Elder, looking him full in the face, reminded him that, two years after the assassination of Joseph Smith, the inspired prophet, Brigham Young, his successor, left Nauvoo for the banks of the Great Salt Lake, where, in the midst of that fertile region, directly on the route of the emigrants who were crossing Utah on their way to California, the new colony, thanks to the polygamy practised by the Mormons, had flourished beyond expectation.

"And this—" added Elder William Hitch, "this is why the jealousy of Congress has been aroused against us! Why the soldiers of the Union invaded the soil of Utah! Why Brigham Young, our chief, has been imprisoned in contempt of all justice! Shall we yield to force? Never! Driven from Vermont, driven from Illinois, driven from Ohio, driven from Missouri, driven from Utah, we shall yet find some independent territory on which to plant our tents. And you, my brother," continued the Elder, fixing his angry eye upon his single listener, "will you not plant yours there, too, under the shadow of our flag?"

"No!" replied Passepartout courageously, who in his turn fled from the car, leaving the Elder to preach in the wilderness.

During the lecture the train had been making good progress, and towards half-past twelve it had reached the northwest border of the Great Salt Lake. From there the passengers could observe the vast extent of this interior sea, which is also called the Dead Sea, and into which flows an American Jordan. It is an admirable lake, framed in lofty crags in large strata, encrusted with white salt—a superb sheet of water, which was formerly larger than now; its shores having risen with time have reduced its width and increased its depth.

The Salt Lake, seventy miles long and thirty-five wide, is situated three miles eight hundred feet above the sea. Quite different from Lake Asphaltite, whose depression is twelve hundred feet below the sea, it contains considerable salt, and one quarter of the weight of its water is solid matter, its specific weight being 1170, and, after being distilled, 1000. Fishes are of course unable to live in it, and those which descend through the Jordan, the Weber, and other streams, soon perish.

The country around the lake was well cultivated, for the Mormons are mostly farmers; ranches and pens for domesticated animals, fields of wheat, corn, and other cereals, luxuriant prairies, hedges of wild rose, clumps of acacias and milk-wort, such would have been the aspect of this region six months later. Now the ground was covered with a thin powdering of snow.

The train reached Ogden at two o'clock, where it stopped for six hours. Mr. Fogg and his party had time to pay a visit to Salt Lake City, connected with Ogden by a branch road. They spent two hours in this strikingly American town, built on the pattern of other cities of the Union, like a checkerboard, "with the somber sadness of right angles," as Victor Hugo expressed it. The founder of the City of the Saints could not escape from the taste for symmetry which distinguished the Anglo-Saxons. In this strange country, where the people are certainly not up to the level of their institutions, everything is done "squarely"—cities, houses, and follies.

The travelers, then, were strolling, at three o'clock, about the streets of the town built between the banks of the Jordan and the spurs of the Wasatch Range. They saw few or no churches, but the prophet's mansion, the courthouse, and the arsenal, and blue-brick

houses with verandahs and porches, surrounded by
gardens lined with acacias, palms, and locusts. A clay
and pebble wall, built in 1853, surrounded the town,
and in the main street were the market and several
hotels adorned with pavilions. The place did not seem
thickly populated. The streets were almost deserted,
except in the vicinity of the Temple, which they only
reached after having crossed several quarters surrounded by palisades. There were many women, which
was easily accounted for by the "peculiar institution"
of the Mormons; but it must not be supposed that all
the Mormons are polygamists. They are free to marry
or not, as they please; but it is worth noting that it is
mainly the female citizens of Utah who are anxious to
marry, as, according to the Mormon religion, single
women are not admitted to the joys of heaven. These
poor creatures seemed to be neither well-off nor happy.
Some—the more well-to-do, no doubt—wore short,
black silk dresses, under a hood or a simple shawl;
others were dressed only in a cotton print.

Passepartout could not behold without a certain dis-
may these women, several of them devoted to making
one single Mormon happy. His common sense pitied,
above all, the husband. It seemed to him a terrible
thing to have to guide so many wives at once across
the vicissitudes of life, and to conduct them, as it were,
in a body to the Mormon paradise, with the prospect
of seeing them in the company of the glorious Smith,
who doubtless was the chief ornament of that delightful place, to all eternity. He felt indeed repelled from
such a vocation, and he imagined—perhaps he was
mistaken—that the fair ones of Salt Lake City cast
rather alarming glances on his person. Happily, his
stay there was but brief. At four the party found themselves again at the station, took their seats in the train,
and the whistle sounded for starting. However, just as
the locomotive wheels began to turn, cries of "Stop!
Stop!" were heard.

Trains, like time and tide, stop for no one. The gentleman who uttered the cries was evidently a belated Mormon. He was breathless with running. Happily for him, the station had neither gates nor barriers. He rushed along the track, jumped on the rear platform of the train, and fell exhausted into one of the seats.

Passepartout, who had been anxiously watching this amateur gymnast, approached him with lively interest, and learned that he had taken flight after an unpleasant domestic scene.

When the Mormon had recovered his breath, Passepartout ventured to ask him politely how many wives he had. From the manner in which he had decamped, it might be thought that he had at least twenty.

"One, sir," replied the Mormon, raising his arms heavenward—"one, and that was enough!"

CHAPTER XXVIII

In Which Passepartout Does Not Succeed in Making Anyone Listen to Reason

The train, on leaving Great Salt Lake at Ogden, went north for an hour as far as Weber River, having completed nearly nine hundred miles from San Francisco. From this point it went east again toward the jagged Wasatch Mountains. It was in the section included between this range and the Rocky Mountains that the American engineers found the most formidable difficulties in laying the road, and that the government granted a subsidy of forty-eight thousand dollars per mile, instead of sixteen thousand allowed for the work done on the plains. But the engineers, instead of violating nature as we said before, avoided its difficulties by winding around, instead of penetrating the rocks. One tunnel only, fourteen thousand feet in length, was pierced in order to arrive at the great basin.

The track up to this time had reached its highest elevation at the Great Salt Lake. From this point it described a long curve, descending toward Bitter Creek Valley, to rise again to the dividing ridge of the waters between the Atlantic and the Pacific. There were many creeks in this mountainous region, and it was necessary to cross Muddy Creek, Green Creek, and others, upon culverts.

Passepartout grew more and more impatient as they went on, while Fix longed to get out of this difficult region, and was more anxious than Phileas Fogg himself to be beyond the danger of delays and accidents, and set foot on English soil.

At ten o'clock at night the train stopped at Fort Bridger station, and twenty minutes later entered Wyoming Territory, following the valley of Bitter Creek throughout. The next day, December 7th, they stopped for a quarter of an hour at Green River station. Snow had fallen abundantly during the night, but, being mixed with rain, it had half melted, and did not interrupt their progress. The bad weather, however, annoyed Passepartout. The accumulation of snow, by blocking the wheels of the cars, might have certainly endangered Mr. Fogg's trip.

"What an idea!" he said to himself. "Why did my master make this journey in winter? Couldn't he have waited for the good season to increase his chances?"

While the good Frenchman was absorbed in the state of the sky and the dropping of the temperature, Mrs. Aouda was experiencing fears from a totally different cause.

Several passengers had got off at Green River, and were walking up and down the platforms; and among these Aouda recognized Colonel Stamp Proctor, the same who had so rudely insulted Phileas Fogg at the San Francisco meeting. Not wishing to be recognized, the young woman drew back from the window, feeling much alarm at her discovery. She was attached to the man who, however coolly, gave her daily evidences of the most absolute devotion. She did not understand, perhaps, the depth of the sentiment which her protector inspired in her, which she called gratitude, but which, though she was not aware of it, was really more than that. Her heart sank within her when she recognized the man whom Mr. Fogg wanted, sooner or later, to call to account for his condur' Chance alone, it was clear, had brought Colonel Proctor on this train; but there he was, and it was necessary, at all cost, that Phileas Fogg should not see his adversary.

Aouda seized a moment when Mr. Fogg was asleep, to tell Fix and Passepartout whom she had seen.

"That Proctor on this train!" cried Fix. "Well, don't worry yourself, madam; before he settles with Mr. Fogg, he has got to deal with me! It seems to me that I was the more insulted of the two."

"And besides," added Passepartout, "I'll take care of him, colonel as he is."

"Mr. Fix," resumed Aouda, "Mr. Fogg will allow no one to avenge him. He said that he would come back to America to find this man. Should he see Colonel Proctor, we could not prevent an encounter which might have terrible results. He must not see him."

"You are right, madam," replied Fix; "a meeting between them might ruin everything. Whether he were victorious or beaten, Mr. Fogg would be delayed, and—"

"And," added Passepartout, "that would be to the advantage of the gentlemen of the Reform Club. In four days we shall be in New York. Well, if my master does not leave this car during those four days, we may hope that chance will not bring him face to face with this confounded American. We must, if possible, keep it from happening."

The conversation dropped. Mr. Fogg had just woken up, and was looking out of the window. Soon after, Passepartout, without being heard by his master or Aouda, whispered to the detective, "Would you really fight for him?"

"I would do anything," replied Fix, in a tone which betrayed determined will, "to get him back, living, to Europe!"

Passepartout felt something like a shudder shoot through his frame, but his confidence in his master remained unbroken.

Was there any means of detaining Mr. Fogg in the car, to avoid a meeting between him and the Colonel? It ought not to be a difficult task, since that gentleman was naturally sedentary and little curious. The detective, at least, seemed to have found a way. After a few moments, he said to Mr. Fogg, "These are long and slow hours, sir, that we are passing on the railway."

"Yes," replied Mr. Fogg; "but they pass."

"You were in the habit of playing whist," resumed Fix, "on the steamers."

"Yes; but it would be difficult to do so here. I have neither cards nor partners."

"Oh, but we can easily buy some cards, for they are sold on all the American trains. And as for partners, if madam plays—"

"Certainly, sir," Mrs. Aouda quickly replied; "I understand whist. It is a part of an English education."

"I admit I do play a good game." said Fix. "Well, here are three of us, and a dummy—"

"As you please, sir," replied Phileas Fogg, heartily glad to resume his favourite pastime—even on the railway.

Passepartout was sent in search of the steward, and soon returned with two packs of cards, some pins, counters, and a shelf covered with cloth.

The game began. Mrs. Aouda understood whist sufficiently well, and even received some compliments on her playing from Mr. Fogg. As for the detective, he was simply first class, and worthy of being matched against his present opponent.

"Now," thought Passepartout, "we've got him. He won't budge."

At eleven in the morning the train had reached the dividing ridge of the waters at Bridger Pass, seven thousand five hundred and twenty-four feet above the level of the sea, one of the highest points attained by the track in crossing the Rocky Mountains. After going about two hundred miles, the travelers at last found themselves on one of those vast plains which extended to the Atlantic, and which nature has made so favorable for laying a railroad.

At the low point of the Atlantic basin the first streams, branches of the North Platte River, already appeared. The whole northern and eastern horizon was bounded by the immense semicircular curtain which is formed by the southern portion of the Rocky Mountains, the highest being Laramie Peak. Between this and the railway extended vast plains, plentifully irrigated. On the right rose the lower spurs of the mountainous mass which extends south to the sources of the Arkansas River, one of the great tributaries of the Missouri.

At half past twelve the travelers caught sight for an instant of Fort Halleck, which commands that section. In a few more hours the Rocky Mountains would be crossed. There was reason to hope, then, that no accident would mark the journey through this difficult country. The snow had stopped falling, and the air became crisp and cold. Large birds, frightened by the locomotive, rose and flew off in the distance. No wild beast appeared on the plain. It was the desert in all its nakedness.

After a comfortable lunch, served in the car, Mr. Fogg and his partners had just resumed whist, when a violent whistling was heard, and the train stopped. Passepartout put his head out of the door, but saw nothing to cause the delay; no station was in sight.

Aouda and Fix feared that Mr. Fogg might take it into his head to get out; but that gentleman contented himself with saying to his servant, "See what is the matter."

Passepartout rushed out of the car. Thirty or forty passengers had already left their seats, among them Colonel Stamp Proctor.

The train had stopped before a red signal which

blocked the way. The engineer and conductor were talking excitedly with a signal man, whom the station-master at Medicine Bow, the next stop, had sent on to meet the train. The passengers gathered around and took part in the discussion, in which Colonel Proctor, with his insolent manner, was conspicuous.

Passepartout, joining the group, heard the signal-man say, "No! You can't pass! The bridge at Medicine Bow is shaky, and would not bear the weight of the train."

This was a suspension bridge thrown over some rapids, about a mile from the place where they now were. According to the signal man, it was in a ruinous condition, several of the iron wires being broken; and it was impossible to risk the passage. He did not in any way exaggerate the condition of the bridge. It may be taken for granted that, rash as the Americans usually are, when they are prudent there is good reason for it.

Passepartout, not daring to inform his master of what he heard, listened with set teeth, still as a statue.

"Hum!" cried Colonel Proctor; "but we are not going to stay here, I imagine, and take root in the snow?"

"Colonel," replied the conductor, "we have tele-graphed Omaha for a train, but it is not likely that it will reach Medicine Bow in less than six hours."

"Six hours!" cried Passepartout.

"Certainly," returned the conductor. "Besides, it will take us as long as that to reach Medicine Bow on foot."

"But it is only a mile from here," said one of the passengers.

"Yes, but it's on the other side of the river."

"And can't we cross that in a boat?" asked the Colonel.

"That's impossible. The creek is swollen from the rains. It is a rapid, and we shall have to make a ten mile detour to the north to find a ford."

The colonel launched a volley of oaths, denouncing the railway company and the conductor; and Passepartout, who was furious, was not far from joining him. Here was an obstacle, indeed, which all his master's bank notes could not remove.

There was a general disappointment among the passengers, who, on top of the delay, saw themselves compelled to trudge fifteen miles over a plain covered with snow. They grumbled and protested, and would certainly have thus attracted Phileas Fogg's attention, if he had not been completely absorbed in his game.

Passepartout found that he could not avoid telling his master what had occurred, and, with hanging head he was turning toward the car, when the engineer—a true Yankee, named Forster—called out, "Gentlemen, perhaps there is a way, after all, to go over."

"On the bridge?" asked a passenger.

"On the bridge."

"With our train?"

"With our train."

Passepartout stopped short, and eagerly listened to the engineer.

"But the bridge is unsafe," urged the conductor.

"No matter," replied Forster; "I think that by putting on the very highest speed we might have a chance of getting over."

"The devil!" muttered Passepartout.

But a number of the passengers were at once attracted by the engineer's proposal, and Colonel Proctor was especially delighted, and found the plan a very feasible one. He told stories about engineers leaping their trains over rivers without bridges, by putting on full steam; and many of those present fell in with the advice of the engineer.

"We have a fifty-fifty chance of getting over," said one.

"Eighty! ninety!"

Passepartout was astounded, and, though ready to

attempt anything to get over Medicine Creek, thought
the proposed experiment a little too American. "Besides," he thought, "there's a much simpler way, and
it does not even occur to any of these people! Sir,"
said he aloud to one of the passengers, "the engineer's
plan seems to me a little dangerous, but—"

"Eighty chances!" replied the passenger, turning
his back on him.

"I know it," said Passepartout, turning to another
passenger, "but a simple idea—"

"Ideas are no use," returned the American, shrugging his shoulders, "as the engineer assures us that
we can pass."

"Doubtless," urged Passepartout, "we can pass,
but perhaps it would be more prudent—"

"What! Prudent!" cried Colonel Proctor, seemingly prodigiously excited by this word. "At full
speed, don't you see, at full speed!"

"I know—I see," repeated Passepartout; "but it
would be, if not more prudent, since that word dis-
pleases you, at least more natural—"

"Who! What! What's the matter with this fellow?"
cried several.

The poor fellow did not know to whom to address
himself.

"Are you afraid?" asked Colonel Proctor.

"I afraid! Very well; I will show these people that
a Frenchman can be as American as they!"

"All aboard!" cried the conductor.

"Yes, all aboard!" repeated Passepartout, and immediately. "But they can't prevent me from thinking
that it would be more natural for us to cross the bridge
on foot, and let the train come after!"

But no one heard this wise reflection, nor would
anyone have acknowledged its wisdom. The passengers resumed their seats in the cars. Passepartout took
his seat without telling what had happened. The whist-
players were quite absorbed in their game.

The locomotive whistled vigorously; the engineer, reversing the steam, backed the train for nearly a mile—like a jumper, winding up to leap. Then, with another whistle, he began to move forward; the train increased its speed, and soon its rapidity became frightful; a prolonged screech issued from the locomotive; the piston worked up and down twenty strokes to the second. They perceived that the whole train, rushing on at the rate of a hundred miles an hour, hardly bore upon the rails at all.

And they went over! It was like a flash. No one saw the bridge. The train leaped, so to speak, from one bank to the other, and the engineer could not stop it until it had gone five miles beyond the station. But scarcely had the train crossed the river, when the bridge, completely ruined, fell with a crash into the rapids of Medicine Bow.

CHAPTER XXIX

In Which Certain Incidents Are Narrated Which Are Only to Be Met With on American Railroads

The train pursued its course, that evening, without interruption, passing Fort Saunders, crossing Cheyenne Pass, and reaching Evans Pass. The road here attained the highest elevation of the journey, eight thousand and ninety-one feet above the level of the sea. The travelers had now only to descend to the Atlantic by limitless plains, leveled by nature. A branch of the "grand trunk" led off south to Denver, the capital of Colorado. The country round about is rich in gold and silver, and more than fifty thousand inhabitants are already settled there.

Thirteen hundred and eighty-two miles had been covered from San Francisco, in three days and three nights; four days and nights more would probably bring them to New York. Phileas Fogg was not as yet behind.

During the night Camp Walbach was passed on the left; Lodge Pole Creek ran parallel with the road, marking the boundary between the territories of Wyoming and Colorado. They entered Nebraska at eleven, passed near Sedgwick, and reached Julesburg, on the southern branch of the Platte River.

It was here that the Union Pacific Railroad was inaugurated on the 23rd of October, 1867, by the chief engineer, General Dodge. Two powerful locomotives, carrying nine cars of invited guests, among whom was Thomas C. Durant, vice-president of the road, stopped at this point; cheers were given; the Sioux and Pawnees performed an imitation Indian battle; fireworks were let off; and the first number of the *Railway Pioneer* was printed by a press brought on the train. Thus was celebrated the inauguration of this great railroad, a mighty instrument of progress and civilization, thrown across the desert, and destined to link together cities and towns which did not yet exist. The whistle of the locomotive, more powerful than Amphion's lyre, was about to bid them rise from American soil.

Fort McPherson was left behind at eight in the morning, and three hundred and fifty-seven miles had yet to be covered before reaching Omaha. The road followed the capricious windings of the southern branch of the Platte River on its left bank. At nine the train stopped at the important town of North Platte, built between the two arms of the river, which join each other around it and form a single artery—a large tributary whose waters empty into the Missouri a little above Omaha.

The one hundred and first meridian was reached.

Mr. Fogg and his partners had resumed their game. No one—not even the dummy—complained of the length of the trip. Fix had begun by winning several guineas, which he seemed likely to lose; but he showed himself as eager a whist player as Mr. Fogg.

During the morning, chance distinctly favored that gentleman. Trumps and face cards were showered upon his hands.

Once, having plotted a bold stroke, he was about to play a spade, when a voice behind him said, "I should play a diamond."

Mr. Fogg, Aouda, and Fix raised their heads, and beheld Colonel Proctor.

Stamp Proctor and Phileas Fogg recognized each other at once.

"Ah! it's you, is it, Englishman?" cried the Colonel; "it's you who are going to play a spade!"

"And who plays it," replied Phileas Fogg coolly, throwing down the ten of spades.

"Well, it pleases me to have it diamonds," replied Colonel Proctor, in an insolent tone.

He made a movement as if to seize the card which had just been played, adding, "You don't understand anything about this game."

"Perhaps I'll do better at another," said Phileas Fogg, rising.

"You have only to try, son of John Bull," replied the Colonel.

Mrs. Aouda turned pale, and her blood ran cold. She seized Mr. Fogg's arm, and gently pulled him back. Passepartout was ready to pounce upon the American, who was staring insolently at his opponent. But Fix got up, and going to Colonel Proctor, said, "You forget that it is I with whom you have to deal, sir; for it was I whom you not only insulted, but struck!"

"Mr. Fix," said Mr. Fogg, "pardon me, but this affair is mine, and mine only. The Colonel has again insulted me by insisting that I should not play a spade, and he shall give me satisfaction for it."

"When and where you will," replied the American, "and with whatever weapon you choose."

Mrs. Aouda in vain attempted to restrain Mr. Fogg; as vainly did the detective endeavour to make the quarrel his. Passepartout wanted to throw the Colonel out of the window, but a sign from his master checked him. Phileas Fogg left the car, and the American followed him upon the platform.

"Sir," said Mr. Fogg to his adversary, "I am in a great hurry to get back to Europe, and any delay whatever will be greatly to my disadvantage."

"Well, what is that to me?" replied Colonel Proctor.

"Sir," said Mr. Fogg, very politely, "after our meeting in San Francisco, I determined to return to America and find you as soon as I had completed the business which called me to England."

"Really!"

"Will you appoint a meeting for six months hence?"

"Why not ten years hence?"

"I say six months," returned Phileas Fogg, "and I shall be at the place of meeting promptly."

"All this is an excuse," cried Stamp Proctor. "Now or never!"

"Very good. You are going to New York?"

"No."

"To Chicago?"

"No."

"To Omaha?"

"What difference is it to you? Do you know Plum Creek?"

"No," replied Mr. Fogg.

"It's the next station. The train will be there in an hour, and will stop there ten minutes. In ten minutes several revolver shots could be exchanged."

"Very well," said Mr. Fogg. "I will stop at Plum Creek."

"And I guess you'll stay there, too," added the American insolently.

"Who knows?" replied Mr. Fogg, returning to the car as coolly as usual. He began to reassure Mrs. Aouda, telling her that blusterers were never to be feared, and begged Fix to be his second at the approaching duel, a request which the detective could not refuse. Mr. Fogg resumed the interrupted game with perfect calm.

At eleven o'clock the locomotive's whistle announced that they were approaching Plum Creek station. Mr. Fogg rose, and, followed by Fix, went out upon the platform. Passepartout accompanied him, carrying a pair of revolvers. Mrs. Aouda remained in the car, as pale as death.

The door of the next car opened, and Colonel Proctor appeared on the platform, attended by a Yankee of his own stamp as his second. But just as the opponents were about to step from the train, the conductor hurried up, and shouted, "You can't get off, gentlemen!"

"Why not?" asked the colonel.

"We are twenty minutes late, and we shall not stop."

"But I am going to fight a duel with this gentleman."

"I am sorry," said the conductor, "but we shall be off at once. There's the bell ringing now."

The train started.

"I'm really very sorry, gentlemen," said the conductor. "Under any other circumstances I should have been happy to oblige you. But, after all, as you have not had time to fight here, why not fight as we go along?"

"That won't be convenient, perhaps, for this gentleman," said the colonel, in a jeering tone.

"It will be perfectly so," replied Phileas Fogg.

"Well, we are really in America," thought Passepartout, "and the conductor is a gentleman of the first order!"

So muttering, he followed his master.

The two opponents, their seconds, and the conductor passed through the cars to the rear of the train. The last car was only occupied by a dozen passengers. The conductor politely asked them if they would not be so kind as to leave it vacant for a few moments, as two gentlemen had an affair of honor to settle. The passengers granted the request with alacrity, and immediately disappeared on the platform.

The car, which was some fifty feet long, was very

convenient for their purpose. The adversaries could march on each other in the aisle, and fire at their ease.

Never was a duel more easily arranged. Mr. Fogg and Colonel Proctor, each provided with two six-barreled revolvers, entered the car. The seconds, remaining outside, shut them in. They were to begin firing at the first whistle of the locomotive. After an interval of two minutes, what remained of the two gentlemen would be taken from the car.

Nothing could be simpler. Indeed, it was all so simple that Fix and Passepartout felt their hearts beating as if they would break. They were listening for the agreed-upon whistle, when suddenly savage cries resounded in the air, accompanied by shots which certainly did not issue from the car where the duelists were. The shots continued in front and the whole length of the train. Cries of terror proceeded from the interior of the cars.

Colonel Proctor and Mr. Fogg, revolvers in hand, hastily left their prison, and rushed forward where the noise was most clamorous. They then perceived that the train was being attacked by a band of Sioux.

This was not the first attempt of these daring Indians, for more than once they had waylaid trains on the road. A hundred of them had, according to their habit, jumped upon the steps without waiting for the train to stop, with the ease of a clown mounting a horse at full gallop.

The Sioux were armed with guns, from which came the shots to which the passengers, who were almost all armed, responded with revolver shots.

The Indians had first mounted the engine and half stunned the engineer and stoker with blows from their muskets. A Sioux chief, wishing to stop the train, but not knowing how to work the regulator, had opened wide the steam valve instead of closing it, and the locomotive was plunging forward with frightful speed.

The Sioux had at the same time invaded the cars,

thrusting open the doors, and fighting hand to hand with the passengers. Penetrating the baggage car, they pillaged it, throwing the trunks off the train. The cries and shots were constant.

The travelers defended themselves bravely; some of the cars were barricaded and sustained a siege, like moving forts carried along at a speed of a hundred miles an hour.

Mrs. Aouda had behaved courageously from the first. She defended herself, like a true heroine, with a revolver, which she shot through the broken windows whenever a savage made his appearance. Twenty Sioux had fallen mortally wounded to the ground, and the wheels crushed those who fell upon the rails as if they had been worms. Several passengers, shot or stunned, lay on the seats.

It was necessary to put an end to the struggle, which had lasted for ten minutes, and which would result in the triumph of the Sioux if the train was not stopped. Fort Kearney station, where there was a garrison, was only two miles distant; but beyond this garrison, the Sioux would be masters of the train between Fort Kearney and the next station.

The conductor was fighting beside Mr. Fogg, when he was shot. As he fell he cried, "Unless the train is stopped in five minutes, we are lost!"

"It shall be stopped," said Phileas Fogg, preparing to rush from the car.

"Stay, monsieur," cried Passepartout; "I will go."

Mr. Fogg had not time to stop the brave fellow, who, opening a door unperceived by the Indians, succeeded in slipping under the car; and while the struggle continued, and the bullets whizzed across each other over his head, he made use of his old acrobatic experience, and with amazing agility worked his way under the cars, clinging to the chains, hanging by the brakes and the beams, creeping from one car to another with marvelous skill, and thus gaining the forward end of the train.

There, suspended by one hand between the baggage car and the tender, with the other he loosened the safety chains; but, owing to the traction, he would never have succeeded in unscrewing the yoking bar, had not a violent jerk jolted this bar out. The train, now detached from the engine, remained behind, whilst the locomotive rushed forward with increased speed.

Carried on by the force already acquired, the train still moved for several minutes; but the brakes were applied, and at last they stopped, less than a hundred feet from Kearney station.

The soldiers of the fort, attracted by the shots, hurried out. The Sioux had not expected them, and left in a body before the train entirely stopped.

But when the passengers counted each other on the station platform several were found missing; among others the courageous Frenchman whose devotion had just saved them.

CHAPTER XXX

In Which Phileas Fogg Simply Does His Duty

Three passengers—including Passepartout—had disappeared. Had they been killed in the struggle? Were they taken prisoners by the Sioux? It was impossible to tell.

There were many wounded, but none mortally. Colonel Proctor was one of the most seriously hurt; he had fought bravely, and a bullet had entered his groin. He was carried into the station with the other wounded passengers who needed immediate care.

Mrs. Aouda was safe; and Phileas Fogg, who had been in the thickest of the fight, had not received a scratch. Fix was slightly wounded in the arm. But Passepartout was not to be found, and tears ran down Mrs. Aouda's cheeks.

All the passengers got out of the train, the wheels of which were stained with blood. From the tires and spokes hung ragged pieces of flesh. As far as the eye could reach on the white plain behind, red trails were visible. The last Sioux were disappearing in the south, along the banks of the Republican River.

Mr. Fogg, with folded arms, remained motionless. He had a serious decision to make. Mrs. Aouda, standing near him, looked at him without speaking, and he understood her look. If his servant was a prisoner, ought he not to risk everything to rescue him from the Indians?

"I will find him, living or dead," he said quietly to Mrs. Aouda.

"Ah, Mr.—Mr. Fogg!" she cried, clasping his hands and covering them with tears.

"Living," added Mr. Fogg, "if we do not lose a moment."

Phileas Fogg, by this resolution, was inevitably sacrificing himself; he had just pronounced his own doom. The delay of a single day would make him miss the steamer in New York, and his bet would be entirely lost. But as he thought, "It is my duty," he did not hesitate.

The commanding officer of Fort Kearney was there. A hundred of his soldiers had placed themselves in a position to defend the station should the Sioux attack it.

"Sir," said Mr. Fogg to the captain, "three passengers have disappeared."

"Dead?" asked the captain.

"Dead or prisoners; that is the uncertainty which must be ended. Do you propose to pursue the Sioux?"

"That's a serious thing to do, sir," returned the captain. "These Indians may retreat beyond the Arkansas, and I cannot leave the fort unprotected."

"The lives of three men are at stake, sir," said Phileas Fogg.

"Doubtless; but can I risk the lives of fifty men to save three?"

"I don't know whether you can, sir; but you ought to do so."

"Nobody here," returned the other, "has a right to teach me my duty."

"Very well," said Mr. Fogg, coolly. "I will go alone."

"You, sir!" cried Fix, coming up; "you go alone in pursuit of the Indians?"

"Would you have me leave this poor fellow to perish—him to whom everyone present owes his life? I shall go.''

''No, sir, you shall not go alone,'' cried the captain, touched in spite of himself. ''No! you are a brave man. Thirty volunteers!'' he added, turning to the soldiers.

The whole company started forward at once. The captain had only to pick his men. Thirty were chosen, and an old sergeant placed at their head.

''Thanks, captain,'' said Mr. Fogg.

''Will you let me go with you?'' asked Fix.

''Do as you please, sir. But if you wish to do me a favor, you will remain with Mrs. Aouda. In case anything should happen to me—''

A sudden pallor overspread the detective's face. Separate himself from the man whom he had so persistently followed step by step! Leave him to wander about in this desert! Fix gazed attentively at Mr. Fogg, and, despite his suspicions and of the struggle which was going on within him, he lowered his eyes before that calm and frank look.

''I will stay,'' he said.

A few moments later, Mr. Fogg pressed the young woman's hand, and, having confided to her his precious bag, went off with the sergeant and his little squad. But, before going, he said to the soldiers, ''My friends, I will divide five thousand dollars among you, if we save the prisoners.''

It was then a little past noon.

Mrs. Aouda retired to a waiting room, and there she waited alone, thinking of the simple and noble generosity, the tranquil courage of Phileas Fogg. He had sacrificed his fortune, and was now risking his life, all without hesitation, from duty, in silence. In her eyes, Phileas Fogg was a hero.

Fix did not have the same thoughts, and could scarcely conceal his agitation. He walked feverishly up and down the platform, but soon resumed his out-

ward composure. He now saw the folly of which he had
been guilty in letting Fogg go alone. What! This man,
whom he had just followed around the world, he had
agreed now to separate himself from him! He began to
accuse himself, and, as if he were the director of police, gave himself a sound lecture for his greenness.

"I have been an idiot!" he thought, "Passepartout
has told him who I am. He has gone, and won't come
back! But how is it that I, Fix, who have in my pocket
a warrant for his arrest, have been so fascinated by
him? Indeed, I am nothing but an ass!"

So reasoned the detective, while the hours crept by
all too slowly. He did not know what to do. Sometimes
he was tempted to tell Mrs. Aouda all; but he could
not doubt how the young woman would receive his
confidences. What course should he take? He thought
of pursuing Fogg across the vast white plains; it did
not seem impossible that he might overtake him. There
were still footsteps on the snow! But soon, under a
new sheet, they were all wiped out.

Fix became discouraged. He felt a sort of insurmountable longing to abandon the game altogether.
Just then he was offered the chance to leave Fort Kearney station, and pursue his journey so rich in setbacks.

Indeed towards two o'clock in the afternoon, while
it was snowing hard, long whistles were heard approaching from the east. An enormous shadow, preceded by reddish light, slowly advanced, appearing
still larger through the mist, which gave it a fantastic
appearance. No train was expected from the east, neither had there been time for the help asked for by
telegraph to arrive; the train from Omaha to San Francisco was not due till the next day. The mystery was
soon explained.

The locomotive, which was slowly approaching with
deafening whistles, was the one which, having been
detached from the train, had continued its route with
such terrific rapidity, carrying off the unconscious en-

gineer and stoker. It had run several miles, when, the
fire becoming low for want of fuel, the steam had
slackened; and it had finally stopped an hour after,
some twenty miles beyond Fort Kearney. Neither the
engineer nor the stoker was dead, and they had revived
after their faint. The train had then stopped. The engineer, when he found himself in the desert and the
locomotive without cars, understood what had happened. He could not imagine how the locomotive had
become separated from the train; but he was convinced that the train left behind was in distress.

He did not hesitate. It would be prudent to continue
on to Omaha, for it would be dangerous to return to
the train while the Indians might still be engaged in
plundering. So what! He began to rebuild the fire in
the furnace; the pressure again mounted, and the
locomotive returned, running backwards to Fort Kearney. That's what was whistling in the mist.

The travelers were glad to see the locomotive resume its place at the head of the train. They could now
continue the journey so unfortunately interrupted.

Mrs. Aouda, on seeing the locomotive come up,
hurried out of the station, and asked the conductor,
"Are you going to start?"

"At once, madam."

"But the prisoners—our unfortunate fellow
travelers—"

"I cannot interrupt the trip," replied the conductor.
"We are already three hours behind time."

"And when will another train come through from
San Francisco?"

"Tomorrow evening, madam."

"Tomorrow evening! But then it will be too late!
We must wait—"

"It is impossible," answered the conductor. "If you
wish to go, please get in."

"I will not go," said Mrs. Aouda.

Fix had heard this conversation. A little while before, when there was no prospect of proceeding on the journey, he had made up his mind to leave Fort Kearney; but now that the train was there, ready to start, and he had only to take his seat in the car, an irresistible force held him back. The station platform burned his feet, and he could not stir. The conflict in his mind again began; anger and failure stifled him. He wanted to struggle on to the end.

Meanwhile the passengers and some of the wounded, among them Colonel Proctor, whose injuries were serious, had taken their seats in the train. The buzzing of the overheated boiler was heard, and the steam was escaping from the valves. The engineer whistled, the train started and soon disappeared, mingling its white smoke with the whirlwind of snow.

The detective had remained behind.

Several hours passed. The weather was dismal, and it was very cold. Fix sat motionless on a bench in the station; he might have been thought asleep. Aouda, despite the storm, kept coming out of the waiting room, going to the end of the platform, and peering through the tempest of snow, as if to pierce the mist which narrowed the horizon around her, and to hear, if possible, some welcome sound. She heard and saw nothing. Then she would return, chilled through, to come out again after a few moments, but always in vain.

Evening came, and the little band had not returned. Where could they be? Had they found the Indians, and were they having a fight with them, or were they still wandering in the mist? The commander of the fort was anxious, though he tried to conceal his apprehensions. As night approached, the snow fell less heavily, but it became intensely cold. There was absolute silence on the plains. Neither flight of bird nor passing of beast troubled the perfect calm.

Throughout the night Aouda, full of sad forebodings, her heart stifled with anguish, wandered about on the edge of the plains. Her imagination carried her far off, and showed her innumerable dangers. What she suffered through the long hours it would be impossible to describe.

Fix remained still in the same place, but did not sleep. Once a man approached and spoke to him, and the detective merely replied by shaking his head.

Thus the night passed. At dawn, the half-extinguished disk of the sun rose above a misty horizon; but it was now possible to recognize objects two miles off. Phileas Fogg and the squad had gone south; the south was totally deserted. It was then seven o'clock.

The captain, who was really alarmed, did not know what course to take. Should he send another detachment to the rescue of the first? Should he sacrifice more men, with so few chances of saving those already sacrificed? His hesitation did not last long, however. Calling one of his lieutenants, he was about to order a reconnaissance, when gunshots were heard. Was it a signal? The soldiers rushed out of the fort, and half a mile off they perceived a little band returning in good order.

Mr. Fogg was marching at their head, and just behind him were Passepartout and the other two travelers, rescued from the Sioux.

They had met and fought the Indians ten miles south of Fort Kearney. Shortly before the detachment arrived, Passepartout and his companions had begun to struggle with their captors, three of whom the Frenchman had knocked out, when his master and the soldiers hastened up to their rescue.

All were welcomed with joyful cries. Phileas Fogg distributed the reward he had promised the soldiers, while Passepartout, not without reason was muttering to himself, "It must certainly be confessed that I cost my master dear!"

Fix, without saying a word, was looking at Mr.

Fogg, and it would have been difficult to analyze the thoughts which struggled within him. As for Mrs. Aouda, she had taken her protector's hand and was pressing it in her own, too moved to speak.

Meanwhile, Passepartout was looking about for the train; he thought he should find it there, ready to start for Omaha, and he hoped that the time lost might be regained.

"The train! the train!" cried he.

"Gone," replied Fix.

"And when does the next train come through here?" asked Phileas Fogg.

"Not till this evening."

"Ah!" returned the impassive gentleman quietly.

CHAPTER XXXI

In Which Fix, the Detective, Considerably Furthers the Interests of Phileas Fogg

Phileas Fogg found himself twenty hours behind. Passepartout, the involuntary cause of this delay, was desperate. He had ruined his master!

At this moment the detective approached Mr. Fogg, and, looking him intently in the face, said—

"Seriously, sir, are you in great haste?"

"Quite seriously."

"I have a purpose in asking," went on Fix. "Is it absolutely necessary that you should be in New York on the 11th, before nine o'clock in the evening, the time that the steamer leaves for Liverpool?"

"It is absolutely necessary."

"And, if your journey had not been interrupted by these Indians, you would have reached New York on the morning of the 11th?"

"Yes; with eleven hours to spare before the steamer left."

"Good! you are therefore twenty hours behind. Twelve from twenty leaves eight. You must make up eight hours. Do you wish to try to do so?"

"On foot?" asked Mr. Fogg.

"No; on a sledge," replied Fix. "On a sledge with sails. A man has proposed such a method to me."

It was the man who had spoken to Fix during the night, and whose offer he had refused.

Phileas Fogg did not reply at once; but Fix having pointed out the man, who was walking up and down in front of the station, Mr. Fogg went up to him. An instant after, Mr. Fogg and the American, whose name was Mudge, entered a hut built just below the fort.

There Mr. Fogg examined a curious vehicle, a kind of frame on two long beams, a little raised in front like the runners of a sledge, and upon which there was room for five or six persons. A high mast was fixed on the frame, held firmly by metallic lashings, to which was attached a large brigantine sail. This mast held an iron stay upon which to hoist a jib sail. Behind, a sort of rudder served to guide the vehicle. It was, in short, a sledge rigged like a sloop. During the winter, when the trains are blocked up by the snow, these sledges make extremely rapid journeys across the frozen plains from one station to another. Provided with more sail than a cutter, and with the wind behind them, they slip over the surface of the prairies with a speed equal if not superior to that of the express trains.

Mr. Fogg readily made a bargain with the owner of this land craft. The wind was favorable, powerfully blowing from the west. The snow had hardened, and Mudge was very confident of being able to transport Mr. Fogg in a few hours to Omaha. There the trains east run frequently to Chicago and New York. It was not impossible that the lost time might yet be recovered; and such an opportunity was not to be rejected.

Not wishing to expose Mrs. Aouda to the discomforts of traveling in the open air, Mr. Fogg proposed to leave her with Passepartout at Fort Kearney, the servant taking upon himself to escort her to Europe by a better route and under more favorable conditions. But Aouda refused to part from Mr. Fogg, and Passepartout was delighted with her decision; for nothing could have induced him to leave his master while Fix was with him.

It would be difficult to guess the detective's thoughts. Was his conviction shaken by Phileas Fogg's return, or did he still regard him as an exceedingly shrewd rascal, who, his journey around the world completed, would think himself absolutely safe in England? Perhaps Fix's opinion of Phileas Fogg was somewhat modified; but he was nevertheless resolved to do his duty, and to hasten the return of the whole party to England with all his might.

At eight o'clock the sledge was ready to start. The passengers took their seats on it, and wrapped themselves up closely in their traveling blankets. The two great sails were hoisted, and under the pressure of the wind the sledge slid over the hardened snow with a speed of forty miles an hour.

The distance between Fort Kearney and Omaha, as the birds fly, is at most two hundred miles. If the wind held out they might make it in five hours; if no accident happened, the sledge might reach Omaha by one o'clock.

What a journey! The travelers, huddled close together, could not speak due to the cold, intensified by the rapidity at which they were going. The sledge sped on as lightly as a boat over the waves. When the breeze came, skimming the earth, the sledge seemed to be lifted off the ground by its sails. Mudge, who was at the rudder, kept in a straight line, and by a turn of his hand checked the lurches which the vehicle had a tendency to make. All the sails were up, and the jib was so arranged as not to screen the brigantine. A topmast was hoisted, and another jib, held out to the wind, added its force to the other sails.

"If nothing breaks," said Mudge, "we shall get there!"

Mr. Fogg had made it in Mudge's interest to reach Omaha within the time agreed on, by the offer of a handsome reward.

The prairie, across which the sledge was moving in a straight line, was as flat as a sea. It seemed like a vast frozen lake. The railroad which ran through this section came up from the southwest to the northwest by Great Island, Columbus, an important Nebraska town, Schuyler, and Fremont, to Omaha. It followed throughout the right bank of the Platte River. The sledge, shortening this route, took the chord of the arc traced by the railway. Mudge was not afraid of being stopped by the Platte River, because it was frozen. The road, then, was quite clear of obstacles, and Phileas Fogg had but two things to fear—an accident to the sledge, and a change in the wind.

But the breeze, far from lessening its force, blew as if to bend the mast, where, however, the metallic lashings held firmly. These lashings, like the chords of a stringed instrument, resounded as if vibrated by a violin bow. The sledge slid along in the midst of a plaintively intense melody.

"Those chords give the fifth and the octave," said Mr. Fogg.

These were the only words he uttered during the journey. Mrs. Aouda, cozily packed in furs and blankets, was sheltered as much as possible from the attacks of the freezing wind. As for Passepartout, his face was red as the sun when it sets in the mist, and he was inhaling the biting air. With his natural buoyancy of spirits, he began to hope again. They would reach New York on the evening, if not on the morning, of the 11th, and there was still some chance that it would be before the steamer sailed for Liverpool.

Passepartout even felt a strong desire to grasp his ally, Fix, by the hand. He didn't forget that it was the detective who had gotten the sledge, the only means

of reaching Omaha in time. However, checked by some
foreboding, he kept his usual reserve. One thing, however, Passepartout would never forget, and that was
the sacrifice which Mr. Fogg had made, without hesitation, to rescue him from the Sioux. Mr. Fogg had
risked his fortune and his life. No! His servant would
never forget that!

While each of the party was absorbed in such different thoughts, the sledge was flying fast over the vast
carpet of snow. The creeks it passed over were not
perceived. Fields and streams disappeared under a
uniform whiteness. The plain was absolutely deserted.
Between the Union Pacific road and the branch which
unites Kearney with Saint Joseph it formed a great
uninhabited island. Neither village, station, nor fort
appeared. From time to time they sped by some
phantomlike tree whose white skeleton twisted and
rattled in the wind. Sometimes flocks of wild birds
rose, or bands of gaunt, famished, ferocious prairie
wolves ran howling after the sledge. Passepartout, revolver in hand, held himself ready to fire on those
which came too near. Had an accident then happened
to the sledge, the travelers, attacked by these beasts,
would have been in the most terrible danger. But it
held on its even course, soon gained on the wolves,
and ere long left the howling band at a safe distance
behind.

About noon Mudge perceived by certain landmarks
that he was crossing the Platte River. He said nothing,
but he felt certain that he was now within twenty miles
of Omaha. And indeed in less than an hour this clever
guide was leaving the rudder and furling his sails,
while the sledge, carried forward by the great impetus
the wind had given it, went on half a mile further with
its sails unspread.

It stopped at last, and Mudge, pointing to a mass of
roofs white with snow, said, ''We've arrived!''

Arrived! Arrived at the station which is in daily

communication, by numerous trains, with the Atlantic seaboard!

Passepartout and Fix jumped off, stretched their stiffened limbs, and helped Mr. Fogg and the young woman to get off the sledge. Phileas Fogg generously rewarded Mudge, whose hand Passepartout warmly grasped, and the party directed their steps to the Omaha railway station.

The Pacific Railroad proper finds its terminus at this important Nebraska town. Omaha is connected with Chicago by the Chicago and Rock Island Railroad, which runs directly east, and goes through fifty stations.

A train was ready to start when Mr. Fogg and his party reached the station, and they only had time to get into the cars. They had seen nothing of Omaha; but Passepartout confessed to himself that this was not to be regretted, as they were not traveling to see the sights.

The train went rapidly across the State of Iowa, through Council Bluffs, Des Moines, and Iowa City. During the night it crossed the Mississippi at Davenport, and by Rock Island entered Illinois. The next day, which was the 10th, at four in the evening, it reached Chicago, already risen from its ruins, and more proudly seated than ever on the shores of its beautiful Lake Michigan.

Nine hundred miles separated Chicago from New York; but there were many trains in Chicago. Mr. Fogg passed at once from one to the other, and the locomotive of the Pittsburg, Fort Wayne, and Chicago Railway left at full speed, as if it fully understood that that gentleman had no time to waste. It crossed Indiana, Ohio, Pennsylvania, and New Jersey like a flash, rushing through towns with antique names, some of which had streets and streetcars, but as yet no houses. At last the Hudson came into view; and at a quarter-past eleven in the evening of the 11th, the train stopped in the station on the right bank of the river, before the very pier of the Cunard line.

The *China*, bound for Liverpool, had left three quarters of an hour before!

CHAPTER XXXII

IN WHICH PHILEAS FOGG ENGAGES IN A DIRECT STRUGGLE WITH BAD FORTUNE

The departure of the *China,* seemed to have carried off Phileas Fogg's last hope. None of the other steamers were able to serve his needs. The *Pereire,* of the French Transatlantic Company, whose admirable steamers are equal to any in speed and comfort, did not leave until the 14th; the Hamburg boats did not go directly to Liverpool or London, but to Le Havre; and the additional trip from Le Havre to Southampton would render Phileas Fogg's last efforts of no avail. The Inman steamer did not depart till the next day, and could not cross the Atlantic in time to save the wager.

Mr. Fogg learned all this in consulting his *Bradshaw,* which gave him the daily movements of the transatlantic steamers.

Passepartout was crushed; it overwhelmed him to miss the boat by three quarters of an hour. It was his fault, for, instead of helping his master, he had not ceased putting obstacles in his path! And when he recalled all the incidents of the tour, when he counted up the sums spent in pure loss and on his own account, when he thought that the immense wager, added to the heavy expenses of this useless journey, would completely ruin Mr. Fogg, he cursed himself bitterly. Mr.

Fogg, however, did not reproach him; and, on leaving the Cunard pier, only said, "We will consult about what is best tomorrow. Come."

The party crossed the Hudson in the Jersey City ferryboat, and drove in a carriage to the St. Nicholas Hotel, on Broadway. Rooms were taken, and the night passed, briefly for Phileas Fogg, who slept profoundly, but very long for Mrs. Aouda and the others, whose agitation did not permit them to rest.

The next day was the 12th of December. From seven in the morning of the 12th, to a quarter before nine in the evening of the 21st, there were nine days, thirteen hours, and forty-five minutes. If Phileas Fogg had left on the *China,* one of the fastest steamers on the Atlantic, he would have reached Liverpool, and then London within the period agreed upon.

Mr. Fogg left the hotel alone, after giving Passepartout instructions to await his return and inform Mrs. Aouda to be ready at an instant's notice. He proceeded to the banks of the Hudson, and looked about among the vessels moored or anchored in the river for any that were about to depart. Several had departure signals, and were preparing to put to sea at morning tide; for in this immense and admirable port of New York, there is not one day in a hundred that vessels do not set out for every corner of the globe. But they were mostly sailing vessels, of which, of course, Phileas Fogg could make no use.

He seemed about to give up all hope, when he saw, anchored at the Battery, a cable's length off at most, a trading vessel, with a screw, well shaped, whose funnel, puffing a cloud of smoke, indicated that she was getting ready for departure.

Phileas Fogg hailed a small boat, got into it, and soon found himself on board the *Henrietta,* ironhulled, wood-built above. He went up on deck, and asked for the captain, who presented himself immediately. He was a man of fifty, a sort of sea wolf, with

big eyes, a complexion of oxidized copper, red hair
and thick neck, and a growling voice.

"The captain?" asked Mr. Fogg.

"I am the captain."

"I am Phileas Fogg, of London."

"And I am Andrew Speedy, of Cardiff."

"You are going to put to sea?"

"In an hour."

"You are bound for—"

"Bordeaux."

"And your cargo?"

"No freight. Going in ballast."

"Do you have any passengers?"

"No passengers. Never have passengers. Too much
in the way."

"Is your vessel a swift one?"

"Between eleven and twelve knots. The *Henrietta*,
well known."

"Will you carry me and three other persons to Liverpool?"

"To Liverpool? Why not to China?"

"I said Liverpool."

"No!"

"No?"

"No. I am setting out for Bordeaux, and shall go to
Bordeaux."

"Money is no object?"

"None."

The captain spoke in a tone which did not admit of
a reply.

"But the owners of the *Henrietta*—" resumed Phileas Fogg.

"The owners are myself," replied the captain. "The
vessel belongs to me."

"I will freight it for you."

"No."

"I will buy it from you."

"No."

Phileas Fogg did not betray the least disappointment; but the situation was a grave one. Things were not in New York as in Hong Kong, nor with the captain of the *Henrietta* as with the captain of the *Tankadere*. Up to this time money had smoothed away every obstacle. Now money failed.

Still, some means must be found to cross the Atlantic on a boat, unless by balloon—which would have been venturesome, though not feasible. It seemed that Phileas Fogg had an idea, for he said to the captain, "Well, will you carry me to Bordeaux?"

"No, not if you paid me two hundred dollars."

"I offer you two thousand."

"Apiece?"

"Apiece."

"And there are four of you?"

"Four."

Captain Speedy began to scratch his head. There were eight thousand dollars to gain, without changing his route. This was well worth conquering the dislike he had for all kinds of passengers. Besides, passengers at two thousand dollars are no longer passengers, but valuable merchandise. "I start at nine o'clock," Captain Speedy said simply. "Are you and your party ready?"

"We will be on board at nine o'clock," replied, no less simply, Mr. Fogg.

It was half-past eight. To disembark from the *Henrietta,* jump into a carriage, hurry to the St. Nicholas, and return with Mrs. Aouda, Passepartout, and even the inseparable Fix, was short work, and was performed by Mr. Fogg with the coolness which never abandoned him. They were on board when the *Henrietta* made ready to weigh anchor.

When Passepartout heard what this last voyage was going to cost, he uttered a prolonged "Oh!" which extended throughout his entire vocal range.

As for Fix, he said to himself that the Bank of En-

gland would certainly not come out of this affair un-
scathed. When they reached England, even if Mr. Fogg
did not throw some handfuls of bankbills into the sea,
more than seven thousand pounds would have been
spent.

CHAPTER XXXIII

IN WHICH PHILEAS FOGG SHOWS HIMSELF EQUAL TO THE OCCASION

An hour later, the "Henrietta" sailed by the lighthouse which marks the entrance of the Hudson, turned the point of Sandy Hook, and put to sea. During the day she skirted Long Island, passed Fire Island, and directed her course rapidly eastward.

At noon the next day, a man climbed the bridge to ascertain the vessel's position. It might be thought that this was Captain Speedy. Not the least in the world. It was Phileas Fogg, Esquire. As for Captain Speedy, he was shut up in his cabin under lock and key, and was uttering loud cries, which signified an anger at once excusable and excessive.

What had happened was very simple. Phileas Fogg wanted to go to Liverpool, but the captain would not carry him there. Then Phileas Fogg had taken passage for Bordeaux, and, during the thirty hours he had been on board, had so shrewdly managed with his bank notes that the sailors and stokers, who were a shady crew, and were on bad terms with the captain, went over to him in a body. This was why Phileas Fogg was in command instead of Captain Speedy; why the captain was a prisoner in his cabin; and why at last, the *Henrietta* was directing her course toward Liverpool. It was very clear, to see Mr. Fogg manage the craft, that he had been a sailor.

How the adventure ended will be seen later. Aouda

was anxious, though she said nothing. At first Fix was dumbfounded. As for Passepartout, he thought Mr. Fogg's maneuver simply glorious. The captain had said "between eleven and twelve knots," and the *Henrietta* confirmed his prediction.

If, then—for there were "ifs" still—the sea did not become boisterous, if the wind did not veer round to the east, if no accident happened to the boat or its machinery, the *Henrietta* might cross the three thousand miles from New York to Liverpool in the nine days, between the 12th and the 21st of December. It is true that, once arrived, the affair on board the *Henrietta*, added to that of the Bank of England, might create more difficulties for Mr. Fogg than he could desire.

During the first days, they went along smoothly enough. The sea was not too rough, the wind seemed stationary in the northeast, the sails were hoisted, and the *Henrietta* ploughed across the waves like a real transatlantic steamer.

Passepartout was delighted. His master's last exploit, the consequences of which he ignored, enchanted him. Never had the crew seen so jolly and dexterous a fellow. He was friendly with the sailors, and amazed them with his acrobatic feats. He thought they managed the vessel like gentlemen, and that the stokers fired up like heroes. His loquacious good humor infected everyone. He had forgotten the past, its vexations and delays. He only thought of the goal, so nearly reached; and sometimes he boiled over with impatience, as if heated by the furnaces of the *Henrietta*. Often, also, the good fellow revolved around Fix, looking at him with a keen, distrustful eye; but he did not speak to him, for their old intimacy no longer existed.

Fix, it must be confessed, understood nothing of what was going on. The conquest of the *Henrietta*, the bribery of the crew, Fogg managing the boat like a skilled seaman, amazed and confused him. He did not know what to think. For, after all, a man who began by stealing fifty-five thousand pounds might end by stealing a vessel; and Fix was not unnaturally inclined to conclude that the *Henrietta,* under Fogg's command, was not going to Liverpool at all, but to some part of the world where the robber, turned into a pirate, would quietly hide in safety. The conjecture was extremely plausible, and the detective began to seriously regret that he had embarked in the affair.

As for Captain Speedy, he continued to howl and growl in his cabin; and Passepartout, whose duty it was to carry him his meals, strong as he was, took the greatest precautions. Mr. Fogg did not seem even to know that there was a captain on board.

On the 13th they passed the edge of the Banks of Newfoundland, a dangerous stretch, as during the winter, especially, there are frequent fogs and heavy gales of wind. Ever since the evening before, the barometer, suddenly falling, had indicated an approaching change in the atmosphere; and during the night the temperature changed, the cold became sharper, and the wind veered to the southeast.

This was a misfortune. Mr. Fogg, in order not to deviate from his course, furled his sails and increased the force of the steam. However the vessel's speed slackened, due to the roughness of the sea. She pitched violently, and this delayed her progress. Little by little the breeze swelled into a tempest, and everyone feared that the *Henrietta* might not be able to maintain herself upright on the waves.

Passepartout's face darkened with the skies, and for two days the poor fellow was constantly scared. But Phileas Fogg was a bold sailor, and knew how to maintain headway against the sea. He kept on his course, without even decreasing his steam. The *Henrietta,* when she could not rise above the waves, did cross them, swamping her deck, but moving forward safely. Sometimes the propellor rose out of the water, beating the air with its blades when a mountain of water raised the stern above the waves; but the craft always kept straight ahead.

The wind, however, did not grow as boisterous as might have been feared; it was not one of those tempests which burst and rush on with a speed of ninety miles an hour. It remained a strong and steady breeze, but, unhappily, it blew obstinately from the southeast, rendering the sails useless.

The 16th of December was the seventy-fifth day since Phileas Fogg's departure from London, and the *Henrietta* had not yet been seriously delayed. Half of the crossing was almost accomplished, and the worst waters had been passed. In summer, success would have been certain. In winter, they were at the mercy of the bad season. Passepartout said nothing; but he secretly hoped, and comforted himself with the reflection that, if the wind failed them, they could still count on the steam.

On this day the engineer came on deck, went up to Mr. Fogg, and began to speak earnestly with him.

Without knowing why—it was a foreboding, perhaps—Passepartout became vaguely uneasy. He would have given one of his ears to hear with the other what the engineer was saying. He finally managed to catch a few words, and was sure he heard his master say, "You are certain of what you tell me?"

"Certain, sir," replied the engineer. "You must remember that, since we started, we have kept up hot fires in all our furnaces, and though we had coal enough to go on short steam from New York to Bordeaux, we haven't enough to go at full steam from New York to Liverpool."

"I will consider," replied Mr. Fogg.

Passepartout understood it all; he was seized with mortal anxiety. The coal was giving out! "Ah, if my master can handle this setback," he muttered he, "he'll be quite a man!" He could not help imparting to Fix what he had overheard.

"Then you believe that we really are going to Liverpool?"

"Of course."

"Ass!" replied the detective, shrugging his shoulders and turning on his heel.

Passepartout was about to criticize sharply the epithet, the reason of which he could not for the life of him comprehend. But he reflected that the unfortunate Fix was probably very much disappointed and humiliated in his self-esteem, after having so awkwardly followed a false track around the world, and refrained from criticizing him.

And now what course would Phileas Fogg adopt? It was difficult to imagine. Nevertheless he seemed to have decided upon one, for that evening he sent for the engineer, and said to him, "Feed all the fires until the coal is exhausted."

A few moments after, the funnel of the *Henrietta* vomited forth torrents of smoke. The vessel continued to proceed with full steam on. But on the 18th, the engineer, as he had predicted, announced that the coal would give out in the course of the day.

"Do not let the fires go down," replied Mr. Fogg. "Keep them up to the last. Let the valves be filled."

Towards noon Phileas Fogg, having ascertained their position, called Passepartout, and ordered him to go for Captain Speedy. It was as if the honest fellow had been ordered to unchain a tiger. He went to the poop, saying to himself, "He will be like a madman!"

In a few moments, with cries and oaths, a bomb appeared on the poopdeck. The bomb was Captain Speedy. It was clear that he was about to burst. "Where are we?" were the first words his anger permitted him to utter. Had the poor man been apoplectic, he would never have recovered from his paroxysm of wrath.

"Where are we?" he repeated, with purple face.

"Seven hundred and seventy miles from Liverpool," replied Mr. Fogg, with imperturbable calm.

"Pirate!" cried Captain Speedy.

"I have sent for you, sir—"

"Bandit!"

"Sir," continued Mr. Fogg, "to ask you to sell me your vessel."

"No! By all the devils, no!"

"But I shall be obliged to burn her."

"Burn the *Henrietta!*"

"Yes; at least the upper part of her. The coal has given out."

"Burn my vessel!" cried Captain Speedy, who could scarcely pronounce the words. "A vessel worth fifty thousand dollars!"

"Here are sixty thousand," replied Phileas Fogg, handing the captain a roll of bank bills. This had a prodigious effect on Andrew Speedy. An American can scarcely remain unmoved at the sight of sixty thousand dollars. The captain forgot in an instant his anger, his imprisonment, and all his grudges against his passenger. The *Henrietta* was twenty years old; it was a great bargain. The bomb would not go off after all. Mr. Fogg had taken away the firing pin.

"And I shall still have the iron hull," said the captain in a softer tone.

"The iron hull and the engine. Is it agreed?"

"Agreed."

And Andrew Speedy, seizing the bank notes, counted them, and made them vanish into his pocket.

During this scene, Passepartout was as white as a sheet, and Fix almost had an apoplectic fit. Nearly twenty thousand pounds had been spent, and Fogg was leaving the hull and engine to the captain, that is, near the whole value of the craft! It was true, however, that fifty-five thousand pounds had been stolen from the bank.

When Andrew Speedy had pocketed the money, Mr. Fogg said to him, "Don't let this astonish you, sir. You must know that I shall lose twenty thousand pounds unless I arrive in London by a quarter before nine on the evening of the 21st of December. I missed the steamer in New York, and as you refused to take me to Liverpool—"

"And I did well by the fifty thousand devils of hell!" cried Andrew Speedy; for I have gained at least forty thousand dollars by it!" He added, more sedately, "Do you know one thing, Captain—"

"Fogg."

"Captain Fogg, you've got something of the Yankee about you."

And, having paid his passenger what he considered a high compliment, he was walking away, when Mr. Fogg said, "The vessel now belongs to me?"

"Certainly, from the keel to the truck of the masts—all the wood, that is."

"Very well. Have the interior seats, bunks and frames pulled down, and burn them."

One can imagine how much dry wood was needed to keep the steam up to the adequate pressure, and on that day the poop, cabins, bunks, and the spare deck were sacrificed.

On the next day, the 19th of December, the masts, rafts, and spars were burned; the crew worked energetically, keeping up the fires. Passepartout hewed, cut and sawed with all his might. There was a perfect rage for demolition.

The railings, fittings, the greater part of the deck, and top sides disappeared on the 20th, and the *Henrietta* was now only a flat hulk.

But on that day they sighted the Irish coast and Fastnet Light.

However, by ten in the evening they were only passing Queenstown. Phileas Fogg had only twenty-four hours more in which to get to London! With full steam on that amount of time was necessary to reach Liverpool. And the steam was about to give out altogether!

"Sir," said Captain Speedy, who was now deeply interested in Mr. Fogg's project, "I really sympathize with you. Everything is against you. We are only opposite Queenstown."

"Ah," said Mr. Fogg, "is that place where we see the lights Queenstown?"

"Yes."

"Can we enter the harbor?"

"Not under three hours. Only at high tide."

"Stay," replied Mr. Fogg calmly, without betraying in his features that by a supreme inspiration he was about to attempt once more to conquer ill fortune.

Queenstown is the Irish port at which the transatlantic steamers stop to put off the mail. This mail is carried to Dublin by express trains always held in readiness to start; from Dublin it is sent on to Liverpool by the most rapid boats, and thus gains twelve hours on the Atlantic steamers.

Phileas Fogg was counting on gaining twelve hours in the same way. Instead of arriving in Liverpool the next evening by the *Henrietta*, he would be there by noon, and would therefore have time to reach London before a quarter before nine in the evening.

The *Henrietta* entered Queenstown harbor at one o'clock in the morning, it then being high tide; and Phileas Fogg, after being grasped heartily by the hand by Captain Speedy, left that gentleman on the leveled hulk of his craft, which was still worth half what he had sold it for.

The party went on shore at once. Fix was greatly tempted to arrest Mr. Fogg on the spot; but he did not. Why? What struggle was going on within him? Had he changed his mind about "his man?" Did he understand that he had made a grave mistake? He did not, however, abandon Mr. Fogg. They all got upon the train, which was just ready to start, at half-past

. At dawn they were in Dublin, and they lost no
me in embarking on one of these steamers which,
disdaining to rise upon the waves, invariably cut
through them.

Phileas Fogg at last disembarked on the Liverpool
quay at twenty minutes before twelve, December 21st.
He was only six hours from London.

But at this moment Fix came up, put his hand upon
Mr. Fogg's shoulder, and, showing his warrant, said,
"You are really Phileas Fogg?"

"I am."

"I arrest you in the Queen's name!"

CHAPTER XXXIV

IN WHICH PHILEAS FOGG AT LAST REACHES LONDON

Phileas Fogg was in prison. He had been shut up in the Custom House, and he was to be transferred to London the next day.

Passepartout, when he saw his master arrested, would have fallen upon Fix, had he not been held back by some policemen. Mrs. Aouda was thunderstruck at the suddenness of an event which she could not understand. Passepartout explained to her how it was that the honest and courageous Fogg was arrested as a robber. The young woman's heart revolted against so heinous a charge, and when she saw that she could attempt or do nothing to save her protector, she wept bitterly.

As for Fix, he had arrested Mr. Fogg because it was his duty, whether Mr. Fogg were guilty or not.

The thought then struck Passepartout—the terrible thought that he was indeed the cause of this new misfortune! Had he not concealed Fix's errand from his master? When Fix revealed his true character and purpose, why had he not told Mr. Fogg? If the latter had been warned, he would no doubt have given Fix proof of his innocence, and showed Fix his error; at least, Fix would not have continued his journey at the expense and on the heels of his master, only to arrest him the moment he set foot on English soil. At the thought of his errors and his foolhardiness, Passepartout was overwhelmed with remorse. He wept. He felt like blowing his brains out!

Aouda and he had remained, despite the cold, under the portico of the Custom House. Neither wished to leave the place; both were anxious to see Mr. Fogg again.

That gentleman was really and duly ruined, and just at the moment when he was about to attain his goal. This arrest was fatal. Having arrived in Liverpool at twenty minutes before twelve on the 21st of December, he had till a quarter before nine that evening to reach the Reform Club, that is, nine hours and a quarter; the journey from Liverpool to London was six hours.

If any one, at this moment, had entered the Custom House, he would have found Mr. Fogg seated, motionless, calm, and without apparent anger, upon a wooden bench. He was not, it is true, resigned; but this last blow failed to force him into an outward betrayal of any emotion. Was he being devoured by one of those secret rages, all the more terrible because contained, and which only burst forth, with an irresistible force, at the last moment? No one could tell. There he sat, calmly waiting—for what? Did he still cherish hope? Did he still believe, now that the door of this prison was closed upon him, that he would succeed?

However that may have been, Mr. Fogg had carefully put his watch upon the table, and was observing its advancing hands. Not a word escaped his lips, but his look was singularly set and stern. The situation, in any event, was a terrible one, and might be thus stated:

If Phileas Fogg was honest, he was ruined.

If he was a knave, he was caught.

Did escape occur to him? Did he examine to see if there were any practicable outlets from his prison?

Did he think of escaping from it? Possibly; for once he walked slowly around the room. But the door was locked, and the window heavily barred with iron rods. He sat down again, and drew his journal from his pocket. On the line where these words were written, "December 21st, Saturday, Liverpool," he added, "80th day, 11:40 A.M.," and waited.

The Custom House clock struck one. Mr. Fogg observed that his watch was two minutes fast.

Two o'clock! Admitting that he was at this moment taking an express train, he could reach London and the Reform Club by a quarter before nine, P.M. His forehead slightly wrinkled.

At thirty-three minutes past two he heard a noise outside, then a hasty opening of doors. Passepartout's voice was audible, and immediately after that of Fix. Phileas Fogg's eyes brightened for an instant.

The door swung open, and he saw Passepartout, Mrs. Aouda, and Fix, who hurried towards him.

Fix was out of breath, and his hair was in disorder. He could not speak. "Sir," he stammered, "sir—forgive me—a most—unfortunate resemblance—robber arrested three days ago—you—are free!"

Phileas Fogg was free! He walked to the detective, looked him steadily in the face, and with the only rapid motion he had ever made in his life, or which he ever would make, drew back his arms, and with the precision of a machine, knocked Fix down.

"What a hit!" cried Passepartout.

Fix, who found himself on the floor, did not utter a word. He had only received his deserts. Mr. Fogg, Aouda, and Passepartout left the Custom House without delay, and rushed into a cab, and in a few moments arrived at the station.

Phileas Fogg asked if there was an express train about to leave for London. It was forty minutes past two. The express train had left thirty-five minutes before.

Phileas Fogg then ordered a special train.

There were several rapid locomotives on hand; but

the railway arrangements did not permit the special train to leave until three o'clock.

At that hour Phileas Fogg, having stimulated the engineer by the offer of a generous reward, at last set out toward London with Aouda and his faithful servant.

It was necessary to make the journey in five hours and a half; and this would have been easy on a clear road throughout. But there were forced delays, and when Mr. Fogg stepped from the train at the terminus, all the clocks in London were striking ten minutes before nine.*

Having carried out this trip around the world, he was five minutes late. He had lost the wager!

*A somewhat remarkable eccentricity on the part of the London clocks!—TRANSLATOR.

CHAPTER XXXV

IN WHICH PHILEAS FOGG DOES NOT HAVE TO REPEAT HIS ORDERS TO PASSEPARTOUT TWICE

The residents in Saville Row would have been surprised the next day, if they had been told that Phileas Fogg had returned home. His doors and windows were still closed; no appearance of change was visible.

After leaving the station, Mr. Fogg gave Passepartout instructions to purchase some provisions, and quietly went to his house.

He bore his misfortune with his habitual tranquility. Ruined! And by the blundering of the detective! After having steadily made that long journey, overcome a hundred obstacles, braved many dangers, and still found time to do some good on his way, to fail near the goal by a sudden event which he could not have foreseen, and for which he was unprepared; it was terrible! But a few pounds were left of the large sum he had carried with him. There only remained of his fortune the twenty thousand pounds deposited at Baring's, and this amount he owed to his friends of the Reform Club. So great had been the expense of his tour that, even had he won, no doubt it would not have enriched him; and it is probable that he had not sought to enrich himself, being a man who rather laid wagers for honor's sake than for the stake proposed. But this wager totally ruined him.

Mr. Fogg's course, however, was fully decided upon; he knew what remained for him to do.

A room in the house in Saville Row was set apart for Mrs. Aouda, who was overwhelmed with grief at her protector's misfortune. From the words which Mr. Fogg dropped, she saw that he was meditating some fatal project.

Knowing that Englishmen governed by a fixed idea sometimes resort to the desperate expedient of suicide, Passepartout kept a narrow watch upon his master, though he carefully concealed the appearance of so doing.

First of all, the good fellow had gone up to his room, and had turned off the gas burner, which had been burning for eighty days. He had found in the letter-box a bill from the gas company, and he thought it was about time to put a stop to this expense, which was his responsibility.

The night passed. Mr. Fogg went to bed, but did he sleep? Aouda did not once close her eyes. Passepartout watched all night, like a faithful dog, at his master's door.

Mr. Fogg called him in the morning, and told him to get Mrs. Aouda's breakfast, and a cup of tea and toast for himself. Mrs. Aouda would excuse him from lunch and dinner, as his time would be absorbed all day in putting his affairs in order. In the evening he would ask permission to have a few moments' conversation with the young lady.

Passepartout, having received his orders, had nothing to do but obey them. He looked at his imperturbable master, and could scarcely bring his mind to leave him. His heart was full, and his conscience tortured by remorse; for he accused himself more bitterly than ever of being the cause of the irretrievable disaster. Yes! if he had warned Mr. Fogg, and had disclosed Fix's projects to him, his master would certainly not have given the detective passage to Liverpool, and then—

Passepartout could hold it in no longer.

"My master! Mr. Fogg!" he cried, "why do you not curse me? It was my fault that—"

"I blame no one," returned Phileas Fogg, with perfect calm. "Go!"

Passepartout left the room, and went to find Mrs. Aouda, to whom he delivered his master's message.

"Madam," he added, "I can do nothing myself—nothing! I have no influence over my master; but you, perhaps—"

"What influence could I have?" replied Mrs. Aouda. "Mr. Fogg is influenced by no one. Has he ever understood that my gratitude to him is overflowing? Has he ever read my heart? My friend, he must not be left alone an instant! You say he is going to speak with me this evening?"

"Yes, madam; probably to arrange for your protection and comfort in England."

"We shall see," replied Aouda, becoming suddenly pensive.

Throughout this day (Sunday) the house in Saville Row was as if uninhabited, and Phileas Fogg, for the first time since he had lived in that house, did not set out for his club when Westminster clock struck half-past eleven.

Why should he appear at the Reform? His friends no longer expected him there. As Phileas Fogg had not appeared in the salon on the evening before (Saturday, the 21st of December, at a quarter before nine), he had lost his wager. It was not even necessary that he should go to his bankers for the twenty thousand pounds. For his antagonists already had his check in their hands, and they had only to fill it out and send it to the Barings to have the amount transferred to their credit.

Mr. Fogg, therefore, had no reason for going out,

and so he remained at home. He shut himself up in his room, and busied himself putting his affairs in order. Passepartout continually went up and down the stairs. The hours were long for him. He listened at his master's door, and looked through the keyhole, as if he had a perfect right so to do, and as if he feared that something terrible might happen at any moment. Sometimes he thought of Fix, but no longer in anger. Fix, like all the world, had been mistaken in Phileas Fogg, and had only done his duty in tracking and arresting him; while he, Passepartout—this thought haunted him, and he never ceased cursing his miserable folly.

When he found himself too wretched to remain alone, he would knock at Mrs. Aouda's door, go into her room, sit without speaking in a corner, and look ruefully at the young woman. Mrs. Aouda was still pensive.

About half-past seven in the evening Mr. Fogg sent to know if Aouda would receive him, and in a few moments he found himself alone with her.

Phileas Fogg took a chair, and sat down near the fireplace, opposite Aouda. No emotion was visible on his face. Fogg returned was exactly the Fogg who had gone away; there was the same calm, the same impassibility.

He sat several minutes without speaking; then, raised his eyes to Mrs. Aouda, "Madam," said he, "will you pardon me for bringing you to England?"

"I, Mr. Fogg!" replied Aouda, clutching her chest.

"Please let me finish," returned Mr. Fogg. "When I decided to bring you far away from the country which was so unsafe for you, I was rich, and counted on putting a portion of my fortune at your disposal; then your existence would have been free and happy. But now I am ruined."

"I know it, Mr. Fogg," replied Mrs. Aouda; "and I ask you in my turn, will you forgive me for having followed you, and—who knows?—for having, perhaps, delayed you, and thus contributed to your ruin?"

"Madam, you could not remain in india, and your safety could only be assured by bringing you to such a distance that your persecutors could not take you."

"So, Mr. Fogg," resumed Mrs. Aouda, "not content with rescuing me from a terrible death, you thought yourself bound to secure my comfort in a foreign land?"

"Yes, madam; but circumstances have been against me. Still, I beg to place the little I have left at your service."

"But what will become of you, Mr. Fogg?"

"As for me, madam," replied the gentleman, coolly, "I have need of nothing."

"But how do you look upon the fate, sir, which awaits you?"

"As I am in the habit of doing."

"At least," said Mrs. Aouda, "want should not overtake a man like you. Your friends—"

"I have no friends, madam."

"Your relatives—"

"I have no longer any relatives."

"I pity you, then, Mr. Fogg, for solitude is a sad thing, with no heart to which to confide your griefs. They say, though, that misery itself, shared by two sympathetic souls, may be borne with patience."

"They say so, madam."

"Mr. Fogg," said Aouda, rising, and seizing his hand, "do you wish at once a kinswoman and a friend? Will you have me for your wife?"

Mr. Fogg, at this, rose in his turn. There was an unusual light in his eyes, and a slight trembling of his lips. Mrs. Aouda looked into his face. The sincerity, rectitude, firmness, and sweetness of this soft glance of a noble woman, who could dare all to save him to whom she owed all, at first astonished, then penetrated him. He shut his eyes for an instant, as if to avoid her look. When he opened them again, "I love you!" he said, simply. "Yes, by all that is holiest, I love you, and I am entirely yours!"

"Ah!" cried Mrs. Aouda, pressing his hand to her heart.

Passepartout was summoned and appeared immediately. Mr. Fogg still held Aouda's hand in his own; Passepartout understood, and his big, round face became as radiant as the tropical sun at its zenith.

Mr. Fogg asked him if it was not too late to notify the Reverend Samuel Wilson, of Marylebone Parish, that evening.

Passepartout smiled his most genial smile, and said, "Never too late."

It was five minutes past eight.

"Will it be for tomorrow, Monday?"

"For tomorrow, Monday?" asked Mr. Fogg, turning to Aouda.

"Yes; for tomorrow, Monday," she replied.

Passepartout hurried off as fast as his legs could carry him.

CHAPTER XXXVI

In Which Phileas Fogg's Name Is Once More at a Premium on 'Change

It is time to relate what a change took place in English public opinion when it transpired that the real bank robber, a certain James Strand, had been arrested, on the 17th of December, at Edinburgh. Three days before, Phileas Fogg had been a criminal who was being desperately followed up by the police; now he was an honorable gentleman, mathematically pursuing his eccentric journey around the world.

The papers resumed their discussion about the wager; all those who had laid bets, for or against him, revived their interest, as if by magic; the "Phileas Fogg bonds" again became negotiable, and many new wagers were made. Phileas Fogg's name was once more at a premium on the stock exchange.

His five friends of the Reform Club spent these three days in a state of feverish suspense. Would Phileas Fogg, whom they had forgotten, reappear before their eyes? Where was he at this moment? The 17th of December, the day of James Strand's arrest, was the seventy-sixth since Phileas Fogg's departure, and no news of him had been received. Was he dead? Had he abandoned the effort, or was he continuing his journey along the route agreed upon? And would he appear on Saturday, the 21st of December, at a quarter before nine in the evening, on the threshold of the Reform Club salon?

The anxiety in which, for three days, London society existed, cannot be described. Telegrams were sent to America and Asia for news of Phileas Fogg. Messengers were despatched to the house in Saville Row morning and evening. No news. The police were ignorant what had become of the detective, Fix, who had so unfortunately followed up a false trail.

Bets increased, nevertheless, in number and value. Phileas Fogg, like a racehorse, was drawing near his last turning point. The bonds were quoted, no longer at a hundred below par, but at twenty, at ten, and at five; and paralytic old Lord Albermarle bet even in his favor.

A great crowd was gathered on Saturday evening in Pall Mall and the neighboring streets. It seemed like a multitude of brokers permanently established around the Reform Club. Circulation was impeded, and everywhere disputes, discussions, and financial transactions were going on. The police had great difficulty in keeping back the crowd, and as the hour when Phileas Fogg was due approached, the excitement rose to its highest pitch.

The five colleagues of Phileas Fogg had met in the main salon of the club. John Sullivan and Samuel Fallentin, the bankers, Andrew Stuart, the engineer, Gauthier Ralph, the director of the Bank of England, and Thomas Flanagan, the brewer, one and all were waiting anxiously.

When the clock indicated twenty minutes past eight, Andrew Stuart got up, saying, "Gentlemen, in twenty minutes the time agreed upon between Mr. Fogg and ourselves will have expired."

"What time did the last train arrive from Liverpool?" asked Thomas Flanagan.

"At twenty-three minutes past seven," replied Gauthier Ralph, "and the next does not arrive till ten minutes after twelve."

"Well, gentlemen," resumed Andrew Stuart, "if Phileas Fogg had come in the 7:23 train, he would have got here by this time. We can therefore regard the bet as won."

"Wait; don't let us be too hasty," replied Samuel Fallentin. "You know that Mr. Fogg is very eccentric. His punctuality is well known; he never arrives too soon or too late; and I should not be surprised if he appeared before us at the last minute."

"Why," said Andrew Stuart nervously, "if I should see him, I should not believe it was he."

"The fact is," resumed Thomas Flanagan, "Mr. Fogg's project was absurdly foolish. Whatever his punctuality, he could not prevent the delays which were certain to occur; and a delay of only two or three days would be fatal to his tour."

"Observe, too," added John Sullivan, "that we have received no news from him, though there are telegraphic lines all along his route."

"He has lost, gentleman," said Andrew Stuart, "he has a hundred times lost. You know, besides, that the *China*—the only steamer he could have taken from New York to get here in time—arrived yesterday. I have seen a list of the passengers, and the name of Phileas Fogg is not among them. Even if we admit that fortune has favored him, he can scarcely have reached America. I think he will be at least twenty days behind, and that Lord Albemarle will lose a cool five thousand."

"It is clear," replied Gauthier Ralph, "and we have nothing to do but to present Mr. Fogg's check at Baring's tomorrow."

At this moment, the hands of the club clock pointed

to twenty minutes to nine.

"Five minutes more," said Andrew Stuart.

The five gentlemen looked at each other. Their anxiety was becoming intense. But, not wishing to show it, they readily agreed to Mr. Fallentin's suggestion of a rubber.

"I wouldn't give up my four thousand of the bet," said Andrew Stuart, as he took his seat, "for three thousand nine hundred and ninety-nine."

The clock indicated eighteen minutes to nine.

The players had taken up their cards, but could not keep their eyes off the clock. Certainly, however secure they felt, minutes had never seemed so long to them!

"Seventeen minutes to nine," said Thomas Flanagan, as he cut the cards which Ralph handed to him.

Then there was a moment of silence. The main salon was perfectly quiet; but the murmurs of the crowd outside were heard, with a shrill cry now and then. The pendulum beat the seconds, which each player eagerly counted, as he listened, with mathematical regularity.

"Sixteen minutes to nine!" said John Sullivan, in a voice which betrayed his emotion.

One minute more, and the wager would be won. Andrew Stuart and his partners suspended their game. They had left their cards, and were counting the seconds.

At the fortieth second, nothing. At the fiftieth, still nothing.

At the fifty-fifth, a loud cry was heard in the street, followed by applause, hurrahs, and some fierce growls.

The players rose from their seats.

At the fifty-seventh second the door of the salon opened; and the pendulum had not beat the sixtieth second when Phileas Fogg appeared, followed by an excited crowd who had forced their way through the club doors, and in his calm voice, was saying, ''Here I am, gentlemen!''

CHAPTER XXXVII

In Which It Is Shown That Phileas Fogg Has Gained Nothing by His Tour Around the World, Unless It Be Happiness

Yes; Phileas Fogg in person.

The reader will remember that at five minutes past eight in the evening—about five and twenty hours after the arrival of the travelers in London—Passepartout had been sent by his master to engage the services of the Reverend Samuel Wilson in a certain marriage ceremony, which was to take place the next day.

Passepartout went on his errand enchanted. He soon reached the clergyman's house, but found him not at home. Passepartout waited a good twenty minutes, and when he left the reverend gentleman, it was thirty-five minutes past eight. But in what a state he was! With his hair dishevelled, and without his hat, he ran along the street as never man was seen to run before, overturning passersby, rushing over the sidewalk like a waterspout.

In three minutes he was in Saville Row again, and was staggering breathlessly into Mr. Fogg's room.

He could not speak.

"What is the matter?" asked Mr. Fogg.

"My master!—" gasped Passepartout, "marriage—impossible—"

"Impossible?"

"Impossible—for tomorrow."

"Why so?"

"Because tomorrow—is Sunday!"

"Monday," replied Mr. Fogg.

"No—today—is Saturday."

"Saturday? Impossible!"

"Yes, yes, yes, yes!" cried Passepartout. "You have made a mistake of one day! We arrived twenty-four hours ahead of time; but there are only ten minutes left!"

Passepartout had seized his master by the collar, and was dragging him along with irresistible force.

Phileas Fogg, thus carried away, without having time to think, left his house, jumped into a cab, promised a hundred pounds to the cabman, and, having run over two dogs and sideswiped five carriages, reached the Reform Club.

The clock indicated a quarter before nine when he appeared in the main salon.

Phileas Fogg had accomplished the journey around the world in eighty days!

Phileas Fogg had won his wager of twenty thousand pounds!

How was it that a man so exact and fastidious could have made this error of a day? How came he to think that he had arrived in London on Saturday, the twenty-first day of December, when it was really Friday, the twentieth, the seventy-ninth day only from his departure?

The cause of the error is very simple.

Phileas Fogg had, without suspecting it, gained one day on his journey, and this merely because he had traveled constantly *eastward;* he would, on the contrary, have lost a day, had he gone in the opposite direction—that is, *westward.*

In journeying eastward he had gone towards the sun, and the days therefore diminished for him as many times four minutes as he crossed degrees in this direction. There are three hundred and sixty degrees on the circumference of the earth; and these three hundred and sixty degrees, multiplied by four minutes, gives precisely twenty-four hours—that is, the day unconsciously gained. In other words, while Phileas Fogg, going eastward, saw the sun pass the meridian *eighty* times, his friends in London only saw it pass the meridian *seventy-nine* times. This is why they were waiting for him at the Reform Club on Saturday, and not Sunday, as Mr. Fogg thought.

And Passepartout's famous family watch, which had always kept London time, would have betrayed this fact, if it had marked the days as well as the hours and the minutes.

Phileas Fogg, then, had won the twenty thousand pounds; but as he had spent nearly nineteen thousand on the way, the pecuniary gain was small. His object was, however, to be victorious, and not to win money. He divided the one thousand pounds that remained between Passepartout and the unfortunate Fix, against whom he held no grudge. He deducted, however, from Passepartout's share the cost of the gas which had burned in his room for nineteen hundred and twenty hours, for the sake of regularity.

That evening, Mr. Fogg, as tranquil and phlegmatic as ever, said to Mrs. Aouda, "Is our marriage still agreeable to you?"

"Mr. Fogg," replied she, "it is for me to ask that question. You were ruined, but now you are rich again."

"Pardon me, madam; my fortune belongs to you. If you had not suggested our marriage, my servant would not have gone to the Reverend Samuel Wilson's, I should not have been informed of my error and—"

"Dear Mr. Fogg!" said the young woman.

"Dear Aouda!" replied Phileas Fogg.

It need not be said that the marriage took place forty-eight hours after, and that Passepartout, glowing and dazzling, gave the bride away. Had he not saved her, and was he not entitled to this honor?

The next day, as soon as it was light, Passepartout rapped vigorously at his master's door. Mr. Fogg opened it, and asked, "What's the matter, Passepartout?"

"What is it, sir? Why, I've just this instant found out—"

"What?"

"That we might have gone around the world in only seventy-eight days."

"No doubt," returned Mr. Fogg, "by not crossing India. But if I had not crossed India, I should not have saved Mrs. Aouda; she would not have been my wife, and—"

Mr. Fogg quietly shut the door.

Phileas Fogg had won his wager, and had made his journey around the world in eighty days. To do this, he had employed every means of conveyance—steamers, railways, carriages, yachts, trading vessels, sledges, elephants. The eccentric gentleman had throughout displayed all his marvelous qualities of coolness and exactitude. But what then? What had he really gained by all this trouble? What had he brought back from this long and weary journey?

Nothing, say you? Perhaps so, nothing but a charming woman, who, strange as it may appear, made him the happiest of men!

Truly, would you not for less than that go around the world?